THE DOGS OF WAR

EMILY HAYSE

CONTENTS

To the little girl who ran barefoot along concrete sidewalks dreaming of heroes and escaping the city.

Just look where your stories have taken you.

COMBAT PERSONNEL

LIEUTENANT: Field commander in the arena. In charge of communication, strategies, and morale. Intelligent, usually non-combat.

FLAG-BEARER: Quick, light, stealthy. Main job is to steal their flag from the enemy's mountain.

COURIERS: The eyes and ears of the arena. Carry orders between the mountain and the offensive fighters. Quick, tall, work closely with the lieutenant. Often used as an in-arena replacement if the flag-bearer goes down.

PHALANX: Protects their mountain, flag, and lieutenant. Heavily armored with shields and sabers. The biggest and strongest fighters in the arena.

VANGUARD: Mobile front for either defense (with the phalanx) or offense (with the chasers). Usually the one who calls orders if the lieutenant goes down.

CHASERS: Tough, faster-moving protection squad. Often matched against enemy phalanxes on offense and in defense, protection for the flag-bearer.

FLANKERS: Quick-moving help to get around slower-moving phalanxes. Often decoys, they scout out and pave the way for the flag-bearer.

NON-COMBAT PERSONNEL

CAPTAIN: Leader of the fighting company. In charge of every aspect in and out of the arena. All masters and fighters report to him.

STABLE MASTER: In charge of training, drilling, and getting the fighters into shape. Makes decisions on injury, fitness, and skill level. Oversees living quarters and rations.

WEAPONS MASTER: Studies strategies, works closely with both the captain and the stable master to draw up war plans. Oversees the armor and weapons maintenance.

They say everything happens for a reason. I believe that with all my heart.

And I believe we were destined, the Iron City Wolves, to be together. Across vast distances, improbable lives, near-misses that a second more or less would have changed forever—we were inevitable.

This I can say about us: We loved each other. And we loved that oak of a man who led us through fire and death.

If they were to give me another chance, I would not change what I did. For these boys, I'd die a thousand times, live a thousand exiles. They would do the same for me.

My name is Jackson Van. And these things I write so that my men will not be forgotten.

ONE
JACKSON VAN

LIEUTENANT, GOLDEN CITY TOROS

I STAND OUTSIDE THE DOOR IN THE DARK hallway. The sound of celebration comes from the other side: the boys shouting, whooping, singing all off-key.

I'm often the last one back to the preparation room after a match. Trying to get through the press is always hard. Most times, I am obliged to stop and talk to them and answer their questions, especially on nights like tonight. It is a necessary evil to be borne. But this—the pride of doing my job and bringing these boys the victory they deserve—is what I love about the Games.

I step into the golden light of the room and I'm immediately attacked by a zealous chaser. He seizes my shoulders and shakes me, whooping.

"It's our lieutenant, boys!" shouts Trace, our lead flagbearer, sitting atop a pile of armor crates. He's wearing someone else's cap, and it's backwards. His shirtsleeve's ripped off, a bloody bandage tied over one arm, and he's drinking out of one of the big water pitchers they give us to wash the dust out of our mouths.

"Trey, what are you doing up there?"

"Celebrating. Get in here, you killjoy." He leans out and pours a little over my head.

He's enjoying himself too much.

I laugh and duck away. "Come on, Trace, I've got to get out of my gear first."

"Look, he laughed! Boys, he's smiling!"

He points at me, giddy.

"Jackson, what's armor when we're going to the Wreath? We've been waiting for you this whole time. Boys, pick him up!" My arms are seized by a couple guys from my phalanx and I'm hauled up in their arms.

Hands pull at the thick leather of my shoulder guards, pulling my uniform askew, and water is dumped over my head. A dozen hands, two dozen faces all around me, shaking me, smacking the hard front of my armor, cheering so loud my ears ring.

I'm embarrassed at the to-do, but I'm warmed.

I get to compete for the Wreath with these boys. My boys. And I'll take them to glory if it's the last thing I do.

"Okay, okay!" Mark Brissinger, our captain, comes into the room, bristling with business. "Quiet down, I have a few things to say to you all."

I escape the boys' grasp and go over to my gear stall to start getting my things off. The room is still quieting down.

"First of all, I want to say how proud I am that the Toros will be representing the Golden City at the fight for the Wreath. This is what we fight for. This is why we are part of the great tradition of the Games."

The boys clap and cheer.

"Trey? You fought like a warrior out there. That's how we take a flag. And phalanx? Good job getting him there. We have a lot of work to do, some things we could be doing better, but we're on our way to Wreath match. That is no small thing."

"Toros! Toros!" the boys chant, jumping up and down.

Mark quiets them down. "Where's Jackson Van?" He begins to crane his neck. The boys part, a few of them pointing.

Mark's eyes fall on me and the light in them cools, even though he is still smiling.

It's coming; he's had it in for me ever since he's become our captain. Just because I'm the son of my father.

Their feud was with each other, years ago when they played the game. Something forgotten by most, but not Mark. I haven't told my father. It would be pointless to. So far it hasn't been public, just private digs.

"Come here, come on up here."

I pause, halfway through unstrapping my armguards.

"Leave those on, Jack. Get over here."

He's mad. This isn't one of his normal barbs. No one calls me Jack, not even him. His tone's lost on some of the boys; they're still murmuring in low approval, ready to cheer again.

I leave the armguards on and go to him in the center of the room.

"What are those for?"

"What? My armguards?"

"What do you think? Yes, your armguards."

"Protection."

"Really, are you sure that's what they're for? Because I didn't see you use them once before you were shocked out."

The quiet murmur of the room stops.

"Can—can we talk about this in private?"

"What you did on that field was not private. I think this is an appropriate place to talk about it." The captain puts his hands on his hips. "You put your teammates at risk by your lack of action. Worse, you reflected badly on the team."

"The phalanx could have done better," says Trace. "He was struck from behind twice. Those chasers were all over him. That wasn't his fault."

"Did I ask you?" Mark turns on him. "I have eyes, I saw what happened on the field."

"Captain, we didn't—"

"Shut up!" he snaps. "I didn't ask any of you!"

I swallow. It's better the boys don't get caught up in this. "I'm sorry, Captain," I say, loud enough for the boys to hear. "It was my fault. I could have done better."

He ignores me and holds out his hand. "Give me that."

Slowly, I unstrap one armguard and set it into the captain's outstretched hand. He thrusts it onto his arm and turns it on.

The bars are gone, but the shocker works fine.

"Block me. Try to block me."

He catches me immediately in the shoulder, the sharp

smack of the shock filling the room. There is an audible catch of breath.

I suck in my own breath quietly, forcing my heart to settle back down, like I do in the arena. I'm not going to block him. He doesn't actually want a demonstration; he wants an example, and I won't shock him in front of the boys.

"Try again, come on—did you lose your guts in here too?"

He tries for me again and I raise my arm just enough for the blow not to take me in the chest, hitting my shoulder again. I take it calmly and don't look him in the eye.

The boys are getting uneasy.

Sweat rolls off Mark's face and down into his collar. His face is red, the veins in his neck standing out.

Again, he comes at me. I just stand where I am.

Seeing I am not going to fight back, he grabs my shirt and pulls me in, the shocker held out, inches from my neck.

"How long are we going to do this, kid?"

I just look at the ground.

He leans up into my face. "Who do you play for?"

"The Golden City."

"Quit mumbling, kid. Who?"

"The Golden City!"

One of the phalanx steps up. "Captain, you know he wouldn't shock out on purpose."

Mark lets me go and throws the armguard on the

ground. "Get out. I don't want to see your face again today."

The room is silent as I calmly, carefully bend down and pick up the armguard. I walk over to my stall and set it gently down with the rest of my things.

The boys resume uneasy conversation. A second later a door slams, and the tension in the room eases.

Mark must have stalked off.

I slide my other armguard off and shove it into my stall, stripping the rest of my armor as quickly as I can.

"Van," murmurs Trey, leaning close, "don't take it personal. Captain's just under a lot of pressure. You got us to the Wreath match."

I look at him quietly. "Thanks, but he meant it to be personal." I pick up my bag and haul it over my shoulder, striding from the room.

The moment the door closes behind me, I am swarmed.

"Jackson Van!"

"Can you spare a word?"

"Jackson Van, how do you feel about getting a chance at the Wreath so young?"

"How do you feel about carrying on your father's legacy?"

The guards that keep the press out of the preparation room step up and push them aside. As we walk down the hall, screaming people with pencils and notebooks and cameras that flash part like water before the prow of a boat.

I'm dead to it.

I know he's never liked me, and I have made my mistakes, but he could have talked to me like a man, on my own. He didn't have to vent his anger on me, in front of everyone, just because I remind him of someone who made him feel inferior.

We step outside and there's a crowd now, lining the way to my waiting automobile, and a television camera, with a host and his loud radio voice. "Jackson Van is the face of the Golden City Toros. And he's taking them all the way to—"

The car door slams behind me, muting the screams of the crowd, the flash of the cameras. On the seat beside me sits the newspaper for the day, its headline screaming with the crowds outside, "Life is Good for the Toros' Golden Boy."

TWO
REMUS BLAKE

CHASER, BLACK TOWN STAGS

FIGHT. CONQUER. WIN HONOR.

I raise my head from between my knees and take a deep breath. My watch sits on the bench beside me. One hour.

One hour and it will all be in our hands, no longer waiting, no longer a circled date on the calendar. It will be us, under the lights of the Iron City arena, man to man, fighting for our shot at glory.

We fight the Iron City Wolves, the lowest team in the empire, for the glory of domination. It's tough luck for the Wolves, who are little better than sacrifices. Even if they win, it means nothing. The Wreath has long been out of their reach. For that reason, the match is not really fair in my mind, but it was decided by the Guild, and I, Remus Blake, journeyman chaser for the Black Town Stags, am but one small thread in the colossal tapestry of history. I do not get a say.

A gong sounds outside the preparation room. It's time.

I stand up and cross the room to where the gear is laid out, numbered by ranks. Couriers here, all between ten and nineteen, vanguards with twenties, chasers with thirties, flankers in the forties. All with the proud emblem of the Black Town Stags emblazoned across them. I pick up my chest armor off the table and heft it over my head, feeling the familiar weight as it drops heavy onto my shoulders.

The rest of the team makes their way to the gear stalls, the latecomers trickling into the preparation room. I glance around for our vanguard. He's a first-year conscriptee, and he has a punctuality problem. Last thing we need is for all of us to get docked because he's not ready for inspection.

His dark head bobs over by the couriers; he's here. Good. Nothing is going to get in our way tonight.

"Remus." One of my fellow chasers comes up and slaps my shoulder. "Glory tonight."

I grin in reply and grab the high cinch on his chest armor, pulling it to the stretched-out notch and buckling it. He turns and I do the other side.

"I got one side," I say, and turn the other towards him. We often do up the buckles on each other's chest armor, the ones that are hard to reach.

We pull on our armbands and fasten them, slip on our numbers for the night and help each other tie them tight. We take our knives—they're for looks and the occasional practical use—and fasten them onto our legs.

Lastly, I take down my boots and go to the bench, lace them high and tight.

"Listen up, Atlas on deck!" our lieutenant shouts. The room stills and any of us on the bench get to our feet as Atlas, our weapons master, walks in.

He's an oak of a man, ex-vanguard—which is where he got the name of Atlas—and even though he was dismissed from the Games over a decade ago after a bad injury, he could still knock a few heads off. I've seen him part fully-armored fighters with his bare hands, seen him shout down a loud-mouthed chaser who'd gotten savage. But he's good to us. Fair. And I've seen him hold the heads of boys hurt so bad they'll never fight again and somehow put the courage back inside them.

I've never known another man like him.

"We're minutes away from glory. So this is your last chance—anyone missing anything?"

His eyes scan us, giving us the opportunity to speak up for ourselves, but not leaving a mistake up to chance.

He pauses in front of our youngest courier and a nervous chuckle runs through the boys. The couriers wear their armor under their uniform; it's light and flexible so they can run fast. It's also a learning curve to put on right, for the new boys.

"Is it in order?" the courier asks, his face solemn. Atlas pulls respect from even the wildest ones.

Atlas's grim blue eyes gentle. "You look good, kid."

The boy grins, quick and relieved.

"We're so close, brother," Atlas says, thumping our lieutenant on the shoulder. "One more match."

"Yes, sir." The man reaches out and clasps his shoulder back.

Atlas pauses in front of Kipling, our main flag-bearer. The center of the storm, as it were.

"No red scarf?" he asks.

"No sir." Our flag-bearer lifts his chin proudly. "I wouldn't miss this for the world."

"Neither would I." Atlas cracks a smile. "Neither would I, kid."

And so he walks through us, his eyes checking every man, stopping now and again to crack a joke or sober a man up or give a little encouragement.

Atlas should have been a captain by now, but our captain is old and beloved and won a fistful of wreaths in his day. Any man that has survived to captain with a gray head deserves to keep his place. And Atlas loves us. He would not upset the delicate political balance of the Black Town Stags. Still, I think if he had a disagreement with the captain, the boys would follow him in an instant. Because Atlas would be right in the matter.

"All right, boys." Atlas raises his voice so that it fills the room. "Get in your places. Captain's coming."

We all line up in front of our equipment stalls, where we keep our boots and our personals. A couple men hike one foot up on the bench behind them, lacing up their boots, their eyes on the door.

The door swings open so hard it hits the wall behind it.

"The Iron City should get that fixed," says the captain in his dry, deep voice, checking the wall.

There's a tight chuckle from the men. The last of them put their boots down before the captain can notice. He's followed by three game keepers with their clipboards.

The room is silent. All the men standing straight and solemn, anticipation hanging over the room, thicker than a cloud.

They take their time, two game keepers starting down one side of the room and the head game keeper, with the captain, down the other.

They pause in front of a few men, but no one is pulled out of line. I let my breath out silently.

"Your team is in order," said the head game keeper.

"Thank you, gentlemen." The captain shakes their hands and they leave.

We stay in our places.

The captain is writing something on his clipboard. "Well, that's done," he says finally.

A relieved laugh spreads along the line.

"What do you say we go pick a fight with some wolves?"

A cheer breaks out, the boys whooping and thumping each other on the backs.

The captain lets us have our moment and then raises his hands for silence.

"Men, I do not have to tell you how important this match is." His eyes whip from Hargrave—our lieutenant—to Kipling, to me. "The Wolves are fighting for pride. We fight for glory. Glory that is going to stick with you for the rest of your life."

Beside me, one of the chasers sucks in his breath with

a hiss. We can all taste it: one game, a game against weak opponents, standing between us and a shot at the highest honor a man can receive.

"You boys have been here before, one match away from the Wreath match. Kipling and Harris have been to the Wreath match. We won it, too."

There's an appreciative whoop, and the boys around Kipling and Harris smack them on the shoulders and shove them out of line. Beaming, they raise their branched-out hands together in the sign of the Wreath and step back in formation.

"We know the Wolves' reputation. They've been put here for us to kick around. The bettors have all picked for us, as they should. But I have news for you boys. I have not picked us. That's something you boys still have to earn."

Lieutenant Hargrave is standing with his hands in his collar, nodding.

"There is one rule we all learn early on in life," the captain goes on. "Never dishonor the Games. Never. They are our history, our tradition, and our future. They existed long before any of us, and they will exist long after our names are lost to time."

He turns to us on the other side of the room, his face lit up, his eyes on fire. "Remember that. Remember that we are the lucky ones, the ones who get to uphold that history and tradition. We might live on a knife's edge, but that also means we live on the cusp of glory. And I don't know about you boys—I wouldn't want to be anywhere else."

A low murmur of agreement is trickling through us, grins starting on solemn faces, eyes lighting with the fire in our captain's face.

"So I want you boys to go out there and fight for that glory. Fight for the memory of the game and bring honor to our city. Prosper the Games."

"Prosper the Games!" we echo, shaking the room.

The captain shoots Lieutenant Hargrave a sharp, proud look. "Dan, they're yours."

Hargrave tilts back his head and lets out a whoop. "Come on, boys, get in rank!"

The gong strikes again, outside our room. The call to arms.

At the exit of the room stands the weapons rack. Vanguards and chasers carry sabers—blunt sticks, but they still deal damage—as do the phalanx. Everyone else is weaponless, unless they can wrest one from us. There's no rules against that.

Atlas stands beside the weapons rack as we take down our weapons and buckle them on. Here and there, he helps someone with a hard-to-reach buckle or with switching out a worn grip, but every one of us he sends off with a nod, a word, or a slap on the shoulder.

"Remus, it's a good day to be alive."

"Yes, sir." I salute him with a grin.

"Go get 'em."

We pour down the hall in our ranks, down to the tunnel and the closed gate. Hargrave is at our head, his back against the big, iron-barred gate. The sharp light of the arena slants in over his shoulder and hits the dust beneath our feet.

I glance through one of the slits into the Iron City's arena. It's like its name—high iron walls pen in the whole place, and a great black banner hangs from the center of the rafters, a snarling wolf standing on ice. The mountains that stand on either end of the dusty arena have been painted black and ice blue. Many arenas leave the grassy mountains natural. Not here.

Here they hold on to their old, shabby pride.

The crowd outside is chanting, impatient for us to take the arena. Even in the Iron City, they love the Game.

We are crowded against the doors so tightly we cannot move without touching one another. A bell tolls in the arena. One minute.

The cheers swell.

"Boys, listen up!" Hargrave shouts. "Listen up!"

The boys quiet down—now it's just the muffled roar of the crowd outside.

"It's just us now. We decide our fate, no one else." His face shifts in and out of a beam of light through the arena gate. "Remember, we are the Stags. They don't own us, they don't scare us, they do not take us down. Let's show the Iron City how we play these war games. Kipling—" He gives our flag-bearer a nod. "Bring it home."

The bars are dropped on the heavy gate and it swings wide.

We follow him out into the wide arena, running, shouting, brandishing our sabers. Our vanguard hits his shoulder armor with his, like a fierce drum tattoo. The far side of the arena is marked clearly with our colors, and the war zone in the middle is strewn with ditches, crates, wide puddles, and stacked branches. The phalanx has picked up on our vanguard's excitement; they're pounding their chests with their sabers too.

The crowd above the arena has fallen silent—silence is what you give your enemies—so our entrance is the only sound filling our ears. I wouldn't have it any other way. This is our moment. And we are happy, all of us, to stand together against the opposing silence.

Above us, from the loudspeaker, the Iron City Wolves are introduced. The bars are dropped on their gate and they burst into the arena, loping like a wolf pack, their lieutenant, Luke Sheppard, at their head. The cheers for him are deafening.

I have no trouble admitting that Luke Sheppard is an inspiring sight. Conscripted by the Wolves five years ago, he's never known anything but the grime and poverty of the Iron City. He doesn't seem to mind.

He pumps his fist to the crowd and they respond with a loud, rippling cheer. I can say this: they love the man, and he loves them back.

The bell tolls again. We will have five minutes to take our places, finalize anything we want, and familiarize ourselves with the terrain.

I bend down and rub my hands in the dirt. It's a dry arena, which means dust. They've tried to wet it down, but it hasn't taken. Before the end, we will all be dust-covered, dirt clotted in our blood.

I reach up and tie my hair back, out of my face.

Hargrave is over by the captain's box, talking through something, probably a change in strategy. I wonder what the captain saw.

I jog over to the far end of the arena, to the foot of our mountain where we wait for orders.

The conversation between captain and lieutenant is short. Hargrave comes my way, followed by the phalanx, the couriers, flankers, and the rest.

"We're going to keep it simple tonight. Flood them, straight across the arena. Nice and hard. Flag-bearer will make the steal, and if any of you chasers are left after the first onslaught, you'll cover his retreat. Flankers and couriers will be on hand for a relay if it's needed. Phalanx will guard our mountain. Keep a sharp eye for changes."

And that's that.

I know my place. I walk out to the edge of the mountain, where I'll start. Chasers aren't usually allowed in the starting boxes, because we don't need the extra help. It's too easy for us to run people over.

I flex my shoulders, make sure there's enough range of movement under my armor. I tighten my armbands another notch, turn them on. The blue bars light up.

Everything's in order.

The standing gallery is level with me, packed with the working men. A little boy stares at me with dark eyes, his cap almost swallowing his face. An ice-blue and black banner hangs from his dirty hand.

I give him a little smile, and his eyes widen. He looks away quickly.

I can hardly blame him—I'm the enemy.

"Remus!" Grant, one of my fellow chasers, jogs up and smacks me on the shoulder.

"You ready?" I can't help smiling. Right before the horn blows, my blood always rises. With the crowds standing, screaming, your comrades next to you under lights brighter than sunshine—there's nothing like it in the world.

Grant tightens the belt on his armband and checks to make sure the thing is working. It hums and shocks him. "Ah—" He spits out an uncouth word and grins sheepishly. "Let 'em come."

The game keepers stand beside the box, eyes watching to make sure everything is legal. There won't be any tricks tonight. We've got one thing on our minds, and that is getting to the Wreath match.

The lieutenants exchange the typical formalities before returning to their respective starting boxes. As the hosts, the Wolves will open the Games.

I take a deep breath.

Fight. Conquer. Win honor.

Grant shoots me a steadying look from his post, ten paces away.

Luke Sheppard raises his fist in the air, the signal for the countdown. The clock strikes—one, two, three, four—

I suck my breath in between my teeth and grin.

Five. They break from the starting box like water from a dam.

These are the War Games, the beginning and the end of the great Empire of Wroth.

THREE
LUKE SHEPPARD

LIEUTENANT, IRON CITY WOLVES

I KNOW THE CROWD IS SHOUTING MY NAME, BUT I hear nothing. Nothing but my heartbeat and the breath in my lungs.

Dust flies from the boots of my phalanx, rising slow and clear, caught in the harsh light of the arena. They're locked with the first rush of chasers from the Black Town, sabers falling heavy on armored shoulders.

They're coming through our line too fast. Our flag-bearer is out there somewhere, but I can't see him and our flag still flies over the enemy's mountain.

We've got to buy some time.

"Fall back!" I shout. "Re-form!"

Peter Hope, our phalanx anchor, hears me.

The phalanx line bends inward, raising shields, circling to protect us. Outside, the couriers circle, tussling a little with a couple hot flankers, ready in case they're needed for a hand-off.

The chasers back off; they're not equipped to take the Phalanx in full turtled defense. My boys aren't afraid to beat them off.

"We go when you say," says Peter Hope, over his shoulder.

My eyes go to the field ahead of us. I see just a glimpse of a movement—I hope it's our flag-bearer. It's not the best set-up I've seen, but if we wait, we might not go at all.

I put my hand on his shoulder. "Go."

They rush as one, plowing straight towards the foot of the hill where the chasers have fallen back, waiting for us like hounds for the kill.

They clash, sabers upon shields, and I see it across the arena: Sampson making for the narrow gap between the war zone and the Black Town's mountain.

A deep horn sounds—halt of game. Someone's been shocked out already.

"Cool it, boys," I mutter. Just as we were getting somewhere.

It's one of their couriers and a chaser of ours. At least it was an even trade. We've already lost three of our men. These big teams will just bully you into the ground.

I lean my hands on my thighs and take a breath.

The clock is set for a minute while they verify that they are removing the right men. I jog over to the edge and one of the attendants hands me water from the big pitchers they keep off to one side, by the medics.

"Keep at it, you're making ground," he says. I drink it

and take another cup, pouring it over my head. The count-down warning rings.

Back to our places.

The phalanx reforms around me and now that the forward momentum is lost, Sampson comes back into the circle to restart. He's lost the element of surprise. I motion the men in for a quick word.

"All right, chasers, flankers. Two of you stick with Sampson, nice and close. Just get your hands on the flag. Get it off that mountain and we'll deal with the repercussions, whatever those are. I want you other two making a feint ahead of them to draw off the left front. The Black Town line is hitting us hard. If we don't stop them here, we will not have time to run our flag back. Phalanx—just like we did before, if you hit them hard enough, they'll have to break. They're not going to expect the same rush twice in a row. Sampson—"

I turn to him and stop.

"Brother, what's wrong with your arm?"

King opens the buckle on his armguard and cinches it tighter, hiding the bloody bandage underneath. "Nothin's wrong, don't know what you see."

A tight laugh runs around the circle.

"All right. Sampson, Grafton is right out there. If you think they're going to take you down, you pass to him, hear?"

"Got it."

Isaac Grafton, my secondary courier, salutes me—he's balanced on the balls of his feet, ready to take the flag if it comes. His armguard has just a thin blue band across the bottom—he has one hit left before he's shocked out.

I know for a fact he's playing with a wrapped-up ankle too.

The clock strikes its countdown. Five, four, three, two —I suck in a deep breath through my teeth.

Bodies rush forward. My phalanx meets them and I step up behind them, out of the immediate fray, eyes on our forward feint.

A split second before it happens, I catch the chaser out of the corner of my eye. It's too late to do anything, even throw up my hand for protection.

I'm slammed to the ground. Immediate, tearing pain shoots up my arm. I shift and something grinds sickeningly.

I grit my teeth against it as sweat washes over me. It's bad. The arena lights swim in front of my eyes.

Beyond me, I see our feint worked—halfway. Sampson King has the Black Town's flag, but even as I watch, he's shocked out. The flag falls in the dirt.

A deep horn sounds like a train, signifying a stop. It's Peter Hope, holding up his hand in the sign of temporary forfeit. He will lose a blue bar, putting him close to shocking out, and in return, I can leave the arena and see a medic.

He's got to quit doing that.

His big frame looms over me, his red hair dark from sweat. "Shep, can you stand?"

"Just be gentle." I give him my good arm, and he hauls me up. Medics are running to me, meeting me halfway, swarming and bombarding my swimming head with questions. One puts his arm around my waist and hauls me to the side of the arena.

The rest of the team flocks around. The stable master's assistant, Crispin, comes down to meet us. Ed Barbara, our stable master, cannot usually be bothered to come down.

"How many?" I ask him.

"Five." He glances around at the men gathered, his dark eyes concerned. "Six, with you."

"Is it the arm?" one medic asks.

I grit my teeth. "Yeah."

Gently, his fingers start at my wrist.

"Did anyone get their hands on the flag?"

"The Stags didn't. Peter called it just in time." This is Jim Danforth, part of the phalanx.

"Good."

Since the flag carrier was shocked out but our flag wasn't stolen, it'll be placed back ten feet and given to our next appointed carrier.

"Easy, easy—" I grit my teeth as they feel up my arm. I look at Crispin. "I need a vanguard."

"Vanguards are out."

"Both of them?"

He nods.

"Don't want to get back on the field, do you?" I ask him.

His grim face lights in the barest wry laugh. "For you, Shep, I would."

"What about Isaac?"

"He's out. And you're out. Hope's making the calls. Just lie still."

"Pete's got one bar."

"All I know is you can't go back out there. We'll handle it from here."

The medics bring out a stiff-sleeve to stabilize my arm; they wave Crispin out of the way.

"Easy, Lieutenant." The medic's fingers are gentle as he slides it under my arm. "We'll have you out of here in a minute."

Crispin sits back on his heels and motions Peter Hope down to him. It's too loud in the arena; I can't hear what they're saying. Crispin's pointing, first at the flag, then at Danforth, and then he gestures to the last of our chasers.

He's the stable master's assistant, and he's doing the job of the captain and the stable master right now. We have a whole lot of leaders in the Iron City who can't be bothered to lead.

A horn sounds. The Black Town Stags are using their substitution. If we start now—*now*—they won't have time to regroup or warm up the new man.

"That's it!" I cut Crispin off. "If we go now, we can get out there and end it."

"We don't have enough men," he argues.

"Do you think the boys can hold off the other side?"

"They're going to try, but I think it's a washed game. The priority is getting you out of the arena."

I'm sick of losing again and again. Buried under the might of stronger teams, or losing by the barest tips of our fingers. Tonight is not the night I go down easy.

I lock eyes with Peter. He's with me.

I haul myself to my feet, shaking off the medics. I strap the stiff-sleeve tight, bracing against the swimming darkness at the edge of my eyes.

"Wait." Crispin reaches for me. "Don't do this."

"Get off me."

"Shep, please—"

I ignore him. I will apologize later. It's now or it's never.

I signal the game keepers, cradle my arm carefully against my chest.

There's no time to communicate; every second is time we give our enemies. I walk straight out and pick our flag out of the dirt.

The Stags are caught by surprise. Their couriers and chasers are waving, trying to get their extra men back in from the other side of the arena.

The clock sounds and Peter rushes ahead of me, knocking down the closest chaser with his bare hands. The world narrows to a small, slow gap. I see the future stretched before me like a finished story. If I don't take it now, it will not happen.

I put down my head and rush.

The chaser's fingers grasp and fall off my shoulder. My shoulder cracks against the charging flanker, his attack thrown off by the chaser's failure.

Peter's ahead of me, takes out another man—they fall together.

We're almost to the mountain.

Something hits me from behind, hits me in the broken arm. Stars explode across my vision; my breath is gone.

Without my breath, somehow, I stumble the last ten yards, barely keeping my feet. The world is silent. And I feel nothing.

I shove the flag into the dirt inside the circle.

The arena rises, explodes around me. Deafening. The last of my Wolves are rushing up the mountain to me, the rest flooding the arena below.

I suck in my breath and it feels like I'm dragging it over glass. Pain rushes over me in a sick wave.

My grip loosens on the flag staff. I'm trying to get my fingers to respond and they're slow—like I'm caught in water.

I sink to my knees.

Victory! Victory! Victory!

The chant swells up around me, surrounds me, blocking out my hearing. I'm on the edge of darkness, fighting not to fall in.

"I got you, Shep, I got you."

Peter Hope's arms are around me. I let go and fall into blackness.

FOUR
REMUS BLAKE

CHASER, BLACK TOWN STAGS

It's over. A year of work and years of dreaming, over just like that. Broken to pieces by that broken man, lying beneath his flag, surrounded by team-mates and medics.

I can't hear a thing. This is the loudest I have ever heard an arena. The crowd is on their feet, screaming, shouting, almost pouring out into the arena itself. Shaking the rafters.

I shove one knee up, hands in the dirt, and pull myself upright.

"Tough luck!" Grant stands over me, blood smeared across his cheek. He dusts off his hand and offers it to me.

I take it and haul myself up. Put my mouth to his ear so he can hear through the roar. "I should have had him!"

Grant shrugs. What's he going to say?

"You're bleeding." He gestures to me.

"Where?" I check my hands, then my arms.

He indicates my hairline. Sticky blood is matted along the side of my head, and the sweat running down my face and neck is stained with it. With my pale hair, it's going to stand out.

I pick my saber up off the ground and trudge towards the center box. A match always ends with a meeting of the final men in the center. Sometimes it's one or two men standing against a dozen. Today, there are four Wolves and nine of us Stags. And we still lost.

The last man standing from the Wolves' phalanx, Jim Danforth, steps forward, his face smeared with dirt, his hair damp with sweat. Blood trickles down his neck.

He's a beast of a man, dwarfing even Hargrave's tall, athletic build.

He will do the honors normally reserved for the winning lieutenant—from the looks of it, Sheppard isn't going to be doing much for a while.

Our lieutenant steps up to meet him. I feel for him; we just lost our shot at the Wreath, and it was to the Iron City Wolves. This kind of surrender takes a lot of guts.

But as lieutenant you get the glory, and you take the dishonor too.

Jim draws his knife, little bigger than a pocket blade, and cuts the Black Town Stag emblem off Hargrave's uniform. He raises it high above his head as the arena explodes in fresh cheers.

"Prosper the Games," he says, with the beginnings of a smile but no malice.

"Prosper the Games," repeats Hargrave, with mustered dignity.

We're being herded to the gate now as quickly as possible. The arena is still packed and the noise deafening; it's not a safe place to be. Where you've come into someone's city on top, expected to win, and instead you're taken down, the victorious city won't stop at humiliating you. Men have been hurt from things thrown into the arena, attacked in the halls, or beaten in back alleys.

The latter doesn't often happen, but it does happen. And this one—it's on me.

An arm is thrown over my shoulders, jerking me in. It's Atlas.

"Pick up your head, Remus."

I lift it, and I see he's glancing around at the crowd and the cameras as we exit the arena.

I should know better. They might come for me, but hanging my head's only going to tell them that they should.

Back in the preparation room, everything smells like sweat. There's no air in here. Hargrave peels off his shirt, which is ruined now that the emblem is gone.

A couple men slap my shoulder sympathetically.

The captain pauses in front of me, looks me up and down. "You're bleeding."

"Yeah, I know."

"Anything else?"

"Ribs."

He shakes his head. The man is exhausted. "Kid, get yourself to the medic."

I clean up and change clothes before heading to the

medic. I've done this long enough to know when to go straight to them and when it can wait.

The cut on my head is what I expected. Small—just bleeding a lot, as the head ones do. It had clotted up before I even left the arena.

They check my ribs and I know from the feel that it's not good, but my lungs are clear and they wrap me up tightly. Nothing you can do about ribs except wait them out.

They send me back out to the preparation room. The captain's there, in the center, and the place is quieting down.

"Boys—" He puts his hands on his hips and shakes his head. The silence stretches. "You fought. Fought like devils. We also made some mistakes, ones we paid a dear price for. I hope you think about both of those things on the way home. You'll want to sleep, think of something else, distract yourself, but don't. Grasp this pain and squeeze it tight. Feel it. I want you to remember it next time, and will a different outcome."

"Yes, sir," the murmured reply echoes through the room.

"You're dismissed, boys. The Iron City police have to give us the go-ahead before we head to the trains, so just be patient. They're trying to protect us. Be civil."

He leaves, probably to go talk to the press. Not something I envy: the swarm, the flash of bulbs in your face, and men with notebooks scribbling words they force out of you and will tease at their leisure into whatever meaning they wish.

As soon as we're told we can, we grab our things and head for the train station.

I step out into the cold alley behind the arena, holding the door for the man behind me. The wind swirls between the brick buildings—there are so many of them in the city—and rushes like a freight train against me.

The Iron City is lit with old yellow street lamps; steam rises from manholes and there's a light snow falling over the hollow-eyed automobiles that wait for the streams of people to cross.

I lift my coat collar against the biting wind and brace against the snowflakes hitting my cheeks and neck.

The streets are loud with jubilation. I can be philosophical: matches are won and lost every day, and this one is the biggest thing the Iron City has seen in years. Luke Sheppard earned them a brutal, glorious victory tonight. Thinking of it outside my own disappointment, it's kind of beautiful.

But it's still hard to leave weary and sore, listening to the cheers of the other side, wondering what you could have done differently.

"This way, this way—" The police herd us away from the crowds and toward the station. The smells of soot and acrid steam fill the cold night air.

None of us talk. We move into the station quick and sullen and cowed, past the travelers who stop to watch. Our cars have been cordoned off from the rest of the station, and it's a blessed relief, as the city seems alive and seeking blood.

"Watch your step," the conductor intones. I duck as I

step up into the train, and I keep moving for the men behind me.

The doors slam shut on the city noise.

In front of me, the men are backed up, voices raised in consternation. Some of the men are turning around, coming back up the aisle way.

"Sleeper cars aren't ready," says Hargrave with disgust. "As if it couldn't get worse."

Gingerly I make my way to the parlor cars and find an empty compartment.

It's decked out for us—a couple blankets, an evening newspaper, a bottle of mineral water.

I reach down and toss the newspaper onto the bench across from me. I check my boots for excessive dirt and then put them up next to the newspaper. I wouldn't normally—kind of bad form, isn't it—but I am alone and unbearably sore.

I lean back against the cushioned bench with a sigh.

Grant drifts in. "You're looking how I feel," he says, pushing my feet over and sitting down.

I take my feet down and sit up with a groan.

"You should lie down," he says.

"Can't. Beds aren't ready."

"Tough luck." He folds his arms. "How's the head?"

"It's all superficial. Just got a little plaster from the medic." I lift the edge of my hair to show him. "But I took a good hit to the ribs. Probably cracked one or two."

"Man." He whistles sympathetically. Ribs are common, but they hurt like fire, nothing you can do about it. No one wants those.

"You're going to have a little something on your face for a bit."

"Don't matter." Grant grins and then winces. "Bella's seen it all. She's stopped counting my scars."

"Yeah, Lucia doesn't care either. I'm lucky." I start to lean forward on my knees and then think better of it.

The train lets loose a long whistle and lurches into motion. My ribs bite again and I shift to find a more comfortable position. I thrust my arms behind my head and take them down immediately. It was a bad idea.

Grant shifts the newspaper over, sparing it a glance, but it seems he's already seen it, as he looks over at me dismally.

"Did you hear the Golden City Toros are going to the Wreath match? Just out on the evening post. Jackson Van is taking them to glory."

FIVE
JACKSON VAN

LIEUTENANT, GOLDEN CITY TOROS

"What is it like, having a chance to represent the Golden City in the battle for the Wreath?"

The question is just like a hundred others I've had to answer this afternoon. "It's an honor. I only hope I can do the city proud."

Another newspaperman raises his pencil. "What about your father? Has he said anything to you?"

I smile. "First thing, he told me to go get a haircut."

This elicits a laugh.

"No, he told me to go do it for the city and the boys in the arena."

They scribble away on their little notebooks and portable typewriters.

"And what do you say to people who think you're too young to handle the pressure of the Wreath match, especially up against seasoned opponents like Lieutenant Cox and the Coventry Watchdogs?"

"Lieutenant Cox is a hero in this empire. It's an honor to play against him. And this is about the Golden City Toros, not me. Every single one of these men has earned the right to be here and I will do everything in my power to do right by them."

It's what every lieutenant says, whether they mean it or not. But I mean it. Every word of it.

The stable master and Captain Brissinger come out. The captain stands impatient, eyes roving over the press.

I'm only too glad to finish this. "I'll take one last question." I point to a short fellow in a fedora.

"Any last words for us before you go into battle?"

I pause and consider. I have given them so many words today.

A quote from an old legend, a once-lieutenant of the Golden City comes to mind. They're not my words, originally, but they're good words. "My glory is not mine, but the Golden City's. The honor is not mine, but my men's. I will fight to my last breath for the Wreath, and may I come home victorious or not at all."

There's a murmur of approval from the press. They know those words. They breathe that sentiment with the rest of the empire. It's the language we all speak.

"Anything from you, Captain Brissinger?"

He puts up his hands in appeasement, shaking his head and smiling. "I'm finished with you gentlemen. Just here to collect my lieutenant." He steps up, putting his hand on my shoulder.

"A photo! Let's have a photo!"

Mark swallows a brief look of distaste and grins wide.

"Come here." He pulls me close into an embrace. I have no choice but to go along with it.

"That's great! Keep going!" The cameras keep clicking.

"I'll hold you to that," he whispers. "Next time, you come in on a stretcher or I'll send you out on one."

I keep my face carefully neutral. The cameras continue their clicking, deceived. They can never know.

I step back and give him a nod. "Yes, sir, Captain." I give a wave to the press and head back towards the preparation room. My mind is only on one thing now.

I must win the Wreath.

Preparation is automatic. I'm in a daze. I change into my under-uniform, put on my boots, stand as the armorers help me with the buckles on my armor, brace against the familiar jerk as they pull them tight. I pull my uniform on over all that. The Golden City emblem is fresh and strong on my shoulder, with an embroidered wreath beside it, for the match.

Trey is excited; he comes over and shakes my shoulder. "It's the Wreath, Jackson. We're going to win that wreath."

Inspection time comes and takes longer than normal. With so much on the line, they go over us with a fine-toothed comb, but we are the picture of professionalism. Everything the Golden City can buy, and all in order. We pass with flying colors.

Mark gives us a rousing speech that I cannot hold onto.

Honor to the Games. Honor to the Golden City. We are

the height of the Empire, the ones everyone looks to, and we must not betray that.

Every word is heard but my brain will not engage with it. My heart feels like stone.

When he's done, he hands the room over to me but won't look me in the eye.

"This is it, boys," I tell them. "What we've worked for, what we've dreamed of all our lives. Let's bring honor to our city and to our people. Let's win that wreath."

I lead the way out of the preparation room, past the weapons rack, and down the hallway to the entrance gate.

Light floods the arena. The people are shouting, impatient, stomping in their seats. Chants for the Toros and the Watchdogs mingle.

It's here. It's now.

I look over my shoulders at the boys. My phalanx, armed to the teeth, faces streaked in war paint, the couriers behind them, faces eager. Trey, his eyes sparkling.

The bullhorn sounds.

"Let's go, boys!" I shout.

The bars drop on the gate and they swing wide.

SIX
REMUS BLAKE

CHASER, BLACK TOWN STAGS

"You're not going to watch it? It's the only thing on the television."

Lucia's nephew is sitting on the floor in front of the television, turning knobs, trying to get the thick gray screen to show something other than dark, blurry shapes.

"Paul!" his father snaps. "Turn it off." He looks at me. "We don't have to watch the match."

"It's all right." I stand up from the sofa. "Don't turn it off on my account."

I go outside to the front porch.

Lucia is sitting out on the steps in the falling dusk. Her hands are clasped over her knee, her face tilted up to the low-branched trees. Her light hair catches the last bit of sun, turning it reddish.

We met shortly after I was conscripted, when I was little more than a lost boy in a big, unfamiliar city. She made me feel at home, made her family mine until I could afford to bring my parents here, and the one time I was injured bad enough to need care, she'd arranged for me to stay with her family instead of in my cramped apartment.

I don't know what I'd do without her.

"There you are." She looks up at me with a smile and moves over so I can sit down.

"What are you doing?"

"Watching the fireflies. If we sit still, some deer might come out, down there." She points to the end of the street. "They come to drink at the river and then they cross through here, if it's quiet."

"Sounds perfect." I put my arm around her, but I can't keep the heaviness out of my voice.

"Is it the Wreath match?" She looks up into my face with concern.

"I guess."

Her sweet face sobers. "There's something else bothering you."

"Mhm." I continue staring at the fireflies, gently flickering in and out. Disappearing in one place, reappearing in another.

"Is it something you want to talk about?"

"I don't know." I rest my chin on my hand.

"Try, then." She reaches over and pushes a strand of hair out of my face.

"It was my fault we didn't stop the Iron City's lieutenant. So it's my fault we're not playing. And I will probably have to take the fall for it."

"I saw that moment. It wasn't your fault. There were other men who had chances."

"That's up to the captain and the stable master. They'll need someone to take the fall, and logically, I'm at the top of the list."

"What will they do?"

"Probably dismiss me. Maybe send me to a smaller city. At the very least, dock my pay."

"Oh."

I put my arm around her.

"When will you know?" she asks quietly.

"In a few days."

She rubs my arm. "You still have a bandage there," she says, her head still against my shoulder.

"It's nothing."

"You always say that."

"The day it's worse, I'll tell you."

A loud cheer breaks out from the living room.

"I always thought you should fight each team that still had a chance," Lucia murmurs. "Why fight ones that have nothing to lose?"

"It's the Guild's choice. I think they like watching a good beatdown now and again."

"So much for that."

"That's the thing about the Iron City. They're like a dog that's kicked so often it has to snarl and bite back now and again or it'll just give up and die."

"I almost feel bad for them."

I don't. I can't.

Shouts come from the living room again. Escalating. Something's happening. It's happening and I can't bring myself to care.

Lucia looks over her shoulder to the window.

A loud collective gasp.

"It's over!" Lucia's uncle exclaims in disbelief. The living room breaks into talk—earnest, excited, heated talk.

"It's the Watchdogs," Lucia says softly, to herself. "They took it from the Golden City."

I stand up.

"I think I'm going to take a walk. Go, enjoy the rest of the broadcast if you want."

She shakes her head, tearing her gaze from the window. "I'm not interested in it. I'm coming with you."

We walk down the road together, arm in arm. She's right; there are deer down by the edges of the river. They see us and turn back, stepping backwards through the brush and then crashing away.

I'm afraid. Afraid of ruining—or that I have already ruined—this beautiful shot at life. Afraid of disappointing Lucia and being nothing to her.

But it's the Games. They are unkind to imperfect men, and none of us are without weakness.

It's why people watch the Games and love them so madly. They get to see spectacles—men ruined and men raised to glory.

"I know it's not going to help much," says Lucia, twining her fingers into mine. The ring I gave her is warm against my finger. "But you shouldn't worry about something you can't change. Enjoy the evening while we have it."

I lean over and plant a kiss on top of her head. She's right. Worrying will not change what happens at final inspection.

"There. I've put it away. Let's enjoy the walk before it gets dark." I throw a glance over my shoulder at the setting sun.

She leans up and kisses my cheek.

"Don't, I'm all scruffy," I protest sheepishly, reaching up to feel my rough cheek.

"You think I care?" Her eyes are sparkling. "You're smiling now."

SEVEN
JACKSON VAN

LIEUTENANT, GOLDEN CITY TOROS

THERE'S A SCRAPE DOWN MY RIGHT SHOULDER where my uniform should have been. Fresh and hot and starting to bleed. Sand grits in my tightly tied boots. Something's wrong with my left ankle and if I take off my boot, it might not go back on.

My boys are defeated. Some openly crying, tears streaming down their dusty faces, some numb, more than a few angry.

One of them collars a gloating Coventry player and the two start slugging it out. Game keepers rush to part them.

"You're limping bad, brother," says Trey, coming up, shoulder brushing mine, to see if I need to be helped off.

"I'm all right. I'll go to the medic." I'm trying to hide it, trying to get out of the arena fast, but there's no fooling Trey.

"Come on, Jackson, let me help you."

I shake my head. "Not this time, Trey. Let me go in alone."

He gives me a troubled look but leaves me be. As I approach the gate, the spectators start jeering and booing, throwing their flags and armbands and trash at us. A wadded-up paper bag bounces off my shoulder, and Trey picks it up and launches it back at the assailant.

The way back to the preparation room and the press area is a mass of voices and flashing bulbs. A crowd of reporters spills out of the roped-off press area, pushing towards me. Their voices mix together in a frantic cacophony—I can't make out a word of it.

The stable master appears, putting himself between me and the crowd of reporters. "Jackson, you can't go out to the press until you change." He nods to my uniform.

It is torn where Lieutenant Cox cut the emblem from my chest.

"Very well."

I go to move past him, towards the door to the preparation room.

"Get your foot seen to, also. Before you go. I don't care if this year is over, you shouldn't be walking on that."

I don't answer him. It's his job, but I don't feel like being looked out for right now.

The preparation room is stony and cold. Some of the boys are just sitting on the benches, staring at the wall. In the corner, one of the chasers is stripping his gear violently.

No one is talking.

I peel off my ruined uniform and armor, unstrap my armguards, leave them all in the gear stall. Pull a fresh shirt over my head. The boots and the rest will have to wait until after the medic.

I limp down to the adjacent room where one of the chasers is coming out. He gives me a grim look and claps my shoulder. "It wasn't your fault, Van."

I acknowledge him, but I know better. This match is going to haunt me all summer.

The medic taps his table without more than a glance at me, and goes to get his bandages. "They told me I'd be seeing you. How long ago was this?"

"Half an hour, maybe?" I settle onto the table and move my ankle gingerly into place.

The medic looks at me. "Swelling?"

I nod.

"You want to save the boot?"

"If you can."

"All right. We'll do this as gently as possible."

He starts untying the tight laces, teasing the boot open bit by bit.

"Does it hurt when I do this?" He looks at me, tugs at the heel of the boot.

I nod. "But it's okay."

He reaches his fingers in, feeling around the ankle carefully. Then he pulls the boot firmly with his other hand and it's off.

"It's going to be crutches for you for a week," he says, fixing me with a stern look. "If you want to come back from this quickly, crutches."

"All right, all right." I wave him off in defeat, too numb to care this time.

"I'll wrap it and you can go talk to the press. I'll leave the crutches with your gear."

The medic is wrapping my ankle when Mark comes in, white with rage. I think what he wants to do he cannot do with the medics here, and me on their table.

I don't know what to say. Nothing will suffice to satisfy him—I know nothing will suffice for me either.

"Jackson—"

"I'm sorry, Captain."

He looks at me with dead eyes. "You'll pay," he breathes. "You did this."

He cannot be angrier at me than I am at myself, yet I think he's afraid in a way that I am not. Captains get their heads taken fast in the Games, and he's the captain of the Golden City.

Again, I don't have words.

He leaves.

"There you are," says the medic, tying off the bandage. "Let's look at that shoulder while you're here. Won't take more than a minute."

He cleans the shoulder, clears away the gritty sand and clotted blood and curled, scraped skin. He spreads ointment over the slick, raw skin and wraps it firmly.

"Don't get it wet for a day or two, if you can manage that."

"Thanks."

He gives me a grim smile. "Don't beat yourself up, kid.

There will be many more Wreath matches for a man like you."

I can't quite bear to answer him. I ease my leg off the table and leave.

The press room is a madhouse.

I take a deep breath, glance at the upturned faces once. Looking them in the eyes is too much.

Just hours ago, I'd spoken with such confidence, such hope. There will be many questions and I will answer them all. But one thing sums it all up. Everything else will be just noise.

I clear my throat.

"The blame rests with me. As lieutenant, I failed my men, and I failed the Golden City."

By the time they let me go, the preparation room has cleared. It stands silent and empty, everyone's gear gone. I can hear the distant sound of celebration from the Watchdogs.

An empty room. That's all that's left of the Golden City Toros and our glorious ambition.

That's the Games for you. You come in so full of hope, with so much joy and expectation for what could be, how this might change your life forever, and a matter of an hour or two decides it all with such finality.

My things have been packed neatly into my bag and the crutches from the medic are leaned up against the wall beside my stall. I pick up the bag and sling it over my good shoulder, then grab the crutches.

I'll use them for a few days—I'm not an idiot—but I am not walking out of here on them. I switch off the lights and head out.

The back street where the exits lead is quiet. The reveling of Coventry fans can be heard in the distance, but here, it is dreamlike. A warm wind blows through, bringing on it the smell of hot street food and automobiles.

I cannot see any automobiles from here, so I start up the street to the empty lot where I know my driver will be parked. I don't think he expected everything to clear up this quickly.

Overhead comes the scream and crackle of victory fireworks. Green and blue and red flash against the white stone walls of the buildings around me and illuminate the pavement beneath my feet. Cheers rise with the falling of the dying ash.

Another round of fireworks shoots through the air: blue, and blinding white. Coventry colors.

Red and gold. Ours.

Victory fireworks that could have been ours.

They go on and on, searing the darkness as I make my way slowly to the street over.

"Jackson!" My driver gets out and runs to my side, opens the door hastily. "I didn't know they'd let you out yet. Normally someone tells me—I am so sorry."

"It's not your fault." I wave him off and throw my bag in.

"And on your ankle too."

"It's not that bad." I hand him my crutches and climb in, careful not to put too much weight on my bad foot.

He shuts the door after me and takes the crutches up front with him.

Good riddance. I can't look at them right now.

He pulls away, out onto the main street and through the pressing crowds. The automobile is not mine, so they don't recognize me.

The crowd is mostly Coventry fans, holding up their hands in the sign of the wreath or waving wreaths hawked by street sellers, cheering as the fireworks light up the streets like lightning.

It's striking how a simple loyalty can create such a clear line between one's joy and one's devastation.

I can pick myself back up, yes, but I feel it in my bones —we will never get back what we lost today.

EIGHT
REMUS BLAKE

CHASER, BLACK TOWN STAGS

Final inspection always begins at the crack of dawn. No drills, as most of us are usually too beat up for that, but every piece of armor and battle equipment you used on the field must be laid out and accounted for.

As the captain said, you never dishonor the Games.

The morning is still dark, but lamps are lit around the sides of the arena. Atlas is over by the equipment racks, helping the phalanx count out their sabers. He's probably been here for hours.

The phalanx is laughing and ribbing each other.

"Well, next year maybe you'll actually catch one," Atlas comments over his shoulder.

"Oh!" hoots one of them, slapping another.

Atlas chuckles to himself, his back still to them.

I swing my bundle of equipment off my shoulder and pull out my practice saber. Our war sabers are kept by the city, so this is the only one I have.

I rack it next to the ones Atlas is counting. It's the only blue-handled one; I'm here earlier than the other chasers.

"Morning, Remus." He gives me a nod, a sad fondness in his eyes. I think he knows what I suspect already.

I am getting the axe and there is nothing I can do about it.

"Morning to you," I reply.

I walk the rest of my things over to the long tables that have been put up for inspection. My chest armor with the proud stag emblem of the Black Town, my arm guards, my shoulder pads, my boots.

Some of these things are my own, but it doesn't mean they're exempt from inspection. The Guild keeps a tight rein on everything.

"Are you set?" Atlas comes up beside me.

"I think so." I muster a smile.

"Chin up," he says. "Everything's going to work out."

The morning sun is in our eyes as we stand for inspection. Captain Marcellus comes out scowling, all business.

I don't think he likes inspection days. Too much to go wrong, too many ways the Guild can find fault with you and dock you something for next year.

There are inspectors from the War Games Guild and our own Black Town inspectors. Marcellus talks with the Guild inspectors and points out a couple things. Beside me, Grant takes a deep breath and lets it out softly through his nose.

Then Marcellus shakes their hands, nodding respect-fully to each, and they leave.

"All right, Stags!" he barks, stepping out in front of us. "The inspection is finished. They will write up our marks by the end of the day, but I don't see any issues. Good work."

A faint murmur of relief goes through our line.

"Now, to the unpleasant part of my job." Marcellus looks down at a paper in his hand. He doesn't seem to want to look us in the eye. "The loss to the Iron City was unacceptable. The Guild says so and we agree. It should never have happened on our watch."

He glances up at us and then back down to his paper. "Thankfully, the Guild was gracious and gave us leave to deal with it as we saw fit. Which brings me to this announcement." He clears his throat, holding up the paper to read.

I brace myself. If it's over, it's over. I just want to take this with dignity.

"Because of his failures in strategy and preparation, and the subsequent loss to our opponents, it is my unpleasant duty to announce—" He clears his throat loudly. My eyes are fixed on the arena fencing over the captain's shoulder. I can't even look him in the eye.

"To announce the removal of Atlas Bolton from the role of Weapons Master and from the Black Town Stags."

The world around me goes still and hot. I couldn't have heard right. There's no world where you could rightly blame Atlas for what happened.

A murmur breaks over the captain's words, hot and

angry. But Atlas still stands to one side, calm and unmoved. He knew. He'd known this whole time.

Our lieutenant raises his voice in protest. "Captain, whose decision was this?"

Marcellus lifts his hand to quiet the men. "Listen—I'm not finished. He will be taking the position of captain with the Iron City Wolves after the recent resignation of their captain. Please join me in wishing him well."

He thrusts his paper under his arm and begins to clap.

Slowly, reluctantly, the boys clap with him. I join in loudly, leaning into it, changing the tone. Clapping louder and harder and more insistently. Refusing to let this be a moment of shame, as it so often is.

"Speech!" I shout. Our lieutenant echoes it and the boys pick it up, chanting it.

Marcellus steps back, indicating for Atlas to step up. Atlas reluctantly comes to stand in front and waits for us to quiet down.

He clears his throat and his voice is unnaturally deep. "Boys, I regret that I have to leave you under these circumstances. I am sorry I let you down. I truly wish you nothing but the best." He pauses, struggles a moment for words, like he wants to say more. He gives up. "Goodbye, and good luck."

He gives us all a smile and a nod—though he's not quite looking us in the eyes—and turns and walks away, off the field.

"Okay, boys, that's it," Marcellus says. "Two months to do what you like, and then I expect you back for eliminations. Get going."

I stand where I am, unable to move.

"Lucky break," says Grant, roughing up my shoulder.

"Yeah." I can't muster up the energy to head back to the barracks as if nothing has happened. I had dreaded this moment for so long, bracing myself for dismissal in front of my comrades, for breaking the news to Lucia. But watching Atlas walk off the field for the last time, I wish it had been me. He hadn't said a word in his own defense.

He deserved to be a captain, but not like this, cast out and sent to the Iron City Wolves like a punishment. At the very least, he's earned the right to be treated with respect.

I stare down the field where he disappeared. It doesn't make any sense.

"You coming, Remus?" Grant pauses, his gear over his shoulder.

I hesitate. Clarity is stealing over me, thick as the morning sun. The only way Atlas Bolton could have ended up on the chopping block for this is if he'd put himself there.

He put himself there. And the captain let him do it.

"Yeah. Don't wait for me." I head the other way, after Atlas.

He's already to his automobile, his bag over his shoulder. All his things are packed up and in the back seat. He must have had them ready to go before he came out to help us set up for inspection. And still he'd laughed and talked with us boys like nothing was wrong.

"Atlas!" I shout.

He sees it's me; he sets his bag down and waits.

"What is it?" He folds his arms. "Is something wrong?"

The words and feelings that had been so present a moment ago are all tangled up now.

"What happened back there—it's so wrong. Everyone knows it. If you said the word, we'd all fight for you. You don't have to take this."

"That's the Games, Remus."

"But it wasn't your fault."

"When you decide to lead, it doesn't matter. It's your place to take responsibility for these things."

"What about Marcellus, then?"

He sighs, shaking his head. "Remus, don't do this."

"No captain ever comes back from the Wolves. Hang, no one does. You don't have to protect us like this. You don't have to protect me. I'll take the fall. It was mine to take anyway."

He glances away. I've seen this expression before; his mind's made up.

"You shouldn't worry about me. I want to go to the Iron City."

"You do?"

"They're looking for hope, and I think I can give it."

I see it, plain as day, in his face; he's not thinking of the Black Town anymore. Sure, he's sad to leave, but he means it. He wants to go.

"You deserved better for what you gave us," I offer lamely.

"I don't need to tell a fighter in the Games that life

isn't fair. But don't think of me. Go, hold your head up. You deserve to be here." He picks up his bag and tosses it onto the passenger seat.

"It was an honor going to war with you, Remus Blake." He offers his hand.

Numbly, I take it.

"Maybe I'll see you across the arena one day," he says.

I hang on to his hand a second longer. "Would there be room at the Iron City for me?" I don't know where the words came from, but I know suddenly that this is what I want. Win, lose, or draw.

He stops. A hard silence follows, stretches longer than it should. He glances away.

"What?" His voice comes out deeper than normal.

"Let me come with you."

"Remus, I—"

"I want to be there. I want to do it with you. When you get to the Iron City, ask for my transfer. You know they'll give it."

"Are you sure it's what you want to do?"

"I'll follow you anywhere, Atlas."

Something in his face relents. "Then I'll see you in the Iron City." He thumps my shoulder affectionately and gets into the car.

I watch him drive away, expecting regret to steal over me. It doesn't. All I feel is triumph.

NINE
JACKSON VAN

LIEUTENANT, GOLDEN CITY TOROS

The barracks are still and silent when I arrive at half past four by the clock against the wall. They've been scrubbed out in preparation for final review and, in a few weeks, the Conscriptio. When I was a conscriptee living the barracks, I'd get up before the others and study, or start drills. Since then, I've made a habit of being at the headquarters before dawn. Something about having the empty place to myself helps me think.

My gear is laid out; I know better than to leave preparation to the last minute. I've cleaned it and the weapons master's assistants have done their best to repair it. The slash on the right shoulder is still visible, a painful reminder of the failed Wreath match.

I haven't seen Mark since then, and I'm dreading seeing him today.

The door opens and the stable master comes in. "What are you doing in here?"

"Getting ready."

"Didn't you hear the news?"

"No."

"Final review has been put off a day. I guess you got in too soon."

"Huh." It's never delayed.

I take down my notebook from my gear stall and sit back. Strategies have to be gone over and studied, final review or no.

Some time later, Jorge, one of our couriers, wanders through the room.

"Hey, Jorge, would you mind tossing me one of those strategy volumes?" I gesture to the shelf behind him.

He looks at me strangely and keeps walking.

"Jorge?" Something's not right.

I set down my notebook and follow him out into the hall.

Trace and one of the chasers are talking just outside the door in quiet, grim tones.

"Do you guys know what's wrong with Jorge?"

The chaser looks at me, tears in his eyes. "Traitor," he spits quietly.

"Are you talking to me?"

He looks at me as if I was the one saying it to him, and he walks away.

"Trace, what's going on?"

Trace looks at me, his face strangely pale. Sick, almost. He holds out a newspaper: "Breaking: Jackson Van Sold Out Team for Wreath Match."

"What? That's ridiculous. Has Mark heard?"

"Mark knows."

"Did he say anything to you?"

He looks away.

"Trace?"

"He told them. He told the Guild and the press that it was you."

The world stops, tilts a little.

"He what?" The words crack coming out.

"I'm sorry, Jackson. There was nothing I could do."

"I know he was angry. I let the team down, I admit it, but I would never sell out. He knows—I thought he knew that."

Trace shakes his head.

"Where is he?" I drop the newspaper.

"Jackson, wait—"

"Where is he?"

I stride down the hall, towards his office. The door is closed, but I try it and it's not locked. "Mark!"

He stands up quickly from his desk. I see fear in his eyes.

"Mark, what did you tell the Guild?"

He doesn't answer. His eyes harden slowly. Any sympathy I might have gotten from him, from his guilt, is slipping away behind that wall.

"What did you tell them?"

"What I had to," he says slowly. "The truth."

"It's not—" Everything is getting out of hand so quickly. I can't lose my composure too. "Mark, you can say what you want about me to my face, you can do whatever you want in the preparation room, but even you know I would never betray the boys. I'd never betray this city. This—this hurts them too."

"You should have tried harder on that field then," he says distantly, not meeting my eyes. "I can only call it like I see it."

"Like you see it? At what time did I ever put myself before the boys? What evidence do you have that I took money? I can show you every penny. I didn't take a dime that wasn't mine."

"Yeah?" He looks at me, eyebrows raised. "What about fame? A scheme to ruin my career? You don't have to sell out for money to be a traitor, with a name like yours."

I forget my own fear for a moment and lean close, hands pressed on his desk. "You keep my father out of this. I had no feud with you. It's you who dragged your old feud into this. If the newspapermen dig, they'll see which of us has motive."

Mark gives a cold smile. "It's too late. You dug your own grave with that performance at the Wreath match. You're through, Jackson Van."

He drops the damning newspaper on the desk.

It appeared, from the way Jackson Van lost all his former momentum, that something was amiss in the Wreath match—it is clear now that it was something far more sinister than previously suspected. Did he take money? Was there a private vendetta? A formal investigation may bring us answers. Until then, we can only trust that the Golden City Toros know more than we do and are taking the appropriate measures.

"Good luck keeping your father's name out of the mud," says Mark softly. "You know, you keep denying any guilt, they'll probably turn to him next."

I match his look. Tears are beyond me. This nightmare is so complete that I am fearless for a moment. "If I'm ruined, I have nothing to lose. If you go after my father, I swear, I will come for you."

Mark draws back. "Get out," he hisses.

"All right." I lick my lips and straighten.

In the doorway, I pause and look back. "Remember what I said."

He's like iron. I shut the door on him.

In the quiet of the hall, a new noise takes over. Voices raised, screaming.

I run to the front entrance, but Trace is there. "Don't." He steps in front of me. "Don't go outside."

Past his shoulder I see a mob through the glass of the front windows. Shouting, waving sticks and banners.

Shouting for my head.

"Get out of sight." He drags me into the nearest room, throwing a glance over his shoulder.

"What do I do?" My hands find his arms. It's all happened so fast, there's no way to undo it.

"I don't know. But don't go out there now. Wait until dark, maybe."

Dark is hours away. I'm trapped here. A new thought comes. "Will they arrest me? The Guild?" My words sound hollow in my own ears.

Trace shakes his head. "I don't know, brother."

I drop my hands, take a step back. "Look, you

shouldn't be seen with me just now. I don't know what is going to happen, and I don't want you mixed up in this."

He just nods. No protest.

"You let me know when you get home safe, then. If—" He cuts himself off. "If you can. I'm really sorry, Jackson."

He ducks quickly from the room.

TEN
REMUS BLAKE

CHASER, BLACK TOWN STAGS

LUCIA SENSES IT THE MOMENT I ARRIVE, EVEN though I always bring her flowers when I visit. I sit at her parents' kitchen table and watch as she trims the stems and puts them in water.

Looking at her, I'm not sure how I got so lucky.

"Your name wasn't on the cut or transfer list." Her back is to me as she arranges the flowers neatly in the vase. "Remus, I won't know what's on your mind unless you tell me."

"They cut Atlas."

"What for?" She turns to me, concern on her face. "If they couldn't pin it on you, they certainly have nothing to put on him."

"I know." I thumb the edge of the table. "I think he volunteered to take the blame. To protect us, protect Captain Marcellus."

"Really? He'd do that?"

"He would. He's the only man I know who would. That just makes it worse."

She comes over and pulls out the chair across from me, reaching out to take my hands in hers. "I am so sorry, Remus."

I pull one of her hands up to my lips and kiss it.

"I talked to him before he left. Briefly." I drop my eyes to the ground, rub her hand gently. Once I say this, there's no going back. "I asked him to take me to the Iron City with him. Put in a transfer request. They'll probably accept it."

Lucia tilts her head down to meet my gaze.

"But I've promised to marry you, and this is your decision too. I won't take you away from your family, to a rough city, if you don't want to go. I'll phone him, or write him and ask him not to."

"Would it hurt you if you did that? Would it hurt him?"

"Yes. Me more than him. But you're the one person I'd do it for."

"Do you believe in him?"

"Yes. More than any other man in the Games."

"Are you sure this is what you want?"

I nod.

"Then that's enough for me. I want to be with you, and I want you to be where you believe you should be." She leans forward, cupping my face in her hand and kissing my cheek. "We'll move up the wedding. I will come with you when you go."

I catch her up in my arms. She laughs, her arms around my neck.

"You're sure, Lucia?"

"Yes. Yes, Remus, I am sure."

"I'm going to take care of you, I promise."

"Of course you will." Her fingers stroke my hair. "I know that already."

ELEVEN
BLAISE VALENTINO
ASSISTANT TO THE CAPTAIN, IRON CITY WOLVES

The taxi drops me off at the front door of the Iron City headquarters. The building towers over me, heavy with history.

The place is even more decrepit than I had expected. The is architecture is old and proud, but the curved embellishments below the high windows and the pavement leading to the scarred doors are cracked. Dead grass from last fall persists in the crooked lines.

I adjust the strap on my bag and straighten my appearance in a cracked windowpane.

This is it. Though shabby, perhaps, it's a new start. A new chance.

The air crackles with possibility.

I reach for the brass handle on the large double doors. They're oak, or something similarly heavy—they creak as I pull them open.

Inside it is a little improved. The rug is new, and the

golden light is warm and homey compared to the cold, gray exterior.

An old secretary sits at a massive desk. "Good morning. Your name, sir?"

"Blaise Valentino. Assistant to the new captain."

"Valentino...." She has opened a green book and is running her finger down a list written in neat, cursive script. "Your office is on the second floor. Mr. Oliver may still be moving out. I can take you there to show you and then find you an empty room for the meantime?"

"That would be just fine."

"One moment, let me call upstairs."

She picks up her telephone and gives me that universal smile that means to wait a moment.

"Susan, Mr. Valentino has arrived. Do you know if Les is still here?" She taps her pen on the desk. "I see. No, no, that shouldn't be a problem. I will take him to room 215. Thank you."

She puts the phone down serenely. "Mr. Oliver is still packing his things. I will make you as comfortable as possible in another room until then."

"Room 215?" I offer.

"Don't worry, I will take you up myself." She stands up and motions for me to follow.

We pass an elevator, but she leads me to a wide staircase instead. The hallway of the second floor is neat and clean, but every room we pass is a mess. Papers stacked on the floor, chairs upside down on tables, velvet chairs covered in sheets.

She gestures to a large, closed door as we pass it. "This

is the captain's office." Two doors down, she pauses. "This will be your office, when Mr. Oliver has vacated it." She gives the partially open door a push.

I peer in. It is spacious enough. Good windows facing dead trees. I prefer that to the street anyway. The room itself is in disarray.

"It will look better in a couple days," she says, as if reading my mind. "Come, I'll take you to your temporary room."

We head further down the hall, around a corner.

The wall is all wide windows, giving a fine view of the practice arena below. It's a dust arena. A couple men are fighting, hand to hand.

"They're drilling now?" It's almost a month early.

"Some men do, year round. They don't have anywhere else to go. Comes out of their pay during the Games."

"Is it common?"

She shrugs. "It is here."

"Who is that?" I point to a strong-built fellow, up against a man a good head and a half taller.

"That is Phillip Blackstone. The other man is Kenneth June. Both in the doorway, if you know what I mean."

I raise my eyebrows.

"On the trash heap. They'll be gone at eliminations."

"How long have they been with the Wolves?"

"Oh, Phillip only a year. We got him from St. John's, but he's older and the flag-bearers—" She shrugs.

Flagbearers don't last long. Too many beatings.

"And Kenneth?"

"Kenneth comes in and out. I think he's been on and off the team three times already."

I pause a moment longer to watch. They're working hard, for men about to be sacked.

"This is a good view."

"The former owner enjoyed watching the men drill," she explains. "He asked for this to be put in thirty years ago, when they built the indoor arena."

"It must be quite the trick to keep these carpets clean," I chuckle.

She looks at me in surprise.

"The players are never allowed up here. Unless they've been summoned to the head office. And trust me, that's never for a good reason." My guide breezes away from the window before I can see her expression.

When we arrive at 215, she opens the door and switches on a light. "Here is your room for the time being. It is a little musty, but you can open the windows. They just dusted in here at the start of the week."

I step into the room, taking in the wide table and the single bookshelf against one wall with volumes of stratagem from forty years ago collecting dust. Beyond that, I see a wastebasket, four chairs, and nothing else.

"Can I get you something? Water? A pot of coffee?"

"A glass of water." I unbutton my cuffs and start rolling up my sleeves.

"Of course."

"And—who should I ask if I want a pot of coffee?"

"Susan is the one at the desk at the top of the stairs.

You can ask her. And for lunch, they usually bring in sandwiches from the corner shop. If that is all right?"

I nod. My mind is already racing, trying to figure out
where to start—sandwiches are inconsequential.

"Is Atl—William here?"

"Captain Bolton has been working in the west meeting
room, 203. He may be out at the moment, but we'll tell
him you've arrived."

"Thanks."

"Of course. Remember, we are here if you need
anything." She turns and walks away, leaving me in the
heavy silence of the room.

I pull the bag off my shoulder and set it down on the
table. The thud echoes in the room. I go to the windows
and pull back the shades. The sunshine is brighter than
the electric lights, so I go over and switch them off.

Much better.

I empty my bag on the table, item by item. My notebooks, my observations, my ideas. Maps of the arena and
drilling areas, a roster that was sent after Atlas hired me.

It had all been quite a surprise. I knew Atlas a little bit
in Stonington, where we worked in the same division for a
couple years. Then he had called me out of the blue, all
this time later, about coming to the Iron City to be his
assistant.

He knew my situation—I was a nobody in a crowded
room full of ambitious souls, and he knew that I might
agree to a higher position on a lesser team. I'd told him
yes, right there on the phone.

I pick up the roster and glance down the names.

Jim Danforth, Winston Heath, Sampson King, Peter Hope, Phillip Blackstone....

Some of these names I know, others are new to me. Most of us in the business don't pay much attention to who comes and goes from the Iron City Wolves.

I will learn them, though. Inside and out. If there is any advantage to be gotten, any skills yet untapped, I will find them. This might be the Iron City, but there must be some good men here—sent down by injury, perhaps, or trapped by the Conscriptio, and I am determined to make of them what I can.

I wander back out an hour later and find myself watching again from the observation windows. Two more men are drilling: a tall fellow with a red scarf on his arm and a limp, and a strong young man who looks too skilled to be on his way out.

"Mr. Valentino, can I get you anything?" It's Susan, carrying a stack of paperwork.

"Your hands look full."

"On my way back, of course. It's just—if someone leaves their room, they usually want something."

"A pot of coffee?"

"Of course, sir. Delivered to room 215?"

"That would be nice."

"Of course." She gives me a nod that's both deferential and dismissive.

"Could you—"

She turns back around, eyebrows raised.

"Who's the young man drilling down there?"

"That's—" She peers down, lips pursed. "Trenton Fitch. Vanguard."

"He doesn't look in the doorway."

"No." She shakes her head. "He's not. Dirt poor, of course, but he's strong and he's fast. Stable Master thinks he can make something of him."

"Local boy?"

"I think so."

"Interesting."

I turn and nearly run right into Les Oliver. His arms are also full of papers.

"Oh, it's you." He stops and looks me up and down.

"Blaise Valentino. Pleased to meet you."

"Yeah, I know who you are." He shifts the papers as if they're uncomfortable. "I'll be out of your hair soon. I don't want to be here any longer than I need to."

"I am not in a rush," I assure him.

"Yeah, you're not. Get out while you can is what I say, but you're young and fresh and optimistic, so I know you won't listen."

"Well, I'm going to at least try the job they're paying me for."

"That's spirit. I'm telling you though, kid, they don't let the Iron City win. They don't. They break you. Break your spirit. You won't be the same person after that."

I don't know what to say to that.

He gives a bitter chuckle and moves past me towards the elevator.

Susan has her lips pursed. "He came like that. Not that he's lying, but the Iron City didn't make him—that."

I raise my eyebrows and walk away.

The coffee is delivered piping hot and strong, with a worn mug that carries the old emblem of the Iron City Wolves.

I guess I'm not important enough to have a mug with the current emblem.

I pour my first mug and set the pot aside. The table in front of me is covered with the names, charts, and profiles of every single player.

The door bursts open.

"Blaise!" Atlas strides in and catches me in a hug, slapping my shoulder. "Brother, you are looking well."

"Thank you."

"Are you settled? Comfortable?"

"Yes—I mean, they tell me this won't be my office, but it's doing the job."

"We'll get you moved in soon. There's a lot of change happening. I've barely been here—they're keeping me tied up at the Guild with procedure. Now, can I do anything for you?"

"I think I should be asking that question of you. I figured you'd be putting me to work straight away."

"And I am." He gestures to the charts, chuckles, and then sighs. "This isn't like Stonington, you know. The Iron City is a different world."

"I am up for the challenge."

"And Valentino—" He glances around before he speaks, an odd thing since we're alone in the room. "Between you and me, be careful who you trust. At least for now."

"Sure, Atlas."

He gives me a brief smile and a slap on the shoulder. "All right. Drink that coffee before it gets cold."

TWELVE
JACKSON VAN

EX-LIEUTENANT, GOLDEN CITY TOROS

My footsteps echo in the empty halls of the Guild council building. The polished marble reflects myself back at me. Pale hair combed, face drawn, my suit too tight for my shoulders and too loose for my otherwise narrow frame.

I look away.

It's exactly how I'd expect a disgraced fighter to look and I hate it.

The main hall's open windows bring in a warm breeze and the sounds of the city outside. The emptiness of the place is odd—in the few times I've been here, it has never been empty—but it's for the best. I don't want an audience.

Through the windows I hear the quick buzz of excited voices. I pause and go over to the nearest one to see reporters shouting, walking backwards to stay in step with a tall, muscular man, bearded, white smile, arm in a sling.

Luke Sheppard, the current toast of the Empire.

I can't fault the man for being brave. I saw his impossible victory. He is the Golden City's new lieutenant, now that I'm facing the tribunal. Even though I have yet to be officially found guilty, they've moved on. They'll be rid of me even if the Guild isn't—but I know in my gut how it's going to go.

I crane my neck to get a better look. Mark's down there. Luke extricates his good arm from his wife's grasp to shake the captain's hand.

Perhaps Mark will get so caught up with Luke that he won't come to my hearing.

I pull myself away from the window and continue down the hall.

The great doors to the tribunal are closed. An attendant stands outside and looks me up and down. He knows who I am. My face has been splashed across every paper for the last two years.

It's the curse of fame and infamy—there is no place for me to hide.

"They are ready for you," he says coldly. He swings the door open.

I give him a nod of thanks.

The room is high-columned and dim. Five men sit behind a table, papers in front of them, staring at me as I cross the long room.

"Jackson Van." The first man on the tribunal looks at me over his glasses.

"Yes, sir."

"Any relation to Tristan Van?" The man beside him is shuffling papers.

"Yes sir. He's my father."

He looks at me, and I think there's some sort of sadness in his eyes. "That's what I thought. I knew your father."

"Well," says the first man, "let's get this over with, shall we?" He looks down at his paper. "Jackson Van, it is the assertion of the Golden City Toros that you betrayed this city for reasons of personal ambition and gain. This is a grave offense and one that deeply dishonors the Games. We looked into this assertion ourselves and have found what we believe to be sufficient grounds for such an assertion. Do you attest to this?"

"Officially, I have not attested to this."

"Do you today?"

I hesitate. It would be lying, and giving up the last scrap of my integrity, if I attest that I sold my team. If I refuse, they'll likely make the sentence harsher.

"I do not."

"Is there a reason for this refusal?"

"Only that the charges brought against me today are false."

"Do you deny that an anomalous sum of money was deposited to your account, the day before the match, in the amount of ninety thousand dollars?"

"Yes, sir. If it does exist, I never knew and have no idea where it came from. I say again, the charges brought against me today are false."

Eyebrows raise. "You wish to elaborate?"

"I failed my team," I begin, palms sweating, "but I would never sell them out. Look again into my accounts. I took no money. And study what you will, my conversations, my orders in the arena—I will agree to every scrutiny. Please, look again. You will not find me disloyal."

"You are aware that we are free to double the penalties if a fighter refuses to acknowledge his guilt?" The man's voice is dry. No acknowledgment of anything I said.

"Yes, sir." It is as I feared. The tribunal was always, from the beginning, going to find me guilty. I don't know if money changed hands or if my fall is the way they wish it, but it's over for me.

"With that knowledge, do you still wish to refuse?"

My reputation is already ruined. My career is gone. I may as well keep my integrity. "I do."

One of the men raises his eyebrows.

"Stubborn," I catch as one of them leans over to whisper to another.

A knock comes at the great set of doors behind me.

"Enter," calls the first councilman.

The doors swing open to admit one man, walking quickly, hands clenching and unclenching. I know his walk, his mannerisms. It's Mark.

He's tense, I can tell from the way he moves, the way his eyes dart. He's here to make sure he gets away with this, rather than to rub it in. I don't know if that's better or worse. Either way, he's going to get what he wants. These men are ready to eat out of his hand.

One of the councilmen clears his throat.

"Thank you for coming, Captain Brissinger. My understanding is that the Toros have you very busy at the moment."

"Yes. That is why I must apologize for my tardiness. But I do wish to do my duty."

"That being the case, we will see to your part in this tribunal immediately so that we do not take up any more of your time than is necessary."

"You are very kind." Mark gives them the most subservient smile I've ever seen from him.

I look away.

"Captain Brissinger, as the representative of the Golden City, do you wish to vouch or speak on behalf of your former lieutenant?"

"The Golden City does not."

"Do you have anything to add to the statement given us by the Golden City?"

Mark will not look at me. I was ready; I was going to stare him in the eyes and make him feel every second of his lies as he spoke them, but the coward won't even look at me.

"Only that our fighters and the entire city reel from this betrayal. We apologize to you that we did not honor the Games as they should be honored, and we pray you do justice as you see fit. We will not speak for Jackson Van. He is no longer one of us."

"Then, Captain Brissinger, we accept your statement and your apology, and we absolve you of all responsibility in this matter. We expect the Golden City Toros will strive in all ways to honor the Games in the future."

"We will."

"Good. You are dismissed; we have no further need of you at this time."

"Thank you, sirs."

Mark glances at me as he leaves the room. There's triumph in his eyes. In return, I give him nothing to gloat over. Not a hint of fear or regret.

As I live, that man will never have power over me again.

"That's as decided a statement as ever I've heard," murmurs one tribunal member to another.

"I've heard enough," says a third.

I don't know what they've heard. Nothing of substance has been said here. But again, they must, for the show of it, go through the motions.

The first councilman addresses me. "You will wait here at our pleasure as we deliberate."

I clasp my hands behind my back and stand still as they file out into an adjacent room.

Nothing is going to make this nightmare better or rid me of it, but I have, over the last couple weeks, been able to steel myself for this moment. The Games are the lifeblood of the Empire, and no man wants to be caught dishonoring them. I have resigned myself to face with courage whatever verdict they bring, but I hope—pray— that I am not sent to prison or to a work camp over this.

I think it would break my mother.

They don't keep me waiting long. The door opens and they file in again, solemn, to take their seats at the table.

The first councilman clears his throat and holds up a

paper that he must peer at to read. "Jackson Van, hear your sentence."

Please, no prison.

"Jackson Van, you are hereby exiled from the War Games. There will be a price set on your head of one hundred and fifty thousand dollars, should a city wish to re-conscript you before the period of ten years, and fifty thousand for the remainder of your lifetime. Your assets, as they stand, are forfeit to the Empire. In addition, you will make penance to the city by means of public confession at a date decided upon by the council."

I fight to keep my voice steady. "Yes, sir."

"Do you accept the sentence as read?"

Autonomy in the Games is an illusion. I have no choice. "Yes, sir."

"Then, Jackson Van, it is my unpleasant duty to certify your exile from the Games. Your assets are seized as of this moment. However, because of the great esteem in which your father was held, we choose to grant—unofficially, mind you—that you may return to your home and remove such things as may be needed for the immediate future. Your automobile may remain yours if you say nothing of it, either in public or private."

My mouth is dry. "The tribunal is very gracious."

The golden light of the fading sun spreads across the city, falls over the well-kept grounds of the Guild offices.

Walking out of there is a strange feeling. I am utterly desolate. Everything I love and worked for has just been stripped away. But the sun falling over the city and the scrap of integrity I have to call mine, held despite the threat of prison and the work camps, give me heart.

I am still Jackson Van. A broken man, perhaps, but still a man.

I go to Trace because night is coming and I don't know what else to do. I park the car around the block, away from the houses, and pull my collar high against the cooling night air.

He answers when I knock. "Jackson, what is going on? Come in quick, before someone sees you."

He ushers me in and shuts the door, bolting it after me.

"They've confiscated my place. They took everything but the automobile. I don't know where else to go."

Trace hesitates, moving the edge of his window curtain to peer out. "You can stay here for now."

"I'd be really grateful."

He reaches out, about to put his hand on my shoulder, and then stops. His hand falls to his side. "Come on, I'll get a couple blankets for the spare room."

THIRTEEN
REMUS BLAKE

CHASER, BLACK TOWN STAGS

I STAND AT THE FRONT OF THE CHURCH IN MY best suit. I'd bought it after I took up the Black Town colors, with my first real money.

A bead of sweat trickles out of my hair and down my neck, but I resist the urge to pull at my collar. Instead, I straighten my cuffs and take another deep breath.

My family is dressed in beautiful bright colors, and they smile. But their eyes are sad. Lucia's family—I can't look at them.

Lucia has been unwavering as the stars in the sky, and with time to think and prepare, I know I'd make the same decision over again. But it doesn't change the fact that I'm taking their daughter, sister, friend away to a faraway city where I may never compete for a Wreath again.

The door at the end of the aisle opens and there she is, chin up, standing ready. Her arm is in her father's, but her step is the one that's determined, strong.

Her eyes are locked on me.

My heart swells. It takes everything in me not to break down and cry.

I don't know how I got so lucky.

Her lips twist into a little smile, creating the tiniest dimple in her cheek. We may be in the presence of our friends and family, but this moment is for us. She's doing this for me.

She kisses her father's cheek and he kisses hers, and she thanks him softly as he puts her hands in mine.

Gently her cool fingers squeeze my warm ones. She raises her eyes to mine and they're sparkling with excitement, and full of tears.

I press my lips to her hand.

It's simple, yet I can't think of a more beautiful thing— we swear our loyalty to each other, and we are wed.

The hall is full of music and the smell of food that they're clearing away. Lucia is sitting beside me, her hand in mine, her head against my shoulder.

"Are you tired?" I ask. She's been dancing.

"Only a little. I just wanted to be with you."

I gaze at the celebration in front of me. A picture of everything I'm about to leave.

"Am I mad, Lucia? To take us to the Iron City, away from all this?"

"Not mad," she says, squeezing my hand. "But it is not an easy thing to do."

My brother Marcus comes up, grinning. "What, tired already?"

"Just talking."

"Not about the move? It's your wedding!"

I laugh, sheepishly.

"Go on, dance," he says. "Forget all that for a night. You're a groom and you're a beautiful bride, on the edge of your lives forever. Worry about those troubles when they come, not before."

We get up, laughing, and join the dance.

But I can't help it. Just for a moment, I pause, and the world slows before me. Laughter in faces, the joyful abandon of dancing, all of us together for this moment in time. It will probably never come again, all of us here at once, feeling a joy that tomorrow can't steal.

My throat thickens. It's beautiful, in a raw, fleeting way. And it strikes me that perhaps this night would not be so beautiful if it wasn't for the pain of saying goodbye.

The night after the wedding, we say our goodbyes in the half-dark just outside the golden light of her parents' doorway. My brother's automobile is running, waiting on the street. He's written *Just Married* on the back window in white paint. A sweet gesture, as our suitcases are in the back, our train tickets tucked into the side pocket of my bag.

It's not far to the station.

Lucia's mother holds her tight, tears streaming down

her face. "As soon as you get into your new home, call, won't you?"

"You'll be the first call," Lucia promises.

I shake her father's hand, and he leans in. "You take care of her, son."

"I will." I press his hand in both of mine.

"Remus?" Marcus holds up his watch.

"Lucia." I touch her shoulder. "We have to go."

She parts from her mother with one last kiss and hugs her father.

The ride to the station is silent. When we get there, Marcus helps me unload our luggage and haul it onto the platform.

"Well, I guess this is it," he says, setting down my trunk and straightening. We've put off our own goodbyes until now.

"I guess so." I meet his eyes, afraid to see tears. I've held mine back so far.

"Take care of yourself." He clasps my hand firmly and slaps my back in a hug. "We'll come up to see you soon, Katherine and I."

"I look forward to it. Call if you can, write if you can't." I give his shoulders a hard squeeze and step back.

The train whistle blows.

"Goodbye, Lucia. Keep him honest, now." Marcus laughs. "And take care of him." His voice wavers, almost breaks.

I was doing alright until now. I bend down to pick up our luggage. By the time I've straightened, I'm good again. "Give my love to everyone. We'll be just fine."

"Will do." He salutes me with a couple fingers and turns, heading off into the crowd of passengers.

There's an empty feeling in the pit of my stomach. Now it truly feels like stepping away from everything I've ever known. I'm suddenly, intensely grateful for Lucia. Without her at my side, I don't know if I would have had the strength to leave, after all.

"Two minutes," she says, looking up at the station clock. She picks up her carpet bag and puts her arm on mine—lightly, as I have two large suitcases in hand.

The train's close. She reaches the tickets in my pocket and hands them to the conductor.

"The Iron City?" He raises his eyebrows. "Not the time of year for a visit."

"It's a move," I say.

His eyebrows only go up further, and he hands the tickets back.

Inside, there's plenty of room. Even though we will have a few stops, it's clear the passenger line between here and the Iron City isn't a much-traveled one. We find our cabin and stow everything, then go to find seats.

The seating car is worn and smelling of dusty carpet. There's something homey about it, though. Makes me think of traveling with the Trial teams before the Conscriptio. How bursting with hope and optimism I'd been.

For a split second, my heart condemns me as a fool. Walking away from a respected team, however unimportant I was them, to go to a place where they'll only tread you into the dirt?

But Atlas—

"What's the matter?" Lucia looks at me with furrowed brows.

"Just thinking about the game." I lean back and stretch my long legs as far as they'll go in the narrow bench seats.

The train starts with a jerk. We watch together as the station slips past, then the automobiles coming and going from it, Marcus's car somewhere in there. Then the houses, and the banks and grocers, the busy markets—

Our hands twine together.

She sighs and leans against me. "You're worth it," she whispers.

I press my other hand against my mouth and turn my face to the window, watching the blurring buildings of my old life race past.

FOURTEEN
JACKSON VAN

I park my automobile outside the front of my childhood home, which is nearly unchanged after all these years. It's where we played, the neighbor children and I all taking turns being lieutenant and chaser, all saying we'd grow up and play in the Games.

No traces of children linger here. The flowers out front are my mother's doing, the fresh paint on the door my father's.

I am afraid to go in.

It has taken me all these weeks to get up the courage to go see my father. I haven't breathed a word about Brissinger's grudge to him; if he had any idea, it would wreck him. I've been in hiding since the tribunal, mostly because of the mobs and to protect Trey, since I've had nowhere else to go. I know my parents would have wanted me to come to them sooner, but I've already let them down. My father's name is being dragged into every newspaper, people speculating that he must have raised me wrong, talking about his legacy being tarnished—not to mention what they're saying about me.

I get out of the automobile, pocketing the keys, keeping my eyes off the neighboring houses. If they're watching, I won't give them much to look at.

I knock. From the open windows I can hear the sounds of dishes being washed. It's familiar and, oddly, makes me feel hope.

"Jackson?"

The door opens and my dad just stands there, his eyes searching my face. I must look terrible.

The words come that I haven't said to another soul. "I didn't do it, Dad."

He puts his arms around me and hugs me close.

Something breaks inside me, lets loose. I can't speak unless I want my voice to crack, and I know he knows it.

"Come inside, son." He steps back and ushers me in, shutting the door behind me.

I'm trying to hold it all in, the feeling of being back home but back as a broken failure, my life in absolute pieces. It's a jumble of relief and nostalgia and sharp pain.

"You all right, son?"

I swallow and nod, but I can't quite meet his gaze.

He sniffs and rubs the end of his nose. "Let's go to the office. Your mom's out, she'll be back by dinner."

His office is really a trophy room. Growing up, it was my favorite room in the house. The walls are lined with his accomplishments. I used to dream about putting mine up next to his.

"You should have called. I worry about you," he chides, as I take my old seat across from his armchair. "I heard you got the tribunal."

"Yeah. Where'd you hear that?"

"The newspapers."

"Don't read the newspapers, Dad."

"What can they do to an old cuss like me?" he chuckles. He's being brave.

"They exiled me."

My dad's nodding, sadly.

"And took everything of mine. And I had to address the Golden City with an apology."

"They were harsh," he says. "For a first-time offense, on scant evidence. But I've seen worse. I've seen men go to prison and I've seen men die."

A chill runs down my back. "For an offense like—like what they said I did?"

"Not quite the same," he says, staring out the window. "Not quite."

"I haven't figured out what to do with myself. I can't stand to be in the Golden City. I feel like I let these people down, even if I didn't sell them out."

"The Games aren't always kind. The ambition and rivalry they bring is often worse than the glory and the fame."

"You made it out of there," I say, remembering as the words leave my mouth that all this is because of an old rivalry.

"Yes. But things aren't always as clean as they seem. I'm glad to be out of the Games."

I nod, but I am not. I still have red blood pounding in my veins for every match, a pulse that quickens at the thought of laying out a strategy, watching your men run like the wind, the flag unfurling behind them under the lights, and the way it feels to see it planted on top of your mountain in victory. And the sudden warmth when you think of the boys, your boys, who you'd spill your blood for. The thought comes with a stab of pain.

"Jackson, take some time away. Out in the wild country, perhaps. Somewhere people won't know your face. Time covers over many things. Don't torture yourself by staying in the city while you're still in the papers."

"Were you ever part of a scandal?"

"Not quite. Rivalries, though. Plenty of those. When you're on top of the world, you will attract men who want to see you fall. The people are that way too—they love you, but they're just as happy to watch you burn. You are not human to them. You are entertainment." He sighs. "I'm sorry you had to learn that the hard way, and when you'd done nothing to deserve it."

My throat starts to close up. "If I'd played harder, if I'd tried harder—maybe then I wouldn't have deserved it," I say quietly.

"What's that?" He looks at me sharply.

The phone rings.

I stare at him until he gets up to answer it.

I can't help thinking that if we'd won, if I'd managed to pull off that match, it would have patched things up between me and Mark instead of blowing the rift wide open.

The phone stops ringing as my dad lifts it off its cradle.

"Hello? Yes. I see." He glances at me. "One moment." He sets down the receiver gently.

"Is it for me?" I ask softly.

He comes over, nodding. "It's the Iron City."

"Who?"

"Atlas Bolton."

"He's not with the Iron City."

"He is now."

I go over to the phone and pick it up off the counter. "Jackson Van speaking."

"Jackson, this is William Bolton, from the Iron City Wolves. We've been trying to find you."

"Well, they disconnected my phone."

"That's what they told us. Look, I'm not going to mince words. As you know, Luke Sheppard was recently promoted. We are in need of a lieutenant, and I would like you. I have spoken to the Guild, and they will reinstate you if we pay your penalties. There will be a few other things to take care of, but we'll walk you through those."

"I see." The blood pounds in my ears.

"But I wanted to talk to you, ask you first. I know the Guild won't give you any choice in the matter, but I will. If you don't want to fight for us, I am prepared to give you dismissal papers after the transfer is finalized."

Something isn't adding up. That's a lot of money for the Iron City to put up on a risk. Cities do not buy us fighters and then let us make our own choices, and I am certain in no position to bargain.

A few weeks ago, I might have been able to leverage my status, but Bolton knows as well as I that I do not have that power any longer.

I swallow. "You want me there?"

"Unequivocally." His answer comes immediately, firmly.

The Iron City Wolves are the laughingstock of the Games. It's almost worse than exile. But it's a chance, and right now, it's the only thing I've got.

I swallow again. My mouth is dry.

"Then, Mr. Bolton, I would be honored to fight for your city."

FIFTEEN
BLAISE VALENTINO

ASSISTANT TO THE CAPTAIN, IRON CITY WOLVES

It is raining outside. Hard, torrential rain that usually comes with early spring. I cross the room and stand at the window as it lashes the trees, tearing away all the new buds. The street below is running with water. Automobiles make their cautious way through deep puddles, plumes of water rising like wings along the running boards.

Thunder crashes, shaking the whole building.

The news from the Golden City is everywhere, bold words splashed across the morning paper in ink so fresh you can still smell it.

Tarnished Gold: The Unthinkable Betrayal of Jackson Van

I scan the pages. They rehash the failure of the Golden City. The mishandled fight. Jackson Van's failure developing from the press's initial judgment—the freeze of inexperience—to something far more sinister and twisted.

The worst thing about it is now the Wolves have been

dragged into it. Somehow, probably as part of a cruel game the Guild is playing, Jackson has been given to us. As if we weren't already the punching bag of the Empire.

In a shocking twist of events, Jackson Van will not be thrown out of the Games. He has been banished to the Iron City Wolves to replace the newest toast of the Guild, Luke Sheppard. This decision is a far more fitting punishment, in my opinion. In the Iron City he will be slowly forgotten, buried, with the dirt stomped down on him for good measure. Sometimes, a quick death is too good for a traitor.

I drop the paper. I can't read this anymore.

A knock comes at the door.

"Enter."

Not until the door opens do I turn. It's Atlas, his hair still wet from the rain.

"Did you just get here?"

"No—no, I was down at the practice arena. The indoor one flooded." He takes off his coat and shakes himself off.

"The boys practicing in this?"

"Yeah. Weather doesn't stop the Iron City. It can't." He throws his coat over the back of a nearby chair. "So you heard the news." Atlas glances at the newspaper.

"Just now. Whose decision was it?"

"It was mine. The Guild was going to throw him out, but since they are taking Sheppard up to the Golden City, I made them a proposal."

"But do we want him?"

"I want him."

"Even with—the scandal?" Jackson Van had certainly

been sought-after a couple weeks ago, but this kind of fall from grace follows a man for the rest of his life.

Atlas sets a hand on the desk and leans towards me. "Do you know the first time I ever saw Jackson Van?"

"Don't think I do."

"It was four years ago, the fall the Stags had a shot at the wreath. We were beat out by the Golden City Toros. I watched as our chasers tore his phalanx to shreds and hit him again and again. I said that they'd break this kid. He'd last minutes at most, the kind of pummeling our boys were giving. And then I watched as he picked himself up again and again, nose bleeding, armguards all but torn off, and ran his flag up his mountain. That soft kid beat us that day because he wouldn't break and he wouldn't quit."

Atlas picks up my old mug and turns it in his hand as if studying it, then sets it down, turning it a little to straighten it. "I don't know everything we're getting with Jackson Van. But I can promise you, whatever else he may be, that boy is not a coward. And I'm willing to take the chance he's not a sell-out either."

A knock comes at the door. "Come in," I call.

It's Susan. She looks straight to Atlas. "They told me you were in here, sir. The press wants to talk to you." She holds out a newspaper.

The headline declaims boldly: *Golden City – Stop Sending Us Your Trash!*

"Susan, tell them I will talk to them later this afternoon. I'm in a meeting."

"Yes, sir." She leaves, closing the door after herself.

Atlas chuckles wryly and tosses the newspaper down. I reach over and pick it up.

"We're going to have to get used to not reading the news here," he says. "The press is notoriously hard."

"I can see that." A quick glance shows they are as much against Jackson Van's coming as they are against Luke Sheppard's leaving. "When is he coming?"

"He'll be here in a few days. No sense in him staying where he is. I'd like you to come with me to the station to meet him."

"Sure." I toss the paper down on my desk with the others. "I hope it's not publicized, though. I don't want to get shot."

Atlas chuckles. "You learn fast, Valentino. But it'll be fine. It's not as bad as all that."

Jackson Van arrives on the last evening train, one of those nights on the edge of spring when the memory of deep snow hangs around in gray mountains of piled slush on the corners. He is accompanied by an armed escort, probably for his protection, and he has next to no luggage.

His coat's too thin, his face tan, his eyes tired and hollow.

Only Atlas and I are there to greet him. Us and a running automobile, waiting to spirit us away if any rowdies make an appearance. But the station is as empty as a graveyard, and the only sounds to be heard are the hiss and clank of the train and the distant, ever-present hum of the city.

"You must be William Bolton." He musters a smile, which is more of an effort than I expected from him. "I'm Jackson."

"Welcome, son," says Atlas, enveloping the young man's long hand in both his strong ones. "Glad you are here. This is Blaise Valentino, my assistant."

"Pleasure." Jackson holds out his hand.

"You must be tired," says Atlas. "It's a long way from the Golden City."

He only nods.

"I hope you don't mind we're going back to my place for the night. We'll have something set up for you soon."

He smiles, and it's a very normal, pleasant smile for someone first touted as a golden boy, then branded a traitor. "I don't need much. Four walls will do."

"It'll be a little better than that, I promise." Atlas reaches down and shoulders Jackson's luggage himself. "It's cold. Let's get out of here."

SIXTEEN
JACKSON VAN

LIEUTENANT, IRON CITY WOLVES

I DIDN'T HAVE ANY EXPECTATIONS, REALLY, OF the Iron City, or of Atlas Bolton. I'd seen him around, of course—he'd been in the Games much longer than I had. But as he drives through the city streets lined with tired workers and vagrants standing at bus stops, he points out beautiful old buildings that had once been proud, and he talks of them like they're his own.

We drive out of the downtown area to a quiet, dark neighborhood. It's not unlike the ones in the Golden City, save that these are made of brick and shingle and have dead flower gardens and patchy snow.

Atlas pulls into a driveway and shuts off the automobile. He insists on carrying what little luggage I have up the stone steps to the front door. He knocks and the door immediately opens, held by a slim lady with warm eyes.

"This is my wife, Eliza," he says, shouldering my bags and motioning me forward.

"You must be Jackson Van." She takes my hands and I realize how embarrassingly cold they are. "Welcome."

"Thank you." I don't quite know how to process this. They seem kind, but they must understand the recklessness of what they're doing. You don't take in people the Empire has thrown on the trash heap. It's asking for the same to happen to you. And I haven't done a thing for these people.

They have soup on the stove that Eliza has kept warm, and even though I've had almost no appetite for weeks, I eat a bowl at their insistence. I probably don't look well, which is not something you want to see when you've just paid a steep sum to obtain a lieutenant.

They show me to my room, which is modest but clean and welcoming. Someone—Eliza, I assume—has put flowers on the nightstand.

"It's not much, but it's what we've got," says Atlas, dropping my bags next to the bed.

"Don't hesitate to ask for anything if you need it," adds Eliza.

"Thank you," I answer automatically.

I am dazed. It doesn't feel like reality, this small room in the smoky Iron City, so far from every home I've known.

I turn to Atlas as he starts to the leave the room. "I apologize if you find this forward of me to ask in your own house, as a guest, instead of in an office or the barracks, but I have to know what you want with me."

He turns around. "What I want with you? What do you

mean?" His strong fingers tap the wood molding in the doorway.

"No one pays the kind of price the Guild set on my head and doesn't want something back."

"You're going to be our lieutenant. That's all we're asking."

"But you and I both know you could have had someone for much less. Someone who the Guild has not set themselves against. I don't know you, but I've heard that you're straightforward, honest with a man. If I am going to fight for your city, I want to know why."

Something relents in Atlas's face. He comes in, out of the doorway, and shuts the door behind him.

"You tell me this. Did they break you?"

"What?"

"The Guild. Did they break you in that tribunal?"

I can see the stony faces of the council, staring without pity. "No."

"No, they didn't. You took a harsher sentence to stand by your word. I don't think you're afraid of them."

Realization starts to dawn on me.

"Jackson, the Guild is already set against us. I'm not looking for a man who's liked. I'm looking for a man who knows how to make a stand if he needs to."

Bitterness creeps into my tone against my will. "You're not afraid I'll be corrupted?"

His eyes turn serious. "Time will tell."

SEVENTEEN
BLAISE VALENTINO

ASSISTANT TO THE CAPTAIN, IRON CITY
WOLVES

"I THOUGHT YOU WOULD HAVE LEFT ALREADY." Susan is watching me with her arms folded. I have my bag over my shoulder, all packed for Istanwick, and I am watching the rain fall in the doorway.

Tomorrow is the Conscriptio, one of the oldest traditions in the Games: new recruits are brought up and assigned by lots to the teams.

"Any minute," I answer. "Just waiting for the taxi."

"Good luck."

"Thanks." I tap my foot impatiently. Atlas has been out there two days already.

"I don't suppose you have been through a Conscriptio?" One of her eyebrows is raised.

"Not in any major capacity."

"Well, just be glad you aren't the stable master. Here sometimes you have to lock them in at night."

"In the barracks?"

She gives a little laugh. "Almost every year we have an escapee."

"But isn't that—"

"Breaking the code?" She shakes her head. "Welcome to the Iron City."

I must look shocked, because she chuckles again and walks away.

In my experience, the conscriptees are always excited to be called. But this is the Iron City, as I am learning. There are different rules here.

The taxi pulls up and I dash out through the rain.

The Conscriptio is always held in Istanwick, the empire's oldest city, in the old forum just after nightfall. Atlas and I spend the day going over every name we know of, marking the ones we want. While the lots are random, offers are sometimes raised, and trades can be made before dawn of the next day.

With that much at stake and untold amounts of money changing hands, it makes for a wild and ethically dubious night.

"Now," says Atlas as our taxi pulls up in front of the forum, "remember, you bring them straight to me if they want a trade. They'll bully us if they can, and it's easier for them if we're not together."

"I don't plan on going anywhere," I grin.

"Well, then." Atlas gives me a grim look, though his eyes are sparkling. "Let's do this."

The crowd is thickening outside the building already.

The air buzzes with suppressed fervor. It's only going to get louder as the night goes on.

Atlas signals two officers standing in front of a side door and brings out a much-folded letter from his pocket.

They take it, look it over. "William Bolton?"

"That's me. And Blaise Valentino, my assistant."

They look at me and then at the letter again. "All right, go ahead."

Atlas thanks them with a nod. One of them, an older gentleman, opens the door for us. "Prosper the Games," he says solemnly.

It is dim inside the hallway; the lights are flickering bulbs set at distant intervals. Voices echo from the end of the hallway, out of sight.

"Have you ever been here before?" I ask. Atlas is trudging up the rough floor with a determined kind of nonchalance.

"I used to fight for Istanwick. Came here every week."

"Oh."

He's never volunteered information about his past in the Games before. Though I could have looked him up in the annals, I suppose. Those are permanent and public.

Our footsteps echo loudly against the stone walls as we walk down the halls and onto the open floor.

It's lit with torches, giving it an ancient, terrible kind of gravitas. The banners of the twenty-seven cities are hung up along one line of columns, each with the emblems of their teams.

While the emblems are new, these banners are ancient, stitched and repaired carefully over the centuries to preserve them. I wonder how many men have stood just as I am standing now and stared up at them with vaulting ambition and hopes of the glory the Games could bring.

I glance up at the sky outside the forum. It's on the edge of dusk. We have less than an hour.

The captains, stable masters, and weapons masters mill about on the open forum floor. On one end is a gallery that will soon be filled with the public. On the other stand the conscriptees, all with numbers on their arms. They've been put in trials and from those trials they're numbered, ranked by skill: one all the way down to about one hundred and fifty.

Two great glass urns stand in front of the hung banners. The names of the cities are in one, and in the other, the names of the conscriptees.

I wander over to where the conscriptees stand. It reminds me too much of cattle in a holding pen, all those boys standing, milling, with numbers on their arms. But looking at their faces, many of them are excited. Talking, boasting, pointing at different banners, places they've talked to the captains of and where they want to go. It's no secret that strings are pulled behind the scenes to match the powerful cities with the men they want.

The other side of the coin are the boys who stand against the far walls or in the corners, quiet. Waiting with nerves, or perhaps with no desire to be there.

There are those that have played on the Trial teams, waiting for a chance to prove their mettle, and then there are those that are rounded up because they're strong and fit and the Guild wants them.

"Blaise Valentino!" Ray Flint, the captain of the Lichenville Orcas, is coming through the milling crowd towards me.

I put out my hand to shake his.

"Is this your first Conscriptio?" he asks.

"No, but it's the first time I've had this much skin in the game."

He smiles at me a little coldly. "Good luck."

I smile back. "Same to you."

Atlas strides over, all business. "Come on, Valentino. We'll take our places below our banner." He throws a grim look over his shoulder in the direction of Ray Flint.

Drums begin to pound.

Every captain and his entourage take their places below their city's banner. The gallery is filling with the public. The drums, pounding like a heartbeat, drown out everything.

It's all stretched out before me like a map—the cities, the boys, the crowd, the ceremony—all heady with glory. I could do this every day of my life.

The drums stop.

From behind the columns comes Everard Livingstone, the head of the Guild, followed by three Guild members and two attendants who will fill in the large board that tracks the pairings.

Livingstone waits until the loud cheers die and he steps up to the microphone.

"Tonight, we carry on the tradition of our great Empire, a tradition that has stood for hundreds of years. Think with me, for a moment, of all the great fighters that have come up from that gallery and crossed in front of these columns, beginning the greatest careers. Howard Milton, Patroclus Billings, Nathan Quinn, and I could go on. Tonight you will witness history. We will all witness history."

He turns and looks at the Guild members over his shoulder. "Let the Conscriptio commence!"

The applause is deafening.

One of the Guild members steps up into Livingstone's place. "It is my honor to draw the first names of the Conscriptio tonight. I know we have all been waiting long for this moment, so I will not delay you any further with speeches."

He reaches into the first urn. "The first city of the night is—" He pulls a paper out and smooths it. "The Leicester Bloodhounds!"

Their name is dropped into a slot above the banners by a man on a ladder.

"And to the Leicester Bloodhounds goes—" A paper is pulled from the second urn. "Number sixty-eight! Owen Moore!"

A moderate ripple of approval goes through the crowd. I don't know the kid. He's tall and lean and speaks the traditional words of acceptance with some gusto.

A second city is drawn. It's the Stonington Makos with number seventeen, Homer Addington.

This one gets more cheers. He's a strong-looking kid, probably a flag-bearer.

"Next we have—the Iron City Wolves!"

A jolt of ice goes through my veins. Atlas is still, watching the man's fingers.

"And to the Wolves goes—Liam Montgomery, number thirty-five!"

Liam gets shoved up by friendly hands that slap his back and shoulders. He's muscled, with a strong jaw and broad shoulders.

"He's a chaser," Atlas whispers.

"Have you met him?"

Atlas nods. "I like him, too."

Liam clears his throat as he steps up to the microphone. His voice is deep and quiet and touched with an accent, something from the back country. "I hear the call of my captain, and to the Iron City I swear my allegiance."

He comes over and shakes our hands respectfully, then takes his place behind us.

It takes us another twenty-eight draws before we get another one.

Chauncey Boston, number fourteen, tall and lithe, with a smile like a lightbulb. He shakes my hand harder than I think it's ever been shaken before.

He's a courier, and he looks fast.

Another four go by. A high number, two mids, and one hundred and twenty-eight.

The man pulls out the next paper and smooths it in the direction of the light.

"The Iron City Wolves!" he calls.

Something feels different about this one.

My heart is in my throat. I look to Atlas and his face is calm, but the paper in his hand has been crushed.

The second paper is drawn.

"To the Iron City Wolves goes—" He looks down at the paper again. "Number four! Colt Bridgerton!"

A large gasp rises from the crowd. Colt Bridgerton is the son of Senator Bridgerton, a native of the Iron City, but a man with his fingers in every major deal in the Empire. Someone like Colt should be going to the Toros or the Watchdogs, not to us.

The boy's tall and well-built, benefiting from good food and the best training. He comes running, his whole face alight.

He steps up to the microphone and raises a fist in the air. "I hear the call of my captain, and to the Iron City I swear my allegiance."

He comes over to our banner, shaking Atlas's hand, and then mine. "I'm Colt. Proud beyond words to fight for our city."

He accepts the armband from the attendant with our emblem on it, stands as it is tied on. Then he raises his arms in the air, like he's already won something.

The crowd continues to murmur, and there are important faces in the gallery that look grim.

"We will have to fight to keep him," murmurs Atlas behind me.

The next names are a blur. I'm suddenly aware of how many eyes are on us, on our banner, and on the boy beneath it with number four on his arm.

Atlas is all drawn-up and alert, his movements casual but the rest of him looking ready for a fight. Colt is the only one unconcerned; I glance over my shoulder and he's beaming with excitement.

Atlas warned me coming here would be tough. Looking at those faces, I think I'm about to learn just how tough.

Our name shocks me out of my thoughts.

"To the Iron City goes—number one hundred and three! Laertes San Domingo!"

A young man is thrust forward reluctantly from the throng. The flame plays against his face, iron-like, jaw clenched. His whole body is braced, eyes blazing, fists knotted at his sides. Anger and disappointment and hot shame are written across his face. But he looks like a fighter.

As he steps up to the microphone, every line of his body shouts defiance, from his squared shoulders to his lifted chin. "I hear the call of my captain, and to the Iron City I swear my allegiance."

He shakes our hands with dead eyes and goes over to stand with the others.

Our last conscriptee is a boy named Eddie, quiet and respectful. His oath can barely be heard above the noise of the crowd, even with the microphone standing on the stage in front of him.

Afterwards, we go back behind the columns where family is allowed to congratulate and say goodbye to their boys.

If the boys have family.

"Let them have time," Atlas tells me. "But do not talk to anyone from the other cities unless I'm there. We're going to have a whole wolf pack out for Colt. Maybe his father, too."

Liam is saying goodbye to his father. The man looks like a farmer. Chauncey doesn't seem to have anyone, Eddie only an older brother.

Colt is scanning the crowd for his parents, so I go to Laertes. He's got family—a brother and his parents.

"Laertes San Domingo?" I thrust out my hand. "Blaise Valentino. Honored to have you."

He eyes me with distrust, the fire still burning, and slowly extends his hand. "How long do I have?"

"A few minutes. But they'll give you more time tomorrow to pack and say goodbye."

His mother presses her hand to her mouth.

"It's all right, Mama." He turns to her with a mustered smile, the fire gone. "You don't worry about me. I'll be just fine."

She turns away from me, trying to hide the tears that are running down her face. He wraps his arms protectively around her and presses his lips to the top of her head. "Don't cry, Mama, please."

I step aside as he comforts her.

Senator Bridgerton is coming up the steps to our banner. I look around for Atlas.

"Excuse me." Colt moves past me and starts down the steps, meeting his father as the man comes up under our banner.

"You tell them that you want to go to the Golden City,

or Coventry," his father demands under his breath. "You can pick."

"Father, I'm staying."

"That's not your decision. I am letting you pick between the two. They're both prepared to make the offer."

Colt shakes his head. "I'm not changing my mind." The boys stiffens and draws himself up. There's nearly a dozen men coming over, from Coventry, the Golden City, Istanwick, others.

Atlas sees, a hard grim mask coming over him. I've seen his face plenty—this looks like war. He comes over, moving the boy to face away from the men.

"Do you want to stay?" he asks quietly.

"I do."

"Do you want me to speak to them?"

"I want to do it."

"Then I'll back you. To the hilt. Say what you need to say."

Colt draws himself up and raises his voice to be heard. "I am a fighter for the Iron City Wolves. I have been conscripted by them and I'm staying with them. You have a problem with that, you take it up with my captain during the traditional transfer period. I have nothing further to say to any of you tonight."

Atlas takes a step behind him, strong arms folded. For a moment, the air between them all—two against ten—is as tight as a bowstring. Then the men break and leave. A couple make hard eye contact, silent threats, before turning away.

Colt's mother, a pale woman in a dark blue dress, stands beneath the banner waiting for him. "I am proud of you, child, acting a man. If this is what you want?"

Colt reaches to give his mother a hug. "I'm happy, Mother. Don't worry about me."

She pulls his head down and plants a kiss on the side of it. "Darling, you'll write?"

"When I can. When they'll let me."

"I will send some things."

"Thanks, Mother." He parts himself from her and goes over to the others, Liam and Eddie and Chauncey, who are all waiting.

Laertes is still parting himself from his mother, gently, whispering reassurances. She leaves with the family, and Laertes stands, staring down at the marble floor.

"Your name is Domingo?" I ask.

"San Domingo."

"Local boy?" I nod to our banner.

"I joined the Conscriptio to get out of the Iron City, not to be trapped here."

"Ah."

"But I'll fight. You'll see."

"I'm counting on it, kid." I reach out and put my hand on his shoulder. He flinches slightly, but doesn't push it off.

EIGHTEEN
JACKSON VAN

LIEUTENANT, IRON CITY WOLVES

Across the room, my alarm clock sounds. I get up and silence it. Outside it is still dark and the air is cold and crisp. I've been in the Iron City a mere two weeks, kept away from the press, given a place of my own away from headquarters to train and build up my strength. Atlas has been out of town, and the stable master, Ed Barbara, seemed to think it best I stay away from the others.

But today, I'm going to headquarters. Atlas has come back with this year's conscriptees, and he was surprised to hear I hadn't been there yet.

Tests will begin in a couple days, and I need to learn to work with my phalanx and flag-bearers if we are to succeed.

I don't know what they think of me. Likely nothing good. But I'll prove myself.

. . .

The sun is rising as I step out into the outdoor practice arena. The air is so cold I can see my breath in the early morning light. It was never like this in the Golden City.

Press line the far edges of the arena, cameras ready, necks craned. Probably to spot me out.

The men in the arena aren't much different. Eyes follow me as I step out onto the sand. Men lean close to one another, words passing under their breath.

Let them talk about me if they want. I am beyond caring.

"Jackson—" A dark-eyed man runs up to me, holds out his hand to shake mine. "I'm Crispin Teller, Ed Barbara's assistant." He gives a nod to the stable master, who is standing on an observation deck wrapped in a coat big enough to cover an automobile.

"Nice to meet you." I take his hand.

"In light of your—situation—Mr. Barbara thought it would be helpful if I made some introductions."

"Thank you."

"Don't thank me." He looks apologetic.

He leads me up to a couple men drilling. "These are your flag-bearers, first and reserve. Sampson King, first, and Phillip Blackstone, reserve."

Sampson salutes with a couple fingers and Phillip just gives me a blank, hard stare.

"Over there are your couriers." He waves in the direction of a cluster of three men who are gathered talking. "And then there's the vanguard and the phalanx."

The men of the vanguard and phalanx stand around like a group of bulls, talking among themselves, wrapping their hands, comparing and patching up cuts and scrapes. They fall silent as we walk up.

"Boys, here's your lieutenant. Mind you're civil."

A broad-shouldered young man with a wrapped-up wrist looks at me. "I heard you got in two weeks ago, but this is the first time you've come down. What's the idea?"

"Ed Barbara's idea," I say.

The man laughs outright.

"Jackson, this is Peter Hope," Crispin says. "He is part of the phalanx."

The broad-shouldered man steps forward, squinting a little in the sun. "Pleased to meet you," he holds out a large hand. "So you're Jackson Van."

"That's right."

He looks me up and down. "You're from the Golden City, are you?"

"Yes."

He grunts.

"Is—something the matter with that?"

"Yeah, your coat's too thin. It'll never do out here. I can show you where to buy one."

I laugh in sudden relief.

Amusement creeps into his eyes and he smacks me on the shoulder. "Welcome to the Iron City." He bends down and picks up his shield. It's painted with the emblem of the Wolves, but like all the others, it's beat up and the paint is peeling. "We've been running hand-to-hands, I don't suppose you want to partake."

"Ed Barbara would like him to observe and come in behind. You should get a feel for how he moves," Crispin says, turning a spear in his hands. He's been inspecting the worn equipment with concern on his face.

One of the other men salutes him sarcastically.

"Don't shoot the messenger, boys." Crispin looks up sharply. "I'm trying to help."

"Yeah, by bringing us Ed Barbara's trash."

Crispin stiffens. "Van was the captain's choice. Respect it. They're all yours, Jackson." He sets down the spear and thrusts his hands into his coat pockets, striding away back across the arena.

"Well." Peter Hope looks at the ground, his voice quiet. "I suppose you'll want to meet the rest of the phalanx."

"I'd like to."

Clearly, whatever is going on here in the Iron City, there are more problems than mine.

Peter lets his shield fall to the ground and pulls himself together. "There's Jim Danforth, our old man—"

Jim's a tower of a man, covered in scars, with a dark tattoo on his neck. He gives me a brief nod.

"And we've got Ami Pritchard-Allen. He's the kid on the crew, but don't tell him that, he doesn't know."

"Apa," the man corrects, keeping his arms folded. "That's what they call me."

"Apa," I repeat.

"We lost our reserve for good halfway through the calendar games, so this is what we've got."

"Come on, Pete. Let's get back to it," Jim says, reaching down and picking up his shield. "Daylight's wasting."

Apa cups his hand around his mouth. "Hey, Sampson, get over here!"

From across the arena the flag-bearer picks up his head and throws a salute. He comes over at a lope, a young man wearing vanguard armor on his heels.

"You must be the new lieutenant." Sampson gives me the onceover. "Jackson, right?"

"That's right."

"Sampson." He smacks his chest. "And Trenton. Say hello, Trenton."

Trenton seems to be a man of fewer words. He just smiles good-naturedly and shakes my hand.

"We're going to drill, Ed Barbara's orders," interrupts Jim.

"Well, let's get on it." Sampson straightens and smooths out the flag so it isn't tangled.

"All right," I straighten. "Let's do a forward feint and then a right wheel." I turn to Sampson. "When you break, break to the left. We'll block it from the front."

"Understood, Lieutenant." Sampson's face is all grim business.

"Everyone clear?" I look up at the faces.

Reluctant nods. Peter Hope is looking at me, serious. Trenton springs a couple times on the balls of his feet.

"Places," I bark. It comes so naturally, I don't even think about it. "Three, two, one—shove!"

We move as one.

For a moment I forget, and the thrill of the Games comes back over me. I can exist just like this, in a world of strategy and action and watching that beautiful flag unfurl.

.   .   .

Ed Barbara strikes the gong a little after noon and tells us to break for the midday. The boys immediately pick up their equipment and head for the arena's exit.

I go to the cool-down bucket and pour a dipperful over my head. It runs cold through my hair and down my neck and sluices off me all brown with arena dust. I pour another over, then sigh and straighten.

Peter Hope is still standing there, his saber resting on one shoulder. "You fight well. It comes to you natural, like it did Luke."

I peel my gloves off and rub my wet neck. "I appreciate that."

He glances over at the backs of the rest of the phalanx, who are halfway across the arena already. "Forgive the boys if they're cold. We loved our lieutenant."

"As they should. He must have been a hero to this city."

He shakes his head. "This city's not allowed to have heroes. The moment the Guild saw he was one, they took him."

I'm not sure what to say to that.

He's looking at me like he wants to say more, maybe ask something, but he seems to think better of it and starts away across the arena.

I pick up my armguards and follow him.

NINETEEN
REMUS BLAKE

CHASER, IRON CITY WOLVES

I RACK MY SABER OUTSIDE THE ARENA WITH THE rest of them. It's worn, almost past usefulness, and the wrong kind of wood.

Everyone's putting away their equipment, heading off to go clean themselves up and eat. I peel off my armor and heave it up over the arena railing to dry. It dries better this way, and it'll be ready for the afternoon drills.

"It's new blood."

Several of the starters are standing there, watching me. A couple flagbearers, a courier, a couple chasers.

Phillip Blackstone leans on his flagstaff and looks me up and down, no attempt to disguise the fact that he's doing it. "Who are you?"

"Remus Blake. One of the new chasers."

"Where from?"

"The Black Town Stags."

"One of the captain's boys, then. Didn't he tell you he got sent here for no good reasons?"

"I was aware of the politics."

"Huh. You get kicked out too?"

"Phillip, leave him alone." One of the chasers shakes his head and walks away.

"I transferred." I know how these things go; I'm not going to let him intimidate me.

"Transferred?" Blackstone laughs out loud. The boys around him join in. "Now I know you're lying. No one transfers here unless they're dumb or they need to hide why they actually came. Now what's your excuse?"

"I came because I'd go anywhere for Atlas. Take that or leave it."

"I'll have to leave it, for now. I'll figure you out, Remus Blake."

"Have at it. I've got nothing to hide." I bend down and pick up my gear bag, slinging it over my shoulder.

"You see, Blake," continues Blackstone, nodding toward Jackson Van, who is bent down retying his boots, "that's the kind of men the Guild dumps on us. Sorry men, the kind who shouldn't be in the game. It's an insult to us Iron City boys. They say never dishonor the Games, but it don't mean nothing to them when it's us. They'll dishonor our games as much as they want."

I glance at the stable master and his assistant, standing ten feet away. If they heard, they're not saying anything.

The assistant seems to sense my eyes on him and looks my way. There's something conflicted in his eyes, and tough too. I can't read it.

"You worried about them?" Blackstone laughs again. "They don't care. Either that or they can't say nothing. You'll get used to it, if you last that long."

Blackstone pushes past me. I'm not starting a fight, not on my first day, but I don't want him thinking he can do that.

"Hey, Blackstone!" He turns, bristled up, wanting it.

"What about Luke Sheppard? He one of your sorry men?"

Blackstone stiffens like I've hit him. "He was here because the Conscriptio gods were against him. I'd have died for that man."

He walks away, over to the equipment racks, and throws the flag down.

The mess hall is busy, crammed full of damp, half-dusty men who've rinsed but not washed. I had tried to go to the showers, but they were full. I'd stuck my head under a pump outside the barracks instead.

The cooks are filling trays and handing them out. One is thrust into my hands. It's sparse—one slice of bread, a fistful of greens, and a piece of meat that wouldn't feed Lucia, let alone me.

"Is there more?" I ask one of the cooks.

"Be grateful," he snarls. "There's fresh milk and coffee down on the end. Get some of that if you're still hungry."

"Oh."

A tray jams into my back. "Keep moving, pal," says the man behind me.

I go down to the end and pour myself a cup of coffee and a glass of milk, balancing them on my tray. There's definitely room for them.

I look around at the other men getting their trays, finding seats, and I see resignation, discontent, but no surprise.

"Hey, new blood!" A man a couple tables over beckons with two fingers. "Come, sit."

It's the young chaser who'd told Phillip to leave me be. I step over the bench across from him and sit down. He's got a gentle-looking face and a sweet expression, but he's built like he could knock a man out.

He takes a bite of food. "I've heard about you. The transfer. The boys all think you're crazy."

My heart's still sinking, looking at the plate. "Maybe I am."

"Dig in," he urges, pointing to my food. "If you don't look hungry, someone's going to ask you for it."

I pick up the piece of bread and take a bite. "Is this the normal amount you get?"

He nods.

"Where's the rest of it?"

"Not enough money."

"I thought each city was supposed to maintain a minimum standard."

He lowers his voice. "On paper, this one does."

I raise my eyebrows.

He gives me a pointed look and twitches his finger in the direction of Ed Barbara, the stable master.

"He's taking it?"

"Shh." He gives me a warning look and shakes his head. "Not here."

A laugh erupts over in the food line at the expense of one of the conscriptees. It's common for them to get pranked or picked on during their first drills.

My companion's eyes flick to the commotion like he's looking for danger. His gaze comes back to me. "I'll be in preparation room." He shoves his last bite of food into his mouth and licks his fingers.

"I didn't catch your name."

He grins. "Lucius. Lucius Shanahan."

He's scrubbing his boots when I come in.

Without a word, he scoots over to make room beside him on the bench. I sit down and start untying my boots.

"No one's in here," he says under his breath. "I checked. Still, if we talk, it's undertones. It's not a subject you want to be caught discussing. You got it?"

I nod.

"It's the secret everybody knows, that the masters are pocketing the money. The Guild knows it, the keepers know it, the boys all know it."

"The Guild knows?"

"Yeah." He laughs. "They've always known."

"Why don't they do anything? This would be shut down immediately in Black Town."

"In the Black Town, in Coventry, the Golden City, that's the difference, isn't it? They're not us. The Guild has different rules for us."

"Why?"

"It's been this way since long before I came here. Maybe we don't make the Guild enough money. Maybe the city's too corrupt. Maybe there's some old wrong standing between us and those in power at the Guild."

"Does Atlas know?"

Lucius shrugs. "Haven't met the man."

He reaches over and sets his extra brush on the bench between us.

I shake my head. "Atlas isn't going to stand for that. Trust me."

"Well, he'd be the first. Even the ones that come to us with their honor intact end up playing the game. At the least it means turning a blind eye."

"But why?"

"So they don't get shot in a dark alley some night."

"No, I mean why is it not shut down, this stealing from the Games? The Games, they'd never allow this."

Lucius's eyes go dead. "I told you, it's different rules. Now take it or leave it, New Blood."

I set my boot between my knees and reach for the second brush. "So what do you boys do about it?"

"Do? What can we do? Our only real advocate just got sent up to the Golden City. I don't blame him. I told him to get out of here. We all did. We only wish we could go too."

"What he did was valiant."

"Of course it was. That's who he was." Lucius stops scrubbing. "But what I don't get, New Blood, is why you came down here. No one in their right mind chooses this."

"Because of Atlas."

"Just because of him."

"Well." I brush my nose with the back of my hand and think for a moment. "He's not like a common weapons master, or any master. He's going to be the first one to set you right and the last to take the credit. If we fail, he's the first in line to shoulder the blame. Men like him don't show up often."

"And so you came all this way?"

I nod.

"Just you? Not a girl or something?"

"My wife. She married me two weeks ago so she could come with me."

He raises his eyebrows. Starts to laugh, but it kind of dies in his throat. "Brother, I don't know who you are, but I think I want you next to me in a fight."

I grin. "Yeah?"

"Yeah." He smacks my arm and chuckles. "You're something else, New Blood."

I take a deep breath and wipe the rain out of my face. A late afternoon rainstorm blew in an hour ago, and it's settled in to stay. The arena is damp; the dust rose at first with each hard raindrop, then settled down, muted by the damp. I like drilling this way—staying cool and less dusty.

Ed Barbara is out here in a large raincoat, the hood hiding most of his face. He leans against the rails of the arena, peering through the rain at us. He's got a big old-fashioned megaphone that's gone rusty at the edges, but he's not using it.

"Get out! Out!" he shouts, waving an arm. "Who is that?"

"Eddie," says his assistant.

"Who's Eddie?"

"Eddie is one of our conscriptees."

"Huh." He plants his hands on his hips. "Eddie, you need to wheel out to the left, don't undercut that or you'll get your head knocked off by a phalanx club! And you'd deserve it too!"

Ed Barbara resumes chewing his gum fiercely.

We reset, waiting, peering into the rain for the phalanx. A brief shadow flits in the corner of my vision.

"There—over there!" I point. Lucius and Eddie run that way, one swinging out and the other cutting in. I move over a few feet and brace for the phalanx, my fingers working into the worn grip of my saber.

They come like a rush of bulls through the sheeting rain. It's hard to see whether the one behind them is flag-bearer or lieutenant.

Someone whips through the rain right towards me, and I raise my arm and hit his shoulder with a sharp shock. I'm bowled over into the dirt, but the shock registers. One bar disappears on the man's armband as he stops and circles back.

"All right. Stop! That's enough." Ed Barbara's voice comes to us through the pounding rain.

"Who was that?" demands the runner—Tom Cranston, the first vanguard.

"Me. Blake," I say, hauling myself out of the dirt. The dirt has turned to mud and is running off my arm in rivulets.

"New chaser, right?" asks Tom.

"Yeah."

"What's the idea?" asks Ed Barbara, stumping up.

"I shocked him," I say.

"Shocked him?" He repeats this like it's a surprise. "You new?"

"Yes, as a matter of fact, I am."

"Oh, you're the chaser. From where?"

"The Stags."

"Black Town, hm?" He takes a couple steps closer. He's standing too close, but I swallow my discomfort and nod. My conversation with Lucius earlier in the afternoon comes back to me. Heat creeps up my neck.

"What's it like there?"

"It's a town. Hot. Rainy sometimes, like here."

"Hm," he grunts. "How'd you like getting beat by us?"

"It's just how the Games go."

"Funny how you and Atlas come over here at the same time. Did he bring you here to spy out the arena for him? Undermine me?"

"No, sir. What would make you think that, sir?"

He raises his megaphone. "We're out of time for today, hear? Practice is over. Practice is over!"

He waits until it is clear his words have been heard. Men break from their positions, tear off gloves, head for the towels set out under the observation deck.

I start to unfasten my gloves.

"Not you, Blake." Barbara looks at me shrewdly. "You won't be going home tonight."

He goes to the wall and drags over the automaton with some effort, dropping it with a hard thump beside the first marker.

"You are going to run a hundred more pace drills, from marker one to marker three."

He crouches down beside it and starts to set the dials.

I lean down, hands on my knees, and blow the rain out of my face. He's wanting a reaction; some kind of protest or plea for explanation.

I'm not giving him that. However, he's right about not going home. It's already late, the last bus is going to leave in an hour, and it's going to take far longer than that to run a hundred.

"Can I use the telephone first?"

"What?"

"I told my wife I would be home. She'll worry."

"Let her worry!"

"Just let me use the telephone. So I can tell her I won't be home."

"Just let me?" He starts up and leans into my face, veins standing out on his neck. "Are those the words I heard coming from your lips? You play for the Wolves, you do as I say, then you make requests!"

Jackson Van steps up, wiping his muddy hands off on a towel. "It is a reasonable request. A hundred pace drills will take hours."

"And who are you? An outcast from the Golden City,

slinking here with your tail between your legs? Don't you tell me what's reasonable!"

A shadow falls over Jackson's face, but I don't think the dart landed. He only presses his lips together and looks at me. "I'll call her, Blake. Are you in the book?"

I nod.

Barbara rounds on me. "Did I say you could stand around? Get going before I add another twenty on there!"

I trudge over to marker one. The automaton is set now to count down from a hundred. I hit the lever and it begins to tick.

The first bell dings. I take off, sprinting through the wet dirt all the way down to marker three, pivot, and come straight back.

I catch my breath, eyes on the automaton, and it dings again. I run down and back. A couple men are watching, brows furrowed, but most of them have already disappeared. It's cold out here and the sun is going down. No one wants to be out in this longer than they have to, and sticking around might get them roped in.

I run again, and then again. Four down and ninety-six more to go.

The rain is turning the arena into mud. Every time I hit marker three and pivot, the ground gets more and more torn up.

The last sympathizers have retreated; the arena is empty. The daylight has nearly all faded to blue, the only light now coming from the observation deck.

I can see the wide outline of Ed Barbara watching me, hands on his hips.

But Ed Barbara won't last, not even for the satisfaction of watching me run myself to pieces. He'll want to get home out of the cold and have a hearty meal.

I wipe my nose on the back of my hand and line up again at marker one.

The automaton dings again and I sprint, double back.

Two runs later, I glance up. The observation deck is empty.

Yeah, he's gone. But it's not worth it to quit. One, I am not a quitter, even on a pointless drill assigned because the stable master has a fragile ego. Two, there are no secrets in a practice arena. If I skip out, someone would know and it would get back to him.

Eighty-two.

Jackson Van is standing beside marker one. He's still wearing his muddy practice clothes. "I called her."

"Thanks." I hit the lever on the automaton to pause it, and I clasp his hand in thanks. "I owe you."

He shrugs. "Ed Barbara is a first-class fathead."

"Don't let him hear you say that."

"Aww, I'm not scared of Barbara."

"Just wait until he makes you do something like this." I hit the lever and it starts to tick again.

Without a word, Jackson lines up beside me. The automaton dings and as I take off, Jackson goes with me.

We both make it back to marker one, panting, splattered with fresh mud.

"You don't have to stay." I eye the automaton. It's counting down, and we're only at eighty-one.

"I know."

The automaton dings again, and we're off. He sticks with me close this time.

"I mean it," I protest. "The bus is leaving soon. You won't have time to clean up."

"It's too late for the bus anyway." He puts his hands on his hips and rolls his head back. "I was going to sleep here."

Seventy-nine. Down and back.

Seventy-eight. Down and back.

Jackson Van isn't leaving.

"What, are you a glutton for punishment?" I ask.

He straightens, panting. "I don't see you complaining."

I wipe the wet hair away from my mouth and grin.

The rain lets up a bit after sixty. Somewhere beyond the buildings, thunder growls, but I don't see lightning. It must be passing closer to the mountains.

The next hour or so is a heavy blur, made of those moments where the mind has to take over the body and force it on, step after step.

Around ten, I stagger over past the automaton and retch into the grass. That's all the time I have. The automaton dings.

A few later, Jackson is sick too. I hit the lever on the automaton to give him a moment.

"No, no—" He waves me off. "I'm good. Let's get this done."

He staggers up and we run again, stumbling through the deepening mud. It is so worn by our feet now it will be unusable tomorrow.

We make it back just as the automaton dings again.

"Six," pants Jackson.

How we finish the last few, I don't know. I'm past the point where your legs and your lungs burn; I can barely think.

The automaton falls silent and its light shuts off.

I collapse to ground beside it. I'm so covered in rain and mud that it doesn't matter that the puddle is seeping through the knees of my pants or that I'm up to my wrists in a murky puddle.

"Blake—"

Jackson Van is bending over me, holding out his hand. The rain runs off him in rivers.

I grit my teeth and try to move. My legs do not want to respond.

"Come on, man, we've got to go."

I take his hand with an effort and haul myself up, almost bringing him down with me.

The observation deck lights swim a little in the blinding rain, but they're warm and we press on until they're right in front of us.

We stumble up the steps and through the door into the barracks. Jackson Van switches on the light.

It's the quietest I've ever seen the barracks. The door to the conscriptees' room is open and someone is snoring.

Jackson limps over and closes it softly.

Neither of us speak. Our clothes are so plastered to us with sweat and mud and rain we can hardly get them off. My shirt snags on my chest armor and rips. I'm too tired to do anything about it. I let the whole thing tear in half.

My fingers are too numb from the cold to undo the

straps and buckles. I limp over to Jackson, who is painstakingly undoing his boots and pulling them off with a grimace. We don't need words. Jackson unbuckles mine and then I unbuckle his.

I shower in scalding water, my frozen skin stinging, but it's worth it. The deep chill that set into my bones slowly recedes. It is by far the longest shower I've ever taken, but I don't care. Jackson takes just as long.

We take our time drying off and getting into clean clothing. I am almost too tired to move and Jackson looks the same.

He's got the towel balled up in his hands, and he's staring at the floor, dead-eyed.

"Can I ask you a question?"

He slowly drags his gaze up to meet mine.

"Why'd you stay and run the drill with me?"

"Why'd you finish it? Barbara was gone before I finished calling your wife."

"And you didn't say anything."

"Would that have changed it?"

I shake my head ruefully.

He laughs. It's a soft, gentle kind of laugh. Unassuming.

Nothing like a man who would sell his team and the Wreath for money.

"Look, the Iron Wolves are my problem now. And Ed Barbara had no right singling you out because he's got a fragile ego. That's all."

"All, but enough to run pace drills in the rain until you're sick." I reach out and push his arm with my fist.

Something warms in his face, sudden, like he wasn't expecting the gesture. "We should get the cots down," he says, getting up.

We haul them out of a storage closet. They're a little musty but they'll do. The same closet produces less musty bedding.

"Blankets, or just sheets?" I ask.

"Give me blankets. I'm from the Golden City."

I chuck them at his chest. He laughs under his breath and shakes them out over his cot.

I spread mine with a sheet and a single blanket and lower myself gingerly down.

The cot is flimsy and smells like sweat, but I don't care. I could probably sleep on a pile of logs right now. Jackson Van pads over and switches off the light. In the darkness, I hear a thud and a little curse as he runs into a bench on his way back.

That's the last I remember.

TWENTY

JACKSON VAN

LIEUTENANT, IRON CITY WOLVES

THE MORNING AIR HAS A BITE TO IT. EARLY SUN slants over the practice arena as I finish belting on my armguards and stride out onto the damp grass.

It's been two days since the drill with Remus Blake, and the side of the arena by the markers is still chewed up. We've been avoiding that spot, and that's the only thing Ed Barbara has done to acknowledge it.

The trials before elimination start this morning. The conscriptees are coming out to join the rest of us, and they are accompanied by handlers—extra crowd control and strong hands, should fights or escapes break out.

In the Golden City, we didn't have escapes. But in the Iron City it happens from time to time. It's a crime, apparently.

The young courier, Laertes San Domingo, comes out to the flag side, trailed by the other young courier, Chauncey.

They are both untested in a real arena, but they'll give

us a shot. Besides them, we have a small-bodied man, Isaac, and our new down-and-out, Winston Heath, who is coming off a bad injury.

Laertes comes over, stretching his legs out. "I saw you running those idiotic drills," he whispers, with a roguish smile.

"Did you?"

"I won't tell anyone."

"What were you doing that you saw it? I thought you guys were under lights-out."

This gives the boy pause.

"Well?"

"I drill after lights-out sometimes, if I don't get through them all before."

"You drill after our drills?"

He nods. "You can't stop me," he says, bracing his shoulders like he's ready to fight.

I chuckle. "I'm not going to stop you." I lean down and lower my voice. "I'll even help you if you like."

His eyes light up. "You mean it?"

"After Ed Barbara leaves. I'll take you around the side of the equipment shed. No one goes there."

He grins bright. "I like you, Jackson Van." I can hear the part he doesn't say: even if you were a sellout.

"All right!" shouts Ed Barbara through his megaphone. "In your places. Starters, in the box."

He comes out to us, pointing to the dirt in the general area the starting box would be in. I am not even going to try to compare it to the Golden City.

I don't like Ed Barbara. There's something off about

the man. I've worked with hot-tempered masters, egotistical masters, and ones that let public opinion run everything. He acts like a fool, to be sure, but there's something more to him than that.

With the toe of his boot, Jim Danforth begins to drag a line out in the dirt for the starting box.

"Conscriptees, on this side—" Ed Barbara points to the side opposite me. "Fitch, go over there with them."

Laertes and Chauncey cross over and Trenton Fitch follows.

"This is a pretty standard drill," says Trenton under his breath to them. "Nothing to worry about."

Ed Barbara rounds on him. "I will tell them whether this is something to worry about—it's none of your business."

Trenton takes a step aside and puts his hands behind his back. He doesn't seem bothered by the shouting.

"Did you hear me?" demands Ed Barbara.

"I heard you."

"Yes sir, I heard you."

Trenton repeats this in a tone that seems puzzled, like he's not sure why he's being scolded.

"Stable Master is on one," murmurs Peter Hope, pressing his shoulder against mine to whisper. "Don't speak to him today unless you have to. He'll take your head off."

"And you!" Ed Barbara leans into Laertes's face, shoving a thick finger into his chest. "Be prepared for the hardest drills of your life! This is the Iron City you've come to, not some comfortable post in a warm city."

"I'm from here," says Laertes stiffly.

"Don't talk back to me! Do that again and you will drill all night! All night, you understand?" He turns away, flipping through his notebook.

Trenton smiles to Laertes, unbothered, all good nature. "Don't worry about it, kid. He's just angry you're not pulling more Guild revenue. It'll pass."

"What did you say?" Ed Barbara rounds on Trenton. There's more than anger in the stable master's face now. There's fear.

Trenton swallows. "Nothing, sir."

"What did you mean by it?"

"I was telling him not to worry, that's all."

"That is not what you said." Ed Barbara's voice is cold. "Take those off." Ed Barbara points to his arms.

Slowly, Trenton unbuckles his armguards and stacks them together, setting them aside.

"Chest armor too." Trenton peels off his chest armor and sets it next to the armguards.

"Step forward onto this mark." Ed Barbara makes an x in the center of the starting box and backs up, shooing away the phalanx as he goes.

Trenton stands in the middle of the arena, half-confused, half-defiant.

"Phalanx, run a blunt head protection."

A blunt head protection is violent, meant for when the chasers are on the lieutenant and they have to defend him. It's for fully armored men, all carrying sabers.

"Do I get a saber?" asks Trenton.

"I want to see what you can do with your fists," smiles Ed Barbara. "Go ahead."

My blood goes cold. I am not sure what I can do. With a man like this, engaging often makes it worse. But that's a dangerous look in his eye. He's out for blood.

I lean over to Laertes, who is watching with an uncertain scowl starting between his brows. "Can you slip away?"

He looks at me strangely.

"Go get Atlas," I whisper, watching as the phalanx takes their places. "He needs to know this is happening."

"I don't know if they'll let me near him."

"I've no one else to ask. You're from here. I bet you know a few tricks."

I turn to look him in the eye, to convince him. He's already gone.

The phalanx has knocked Trenton down in the dirt. It wasn't even a fight. To their credit, they did it about as nicely as they could.

"Go again."

Ed Barbara circles his finger for a redo.

The same thing happens. Any attempts Trenton makes in defense are useless against the thick armor and shields of the phalanx. They swarm him in seconds and Apa just knocks him into the dirt with a quick shoulder hit.

Trenton bounds back up, but his lip's bleeding now.

"Again. Use those sabers, they're not for decoration."

Same thing. They're still not using their sabers. Trenton gets a piece of someone's uniform and hangs on a few seconds longer, then he's in the dirt again.

Again and again, they go. Each time, Trenton gets back up, but it's slower and he's got more nicks. The rest of us are stuck watching. If any of us had thought this was a normal drill, no one is thinking it now.

He's in the dirt again, panting, and reaches out an arm slowly to pick himself back up.

"Finish it," orders Ed Barbara brusquely.

The phalanx hesitates.

"What are you cowards?" demands Ed Barbara, "Use your sabers. Hit him! Shock him out!"

"He's down," protests Hope. "We've hit him enough."

"That's no excuse. You follow orders! This drill is not over until he's incapacitated."

The phalanx doesn't move. Peter Hope, who I've not seen angry before, faces the stable master with a curled lip. He throws down his saber.

"No, sir."

"Peter Hope, get out of my sight. Danforth, you're up."

"I will run any drill you ask of me," says Danforth, raising his arm and unbuckling his armguard. "But this is not a drill any longer. I won't be part of it."

Ami Pritchard-Allen follows suit. He shakes his head and slides his armguard off. "I won't use a saber on a man who's already down."

Ed Barbara is boiling. He stalks over to Ami.

"You are a fighter for the Iron City Wolves, you'll follow my orders." He smacks him across the face.

It's a reflex; the man hits him right back, knocking him flat in the sand.

The handlers rush the field and it's suddenly chaos.

The handlers are going after the phalanx, and those boys are trained to take down the best of us. They don't hold back.

Every little bit of anger that's been stewing, building under the surface breaks loose. Men are getting hit, knocked down, stepped on. Instinct tells me I need to distance myself—nothing like Jackson Van the disgraced lieutenant caught beating up his stable master in the Iron City, or whatever they'd print about this once it hit the papers.

But I'm the lieutenant. I have a responsibility to set the example.

"Stop! Stop it!" I'm wading in, shouting. I feel like Peter Hope would listen to sense, but I can't reach him. He's somewhere deep in the melee.

Someone's elbow pegs me in the neck and the next thing I'm aware of, I've fallen hard on the ground. I spring back up but a fist plows into my face, skimming my cheekbone and getting the side of my nose good.

I'm bleeding.

"Stop!" A voice roars, not my own.

It's Atlas.

"What is this?"

The place falls silent. Hands gripping the fronts of others' shirts fall to sides. Men step back from each other.

"I thought I was clear on fighting during drills."

Still silence.

"Jackson Van?" His gaze whips over to me. I'm acutely aware of the bloody nose now. "Were you fighting?"

"No, sir. Trying to break it up."

"What was it?"

"The boys, they were up against the Stable Master."

"Why?" He's angry. My answer better be fast, and good.

"He asked the phalanx to run a blunt head protection against Trenton. Just—Trenton."

Atlas's gaze snaps to Ed Barbara, who is still picking himself up off the ground, feeling his jaw. No one's reaching out to help him.

"Why?"

I hesitate. Glance at Trenton, who is standing respectfully with his hands clasped, not quite looking at me or Atlas.

"Mr. Barbara, would you like to explain?" Atlas says it softly.

"He was challenging my authority and mocking me to the conscriptees."

Immediately protest rises from the men.

"And you think that is an appropriate measure for the offense?"

Ed Barbara is dusting off his dignity. He pushes out his chest. "Mr. Bolton—"

"Captain."

"Captain Bolton, you have come from prestigious cities such as Istanwick and Black Town. This place is neither of them. The Iron City needs a rod of iron or else there will be no discipline and no progress."

"I agree that respect and discipline will be upheld. If Mr. Fitch has transgressed, rest assured, appropriate discipline will be given. But tell me truthfully, would he be in a condition to fight in the calendar games after that drill?"

Hard silence.

"That's what I thought. You will leave this practice arena this moment. Anything you can't carry, I'll have shipped, wherever you want it. But you are not stepping foot in the barracks again."

"But I'm—I'm the stable master. You can't just tell me to leave. We have protocol, contracts—"

"Did I not speak loudly enough?" Atlas's voice is calm and almost too quiet.

"It's just not done."

"Well, I am captain here. It's how I'm doing it." He reaches out and picks up the folder Ed Barbara always carries. Calmly, he drops it on the ground. Papers go everywhere. He reaches out and knocks down the automaton that had been set up for the drills. Then he goes over to the blackboard and shoves it over with a crash.

Even the boys recoil.

"You can't do this!" screams Ed Barbara, rushing him like a bull. "This is a travesty! There will be repercussions, on your head and on theirs!"

Atlas stands his ground, coolly. "I don't care if you're the head of the Guild. You should have thought before you tried to abuse my boys."

For a split second the two face each other down, clean anger against hot, purple rage. Then Ed Barbara breaks. He reaches out and knocks the rack of sabers down with a string of oaths. And he stalks away, shoving Sampson in the shoulders on his way by.

It is quiet a moment, a strange thing, with the only sound the heavy tread of Ed Barbara's receding footsteps and the curses still coming out of his mouth, fading away. Sampson's got his hands raised in protest at the parting shove.

Atlas steps out into the arena and strikes the gong so hard it almost flies off its hooks. "Practice is over!" he thunders. "Go home!"

The boys are frozen where they stand.

Atlas looks out at all of us. "Did you hear what I said? You're free. Go home. Van, Hope, and Fitch—you three report to my office as soon as you're cleaned up."

"Yes, sir," I answer loud and clear.

This seems to get through to the boys. They break and head for the racks.

Ami Pritchard-Allen lingers, coming up behind Atlas.

"Do you have something to say?" Atlas demands. His face is still like thunder.

"I'm sorry, Captain," mumbles Ami. "I hit the stable master."

Atlas's face goes blank and his eyebrows go up. Then he sniffs and squares his shoulders grimly. "That's a very serious offense, son."

"Yes, sir."

Atlas puts his hand on the man's shoulder and leans close. "It's a good thing he's not the stable master anymore."

Ami looks over at him, surprised. "I'm not—?"

"Practice is over. Get back to the barracks and clean yourself up, kid."

Not until Ami has turned to catch up with the others does Atlas turn away, and I see a smile twitching beneath his beard.

The whole place is quiet and subdued as we hang up our gear and shower. The three of us head to the headquarters in our street clothes.

Trenton's got a split lip and a big dark bruise starting on one cheekbone.

"Hope we didn't hurt you too much," says Peter in the silence of the elevator.

"Naw." Trenton touches the bruise gingerly. "This could have been from the dog pile after Apa hit Ed Barbara."

"Wish I could've done that just once," murmurs Peter. "How is your nose, Jackson?"

"I don't think it's bad. Not much swelling."

"Thank goodness. We got ourselves a good-looking golden boy, we've got to keep you that way." I look over at him quickly, but there's no trace of mocking in his face.

Atlas is waiting for us in his office, standing at the window, like he can't sit still. "Have a seat, gentlemen."

We take our seats, but it's uncomfortable sitting here while he's standing—almost pacing—by the window. It feels like I'm in school again.

"Trenton, I am going to start with you. I need you to be honest. How did that out there start?"

"I made a comment, and I did not realize that the—that Ed Barbara heard." Trenton's lacing and unlacing his fingers in his lap.

"And it was derogatory?"

"It referenced the funds—a little."

"The funds?" Atlas looks at him sharply. I look over at Trenton, and then Peter. Peter's just sitting with his brows knitted, not looking surprised.

"The funds Ed Barbara takes from the food and equipment allowances. Everyone knows that it's happening. I didn't even say it directly."

"I didn't." Atlas looks at him straight.

"Oh."

"Peter, did you know about this?"

"Yes."

"How long has it been going on?"

"Since before I came."

"Is he the only one doing it?"

Trenton glances at Peter Hope. Peter shifts in his chair.

"I need the truth. Are you worried this will put you at risk?"

"Ed Barbara was one of the biggest," ventures Peter, "but there are others. And yes, there is risk. The captains couldn't speak out because it was silence or you get jumped in some dark alley. Maybe even a bullet."

"You tell me, and I promise you, your name will not be anywhere near this matter."

Peter clears his throat. "The weapons master is in on it. The co-equipment handler, most of the armed handlers

—I don't know them all well enough to be sure—and half the assistants."

"Ed Barbara's assistant?"

"No, not Crispin. He's been against it since he was a fighter, but like the rest of us, he can't really speak out."

"Is it in the books at all?"

"I doubt it. They falsified those. The food delivery men could be in on it too, for all I know."

Atlas pulls gently at his beard. "Well, thank you for telling me." He sighs. "Go. You boys get some rest." He looks at me. "Jackson, if you could stay, please."

Peter and Trenton get up and head out, shutting the door after them.

Atlas comes over and sits across from me. The silence in the room fills it. I brace myself for whatever he is going to say.

"I heard you ran pace drills in the rain."

"Yeah, we all did."

"That's not what I mean." There's a sharp edge in his voice.

He means with Remus. I don't answer.

"It's true, isn't it?" he presses.

"Yes, it is."

"Why?"

"Well—" I'm looking for words, but none of them seem like the right answer exactly. It was just the way it happened, how Remus took the punishment and didn't complain, didn't make it worse, when it was all pettiness that shouldn't have happened in the first place.

"Ed Barbara didn't force you to do those drills. It wasn't your problem."

"With all due respect, sir—"

"Just Atlas, when we're together, please."

"Atlas," I echo. "With all due respect, it is my problem."

"Really?" He leans forward a little, raising his eyebrows. I can feel the sweat collecting on the back of my neck.

"I'm the lieutenant. I don't leave my men in those situations alone."

"What about the men who fought for you with the Toros?"

A sick feeling starts in the pit of my stomach So that's what he's thinking. I look him right back in the eye. If he wants to sift me, he can go right ahead. I'm not going anywhere. "You want to talk about that?"

"Why not?"

All right. Fine.

"I gave the Golden City everything I could. I was in part to blame for our loss. I will even say I was mostly to blame, but I took that loss. And I took it in front of everyone. The rest—I couldn't save them, but I left them their captain and their dignity. That's more than a lot of men would have left them, considering the circumstances."

"Is that so?" He looks at me quietly. There's none of the flaming passion that was on display a minute ago in the arena, none of the stern edge for sifting truth from lie. He's looking at me thoughtfully, looking at me like he knows the truth.

"That's all, kid. Get out of here before the bus leaves."

TWENTY-ONE
REMUS BLAKE

CHASER, IRON CITY WOLVES

ATLAS IS WAITING FOR US IN THE ARENA WHEN the first of us from the bus arrive at dawn. The sleeves are rolled up on his good shirt, and he's fiddling with one of the resistance targets we chasers use for our sabers.

He looks like the weapons-master Atlas I'm used to. I haven't met a captain who bothers himself with fixing equipment.

He glances up and takes the screwdriver out of his mouth. "Jackson, go get the stragglers, will you? I am running the drills today."

"Yes, sir." Jackson sets down his bag and heads into the barracks.

The sunlight is just lightening the edges of the buildings, and the air is fresh. The dirt of the arena is still damp with dew.

After yesterday, everyone is subdued. Atlas doesn't

acknowledge us further; he's looking over the top of us at the morning light starting to spread.

There's some kind of pathos in the set of his shoulders right now, in the look on his face. Like he sees something we can't, some mountain he's got to climb alone.

For a moment, I feel it again: that strength of resolve. I'm here to follow him—and to do it with him, this thing he wants to do, as much as he'll let me.

He looks down at us, at the rest of the boys coming out with Jackson, and the look disappears, neatly tucked away behind a polite, grim front.

"Men, I want you all to gather around. I have an apology to make to you."

There is a general, uneasy murmur. As much as we don't enjoy being yelled at and drilled into the ground, an apology is stranger. We fighters are never given apologies and do not expect them.

Atlas folds his arms. "I will start with this: I am sorry. Sorry that I did not step in earlier to stop this. Sorry that I did not protect you, that I took these men in power for granted while I was busy. There's no one at blame for this but me. But I promise you, I will make it right."

The men around me shift uncomfortably. The sun is coming up over the high brick buildings, starting to creep across the dirt floor of the arena. Atlas takes a step forward and a bright shaft falls across his face. He doesn't seem to notice or care.

"Right now, you have no reason to trust me. You've been lied to, you've been kicked when you're down. You've been promised food, pay, and a roof over your head, and you've had those promises broken again and again. Some of you have had your captains or one of the masters sell you out to save themselves. To a man, you boys have all seen it and experienced it. And I cannot promise that now that I am here, the hardships will stop. There are twenty-six other cities, and they are coming for our throats. But I can promise you this: I will not sell you out. Here, I will take responsibility for what happens. I will stand between you and them until you can get on your feet and fight back. I mean to earn your trust."

Warm sunlight is stealing over all of us now. Some of the men listen with folded arms, a couple whisper back and forth.

But I nod. I want Atlas to know I am for him, come what may.

"I know we don't have enough staff, enough food, our equipment is broken, and there is not enough pay," continues Atlas. "That will take time to correct. I ask that you remain patient. It will be done."

"How soon?" asks one of the men.

"As soon as I can. Food, we'll fix that first. Then the equipment."

There's a low murmur from the men. Approval and skepticism.

"Also, I've been told that you are not allowed in the headquarters without permission." Atlas raises his voice again. "That's over. As of today, my door is open to you. You want to talk, you have a need, you come find me. My receptionist has orders to let you through." He stops, looking around at us all. When his eyes fall on me, I nod again.

"Any of you who aren't suited up yet, you have ten minutes. Anyone who comes late can pack their bags. Jackson Van?" He raises his chin in a clear beckoning.

Jackson goes over to hold quiet conference with him, and half the men head back to the barracks to get ready.

The rest of us mill around and wait.

"This is a farce," says one of the men. "I don't know what this man's game is."

"He talks big," says another, "but so has every other traitor who comes in here."

I shake my head. I may be new here, but I won't take this. "Hey, you wait and see," I say. "I know Atlas. He means every word of it."

I'm shouted down.

"Wait, wait—boys, come on!" Sampson King pushes his way in. The others are still shouting at me. "Boys, may I say something?" he demands.

One of them gives him a permissive gesture.

"Boys, I been in this city a long time. You know that. Longer than most of you. And we've seen it all. Look, we don't know if he's telling the truth. But I know and you know we haven't heard anyone talk like this, not here. I say give him a chance. We got nothing else to lose right now anyway. So get out your broken sabers and that cracked armor and let's give ourselves a shot."

Finally there are nods, words of agreement.

I give Sampson a long look, acknowledgement passing

between us. He gives me a nod, then shouts out loud, "Let's get to work, boys."

TWENTY-TWO
BLAISE VALENTINO
ASSISTANT TO THE CAPTAIN, IRON CITY WOLVES

CRISPIN TELLER STANDS IN THE MIDDLE OF Atlas's office, dirt still on his boots from the arena.

"Thank you for coming up here on short notice," says Atlas. "I imagine the last twenty-four hours have been chaotic."

Crispin draws himself up, braces himself. "Sir."

"The boys tell me you are an ex-vanguard."

"I was. Played for Pompeii, Leister, and Riverton. The Wolves were my last stop on my way out."

"They tell me you did a lot of Barbara's work for him."

He keeps his eyes forward. "It was inconvenient for him to come down into the arena during games. I carried his orders down for him."

"And in drills?"

"I did what I could. I am only the assistant."

Atlas nods, chuckles a little at all the implications of

that statement. "What about his illicit orders? Did you follow those?"

Something goes still in Crispin's face. He looks down.

"I'm just interested in the truth," Atlas prompts.

"I did only what I had to. To keep the position."

"Your job's that important to you?"

"The boys are. I knew if I lost this job, Ed would just bring in a man who wouldn't think twice about following all his orders. I walked the line carefully."

"So you knew about the stealing?"

"Yes."

"Did you help?"

"No. I mean, I stole for the boys, sometimes. I'm not proud of it, but it seemed the only thing to do."

"What did you steal?"

"Food. That is, food money, but I used it only for food during the calendar games. Ed didn't pay enough attention. I got him to trust me."

"So you did it for the boys."

"Yes."

"And what would happen if I did something you didn't agree with? Would you steal from me?"

Crispin sniffs, looks at his hands and then drops them. "I don't know you well enough, personally, sir, so forgive me if I'm bold, but I don't think you're like Ed at all. He was a brutal man."

"You're saying I'm not?"

"You might be brutal, but I think you're fair. So no. Not the way he was."

Atlas just nods. "So you wouldn't steal from me?"

"It's not that simple. Not here in the Iron City. The rules are broken every day, and honor is as good as a curse. But I hope I'd never have to. I've never stolen a thing except for these boys, and only because—" He breaks off as if he's walked in on a room where he's not supposed to be.

"Go on," Atlas urges.

"Because I couldn't stand watching them beaten in the arena like that. I was sick of it." He leans forward, hand on the table. "They couldn't do their jobs on that food and with that equipment. But they couldn't get out either, and no one cared. Not just the Guild and crowds, but our masters. Our captains, sometimes. The dishonor was not theirs and they were forced to take it anyway, day after day. And I'm telling you, most people I know would have broken. Most fighters in the Games today would break. But not these boys. They're proud. They wouldn't even complain."

He's in earnest, almost to the point, I think, of forgetting his position is on the line.

"Well, Crispin," Atlas says slowly, glancing down and pulling briefly at his nose, "I called you in to tell you that I am taking over the responsibilities of stable master for the time being. I will be dismissing much of the staff that worked under him. That is standard procedure."

"I am familiar with it." Crispin braces himself calmly.

"I asked some of the boys about you. They were honest. I know you stole for them. But they speak highly of you. They say you put yourself between them and Barbara as much you could. I admire that in a person."

"Thank you, sir."

"It's not going to be easy here. I will make changes, but that may mean it gets harder before it gets better. I'll likely have to stand between these boys and some bullets for a while. And I could use men who aren't going to run when the bullets come."

"Sir?" Confusion crosses his face.

"If you can work under me, I would like you to stay."

Crispin's stony expression melts. "Sir, I'd be honored."

"Then it's settled."

Crispin steps forward, takes Atlas's hand across the table, shakes it.

"It's going to be hard work."

"I am not worried about that. These boys, they mean the world to me."

"Good. I want you to lock up the stable master's office until I can get down there. I have, unfortunately, more men to let go."

"I'll bring the key up to you when I'm done."

"Good." Atlas gets up and sees him to the door.

"Thank you again, sir," says Crispin, as he leaves. "You won't be sorry."

Atlas closes the door after him with a sigh and turns to me. "We don't have enough staff as it is, and we definitely won't once I let go the rest of the bad apples. He's one I can keep in good conscience. Thank goodness there are a couple of them."

He comes over and sits down across from me. "Look, Valentino, I'd like to ask a favor of you."

"Anything."

"Hear me out before you say that," he laughs.

"It's still the same answer."

"How would you like to be weapons master?"

The world stops. I'm almost afraid I didn't hear right. But the words are out of his mouth, so he can't take them back now. It's the next step, and sooner than I expected it.

"I'll do it." I smile, though my heart is pounding. "What's more, I'll be the best you've ever seen."

TWENTY-THREE
JACKSON VAN

LIEUTENANT, IRON CITY WOLVES

ATLAS HAS BEEN IN CHARGE OF DRILLS FOR THE past week, but today he meets us in the barracks while we're still getting ready. This is new.

"Boys, we're going to get a later start today. I want to ask you a few questions."

I set down my armguard and turn to face him. The boys follow suit, some a little slower than others. Over the last seven days, the objectors have become less bold. Atlas commands a room, whether you agree with him or not.

"Do you know who makes the best fighters?"

Atlas lets the silence stand for a long moment. His eyes are going over the faces in front of him.

"Those that don't got nothing," ventures Chauncey, one of the conscriptees.

"The ones who don't have anything to lose," adds Phillip Blackstone.

"That's right," says Atlas. "The best fighters are the desperate ones. The ones who are fighting for their lives."

"Or to the death," says Tom, the long-haired vanguard.

"All right, next one. Can anyone tell me what's the main reason an upset happens in a match?"

"Mistakes," offers Remus, his arms folded.

"Pride," Phillip says.

"Or hope," I add.

"All good answers. You've each hit on a piece of it. Upsets happen when one opponent underestimates the other. For any reason."

Atlas looks around the room like he's studying us. "One more question. In a boxing match, who lasts longer, the man who's trained in the best rings, eats well, and sleeps in a good house, or the one who's slept on the street and fought for every scrap of food?"

"If it's lasting longer, it's the man who's been hungry," says Peter.

"Why?" Atlas fires back.

"Suffering isn't a stranger to him. To the well-fed man, suffering comes a lot sooner and feels heavier."

Atlas nods, points to the man. "Well put. Boys, what do these things have in common?"

"They're us," answers Eddie, our new conscriptee, softly.

"What's that?"

"They're us." Eddie raises his voice just barely loud enough to be heard.

Eyes go to the boy—he hasn't spoken more than a dozen words since he's gotten here.

Something warms in Atlas's steely face.

"That's it, kid. We are at the bottom and we face twenty-six cities that would love to keep us there, stomp our faces in the dirt for good measure. And they probably will, for a while. But we'll show them that we've got something they don't, and that's the taste of dirt in our mouths. We don't care what we have to go through to win, and they do. That's going to be the difference."

I look around the room at the men. A few still wear open skepticism, arms folded, heads cocked back, but most of them are listening.

"We are at a disadvantage, naturally. I will give you the best shot I can at facing them. But it's not going to be easy. In order to be able to fight them and have a chance, I will be hard on you. Maybe harder than anyone's ever been. But I swear, it will all be to a purpose."

He looks at me. I nod. I don't mind hard.

"We face the Leister Bloodhounds in two weeks. That doesn't give us a lot of time. Flag-bearers, couriers, phalanx, head out with the lieutenant. Jackson, you're going to work with Valentino on the strategy. The rest of you, we are going over attack formations here, and then we'll meet in the arena in—" he pulls out his watch and checks it "—thirty minutes."

"You heard him." I clap to the starters and pick up my armguards. "Let's get out there."

I'm the first one out in the arena, except for Valentino, who stands on the other side, going through his notebook.

The man is untested as a weapons master, but he seems passionate, and down here, I've already learned to adjust expectations of what's realistic.

The next man out is Winston Heath, the reserve courier, trailed by Isaac and the two conscriptee couriers.

Winston is tall and lanky, clearly older than the others. He's got a big dark scar down one cheek.

"Weren't you a red scarf?" I ask, reaching out to clasp his arm in greeting.

"Just got cleared," he grins shyly. "Reporting for duty."

"You been in the Iron City long?"

He shakes his head. "Naw, I'm fresh from Colchester. I got shipped here after I broke my ankle. They didn't want to pay me to recover."

It's the story of many a man.

"Well, if your ankle can hold up, I'll take anything you can give me."

"Sure." His eyes warm. "Anything you want, Lieutenant."

Within the next few minutes, the rest of my group trickles out. An arena can be run many different ways within tradition, but most commonly, the lieutenant with the ones he works with the closest—phalanx, couriers, and flag-bearers.

Valentino comes striding out towards us, squinting in the bright sun. "We have a lot to work on in the next couple hours, so let's get right to it," he says. "We'll start with the *quintus* defense. Couriers, I want you in for flankers. You touch the lieutenant, it's a point for you, and we reset. Lieutenant and phalanx, my stopwatch is going up to four minutes. You have to last that long."

"Which of us will go in for flankers?" asks Laertes.

"Let's start with you and Winston."

"I'll go in for a flanker," says Phillip, his hands in his armpits, his head cocked back. "I can move quick."

"I will put you in for the next substitution."

"All right," says Valentino briskly. "In your places, the time starts in—five, four, three, two—go."

I step in behind Peter.

Time to see what we've got.

We have drilled some together before, but this is the first time I can feel the phalanx, feel them as strongly as the thick, heavy air that lies over the arena. Ami Pritchard-Allen is quick and hot—I've never seen a man his size move the way he does. It reminds me of the parade horses that are all muscle and hooves, but still move quick as lightning. Jim Danforth is more slow-moving and deliberate, but he has a knack for knowing where I am behind him, anticipating where I want to be. It's as comfortable as slipping into a hot bath. And Peter Hope, he's got an eye on me at all times, yet he never misses when a flanker roars up against him.

We're about evenly matched. I get tagged quite a bit, but we also last until four minutes multiple times.

They substitute. Chauncey and Blackstone come in.

They're both fast, in different ways. When they hit, it

hurts. The hits they take from the phalanx don't seem to stop them, Blackstone especially.

Sweat pours down our faces, and the dust we kick up sticks. I reach up and wipe the grime from my forehead with my wrist, and it just streaks down my face.

We substitute again.

Again, we dodge, move, hold our ground.

Valentino runs us again and again, his face grim, barely changing whether we lose it badly or succeed.

Finally, he wraps things up and lays out the next plan. This one is protecting a retreating flag-bearer after a steal.

It involves me less physically, because we lieutenants wear lighter armor and our hand-to-hand engagement is supposed to be limited. But I'm watching, sending orders through the couriers or giving the order for all-in, which is every man going straight to the flag-bearer's defense.

Sampson is good at handing the flag off to the couriers if he's slowing or if he's caught, but Phillip Blackstone seems to have trouble following orders. He doesn't like to let go of the flag.

I will have to keep an eye on him.

Some of the chasers begin trickling out to the arena to watch. I see Colt and Remus there, arms folded as they stand with their heads tipped back.

Valentino signals that the captain will be out momentarily.

"Atlas will be out in a minute, boys, let's get one more in," I call, clapping my hands. "We better make this quick."

Most of the men move right away, but Blackstone is taking his time.

"Come on, the captain's coming," says Chauncey, glancing over at Blackstone's slow reset.

"You mind your own business, kid. Let the adults work," he retorts.

"Hey, watch who you're talking to!"

Blackstone takes his place across from Chauncey. "You're one to talk, with that conscriptee scarf on. What do you know about the Games?"

"More than a flag-bearer that's fallen down the ranks to the Iron City."

Blackstone seizes Chauncey's collar. "Kid, I'm going to—"

"Let go of him!" demands Laertes, grabbing at Blackstone. Blackstone just pulls Chauncey further in.

"That's enough, that's enough," says Colt, reaching for Laertes's arm.

"Boys, come on," calls Remus. "We've got better things to do."

"Stay out of it, Stag!" shouts Blackstone. "I'm going to rip his head off."

Blackstone grabs a fistful of Chauncey's thick dark hair, jerking him down to his level. It's spark on tinder.

The boys rush each other and we've got a tangle of bodies and sabers and ripped uniforms getting ripped further.

I step forward to break it up, but Apa pulls me back. "Stay clean, Golden Boy," he says, shoving me behind him. "We got this."

They pile in. I think the entire group is in there except for Remus, who's pulling boys back as hard as he can.

Atlas is suddenly here, coming in at a run. "Easy, boys!" he roars. He steps into the middle of them, pulling them apart, throwing them to the ground. "Are you done? The Bloodhounds are more than capable of breaking your thick heads without you getting the job started for them. You'll hit when I say you hit. I see another one of these fights, you're leaving the arena. I don't care who you are."

There's a shocked, half-sullen silence.

"Break into your divisions and take a cooldown. There's water over there under those trees and some apples. Thank Crispin for that, I don't know where he found them."

I reach down and give Laertes a hand up. "We've got to keep the peace."

He casts a dark look in Blackstone's direction. "He can't just mouth off on you and then attack Chauncey."

"We're on the same side."

"Not yet, we aren't." He spits dirt and wipes his mouth, checking for blood. "Captain means well, but look at us, we're not a team. We're just the leftovers."

"That doesn't mean we can't work together."

"I've worked every day of the last fifteen years trying to get out of this city, away from men like these." He strips his armguards angrily.

Apa is at the water barrel, pouring himself water with the dipper. He glances at Laertes. "You got some scrap in you, Tee."

"You talking to me?" Laertes bristles.

"Sure." Apa grins. "Don't take it so personal. I don't give names to guys I don't like."

I pick out an apple and sit down underneath the closest tree, lean back with a sigh. Peter Hope settles on the ground next to me, a gesture that means nothing really, but I'm warmed. It's like he wants to be there.

It's a strange group we have here, but I am starting to like them. The clannish phalanx, the mix of young and veteran couriers and flag-bearers, the scrappy vanguards.

It's not much like the Golden City, where men were picked not just for skill but for looks, and for their ability to praise the Empire and give reporters a good turn of phrase.

I bet these men have different stories, each one.

"Any of you men got a girl?"

Apa's rinsing the dust out of his mouth, and he spits. "Yeah, I got a girl. She's back in Upton. I only got this pair of shoes because I'm sending money back to her. I'll marry her when I can."

"You got family too?" I ask.

"Yeah. Parents and two kid brothers. Send money to them too."

"Anyone else got a girl?"

"Me? No!" Laertes tosses his gloves down. "I wouldn't ask a girl to stick with me in the Iron City."

"That sounds like what a man who's married to the Games says." Winston shoves Laertes in the ribs. "I see you drilling out there after lights out."

"Yeah?" Laertes shoves him back. "What about you?"

"I'm married," laughs Winston. "My money's already all going to her."

"Isaac?"

"No, not yet," he admits sheepishly.

"Sampson? Phillip?"

They shake their heads.

"What about you, Golden Boy?" asks Danforth.

"No."

"What, no Golden City girls wanted you?"

"I was like Laertes. Married to the Games."

"Do you want a girl?" Peter's leaned back against the trunk of the tree, savoring his apple.

"One day. But I don't know of any girl who'd say yes to this, right now."

"You'd be surprised," says Tom Cranston, his eyes on the apple he is peeling with his arena knife. "Standards are low around here."

"I think we're getting some weather," comments Apa, pointing at the horizon with his apple in his hand.

It's hung low with dark blue clouds. I can already feel the breeze cooling.

"Smell like rain," grins Peter, breathing in deep.

Crispin comes over and brings up a dipper of water, first to rinse the dust out of his mouth, then to drink. You can usually tell when a man's been in the arena.

"We've got to get back to it before the weather hits," he says. "Atlas wants five more drills."

"Five?" echoes Cranston.

"The sooner we get to them, the sooner we finish."

"And if we get struck by lightning?"

"We practice in all weather," says Crispin wearily, as if reciting something he's said many times.

"All right, that's enough lounging," I say, getting up and dusting the grass off myself. "Captain's got every right to fit these in."

I reach down and tighten my chest armor again.

The wind sweeps across the arena, brushing up dust into the air. Overhead, dark clouds move across the sun and the sky grumbles.

We don't have much time at all.

"All right!" Atlas cups his hands around his mouth to be heard. "Starting positions! Like we haven't run anything!"

We reset to starting positions, which means we've lost the element of surprise. I will have to change my instructions to the couriers.

I put the flag-bearer in formation behind the chasers, with the vanguard out front. We're doing a traditional spearhead attack, which doesn't need the element of surprise.

Thunder rolls like ceremonial drums across the sky. I glance at Atlas. His face is like stone.

We're staying in.

"Hold positions!" shouts Remus Blake, leaning forward on one knee, head turning to take account of every head.

Rain rushes over the arena in sheets.

"Hold!" calls Remus again, squinting against the rain.

It's completely obscured the boys on the practice mountain, the reserves waiting to tear our formation apart.

Remus turns his head to look at me, waiting for the signal.

I nod.

"Let's go!" he shouts. They rush forward into the pounding rain and turn into nothing but shadows in the gray curtain.

"Be ready," I shout to the phalanx around me. We have a counterattack coming.

Sampson falls shoulder first into the dirt. The chasers around him are smeared in mud, hair soaked through. Remus has a dark streak across his face that continues down his shoulder. Lucius Shanahan is missing—I wonder if they took him out already.

Colt brings up the rear, loping on his long legs, his saber gripped in one hand. He throws a glance over his shoulder every few seconds.

"Get in here! Get in here!" I shout. I can see pursuit coming.

Sampson scrambles up to his feet, shoves the flag into Laertes's hands. The boy, fresh and hungry, runs to the shelter of the phalanx. They engulf him and I step out of the protection to give them freedom to move.

They fight their way up the slippery mountain, boots digging into dirt, hands grasping at the ground for any grip. One of them shoves his shoulder against Laertes's legs, pushing him up.

He reaches the top, muddy, soaked, triumphant.

Lightning flashes, illuminating him in blinding light, and thunder crashes around our ears, shaking the earth.

"All right! Get to cover, boys!" Atlas throws up his arm, signaling the end.

We dash across the open arena for the covered observation deck. The boys push and shove Laertes affectionately as we run. That was an impressive moment; the boy has no small measure of heart.

Crispin has set out towels and blankets. The frontrunners snatch up the towels like it's a competition and leave the moth-eaten blankets for the rest of us.

I hang back with the phalanx, who aren't as fast as the young couriers and chasers. The mud's caked up to their knees as they climb the steps.

"Wish we could get some sand in there," mutters Danforth. "This is getting ridiculous."

I grab a blanket and hold it out to Danforth, then offer a second to Peter. He shakes it out and drapes it over his shoulders.

We're muddy, but we don't care.

"Now that's a storm," says Cranston, settling down on the end of the bench. He's got a towel, a clean-looking one, and he rubs his long hair.

"That arena's going to be no good," sighs Peter. "Just as we were getting comfortable too."

I settle on the bench beside him. "Does it always rain at bad times in the Iron City?"

He looks at me. "Yeah, actually, it does."

"Pity. If it weren't for the lightning, we could be out there."

"One time, we were in a match and they'd called *te mortum* and we had to play through the storm. One of the men got struck. But he was lucky—it hit his shocker and wrecked it, but he was all right."

"When was that?" I hadn't heard of such a match.

"Oh, two, three years ago. They don't usually call *te mortum* though, even on us."

"I've done it once. It's hard."

"One of the meanest matches I ever fought was under *te mortum*. A man played so hard he collapsed and died later that night. But there was nothing the captain could do once it was called." Peter stares at the towel in his hands. "Lucas Hartman. You ever hear of him?"

"No."

Peter makes a regretful sound in his throat. "He was a good man. He'd nearly played out his time. Back when they gave men commissions. Left a daughter, I think."

He pulls himself out of the thought and glances away.

Across the observation deck, Crispin strikes the gong. "We're ending it," he announces. "Go shower and get dry."

We troop into the barracks, boys shouting and shaking the water from their hair, wringing it from their shirts. I follow them quietly and peel off to one side, away from the horseplay.

A hefty parcel sits beside Colt's bunk, "Fragile" and "This Way Up" stamped all over it.

"Look, someone's getting the royal treatment." Phillip

nods to the box. "Kid should tell his daddy to pay off the Guild, not send candy."

Colt walks in rubbing his head with a towel, his light hair darkened by the rain.

"Hey, rich kid, what's the deal with the special treatment?"

Colt goes to the equipment rack and puts up his saber.

"Hey, Bridgerton. I'm talking to you."

Colt stops. This time, the whole barracks go quiet.

"To me?" He hasn't seen the box, and he's surprised, like he's afraid he's done something wrong.

"You're still daddy's favorite," Blackstone chuckles, jerking his head towards the box. "You think this is a game, don't you? You are excited to wear this city's emblem and you still have no idea what it means."

Colt flushes. "Is that what you think of me? That I only love the Iron City because I don't have to suffer with it?"

He crosses the room to the box, pulling his war knife out of his boot. With it, he pries up the slats of the box and unwraps the contents.

It's food. Good food, the sort that a man can fight on. The kind of food I was accustomed to in the Golden City.

A grim look comes over the boy's face, almost sad. He stands up slowly. "I don't want it. You boys help yourselves."

He walks over to the equipment tables and starts to strip his armor.

"Hold on." I hold up my hand to the other boys beginning to circle the food and go over to Colt. His head's down, his jaw clenched.

"Don't let these boys push you around because you're a conscriptee," I say under my breath. "If you don't want it, fine. But don't be afraid to stand up for yourself."

He meets my eyes with sad, sullen blue. "No food's worth losing their respect," he says. "And it's from my mother. Father's written me off because I won't change my loyalties to another city. We had a fight about it. But they don't need to know that."

"These boys are slow to trust," I reply. "I don't think they trust me either. But you'll prove yourself. And they'll have only themselves to live with if they aren't good to you in the meantime. You go tell them, straight up and not ashamed, that you want to give them the food."

He straightens his shoulders and nods. "All right, then."

Everyone's in here now and the room's gotten loud again. "Boys!" Colt turns around and shouts. "See that box over there?" He points it out. "It's full of good food. The best in the Empire. It's for all of you."

A whoop breaks out. Blackstone is still looking at him with a dark expression, but most of the other boys just see food. Heaven knows they're starved enough not to care where it's from.

They fall on the food until Sampson comes in and shoos them off. He gets Peter and Apa to carry it off to the kitchen. But the mood isn't dampened.

It's probably the first time I've seen these boys really happy.

TWENTY-FOUR
REMUS BLAKE

CHASER, IRON CITY WOLVES

THE SUN SPILLS OUT ONTO THE OUTDOOR ARENA, falling over the lines of men standing at attention. The preparation period is over. Today is eliminations.

On the eve of the calendar games, all of us who have drilled and prepared for them line up as the final cohort is selected. Then the reserves will be chosen, and finally, the remaining men are cut.

Many times, a cut fighter may go to another city, as the names are all published to a list. But in the Iron City, it seems no one ever does. To be cut from this team is to be cut from the Games.

Atlas walks down the line, face solemn, trailed by Valentino and Crispin.

"Step out," he orders, motioning to Sampson. The man steps forward.

They move down the line and pull Winston, Laertes, Peter, Jackson.

Atlas makes it down the line to me.

He's been in the role of the hard captain this whole time, and I have answered the call, never depending on my friendship with him or our years together with the Stags.

But now his eyes are sparkling quietly, and he gives me a begrudging smile. "Step out. You're head of the chasers, Remus. You earned it." He slaps my arm and moves on.

Once they make it to the end of us, the men not pulled out—there are a few—are sent away quietly, without the usual fanfare of dismissal.

It does not make it easier for them, I am sure, but I think Atlas was, in his way, trying to protect them from embarrassment.

"Men, you have fought hard in these elimination drills. I am proud of how you have fought. I have worked you hard, but that is needed in the Games. I will not have a man step into the arena who is not prepared, mind and body. It is my honor to introduce our division leaders: for the starters, Jackson Van, forward attack, Remus Blake. Sampson King and Jim Danforth are the reserve leaders."

He pauses a moment to allow the men to acknowledge us. The claps are not as plentiful as I am used to, but the boys around Sampson and Danforth slap their backs and shake them.

I think Jackson is not who they would have chosen, save perhaps the phalanx. They seem to have become fond of him.

"We meet the Bloodhounds in battle in two days. I expect you at the station by eight o'clock tomorrow morning. Get some rest today. You've earned it."

. . .

I climb out of the automobile in front of the Bloodhounds' arena and shoulder my bag. The arena towers over us, high and white-columned.

Colt whistles. "This place is beautiful."

"I think it's among the finest in the Empire," I pull my gaze from the arena to him. "Have you been here before?"

"Once with my father to see the Games. Have you?"

"Often, with Black Town. You'll like fighting in this place."

Inside, white columns ring the sand round, and everything is plated in gold, from the emblem hanging between two pillars to the clock set at the front of the arena. And since it's an open arena, the sun slants down in the evenings and lights everything like fire.

"All right!" Crispin shouts. "No stragglers, get your bags and gather up!"

A group of guards waits to escort us in. With this being the beginning of the calendar games, everyone is in a bit of a frenzy. Crowds have gathered, though we have a while before we take the arena. They crane their necks to look at us as we are herded in by the guards.

Their looks are hungry, expectant. Hoping, knowing that their Bloodhounds will tear us apart today. The Bloodhounds are the heroes, and we are mere spectacle.

Well, we mean to give them a fight for it.

. . .

Captain, lieutenant, and weapons master all meet to go over strategies again. At some point, I'm pulled in as well.

We're going to keep it simple for the most part. Nothing that's going to so wrong that someone gets hurt. A direct attack gives us a chance to catch them unawares. Not likely, but our best chance.

A game keeper comes into the room, glances around, and sees us. "I need to speak to the captain."

Atlas peels away from our conference and goes to talk to them. There's quick, low talk. The game keeper's voice grows firmer and firmer, and Atlas's more agitated.

They part. The game keeper stands back along the wall and Atlas comes back over. His mouth is set in a hard, straight line. It's never a good thing.

"Jackson, I am afraid I have some bad news."

"Tell me." Jackson braces himself.

"The game keepers inform me that you are ineligible."

"What do you mean he's ineligible?" Valentino breaks in, his face going slowly blank.

"They've told me—just told me, mind you—that he hasn't cleared every protocol. Or the Iron City hasn't on his behalf."

"That is ridiculous," spits Valentino, "and they know it. Everything was accounted for."

"Then they're moving the standard on us. All I know is they have handlers ready to pull him out."

"It's not something we can do now? Some papers we can sign?" Jackson asks.

"No."

"What's the penalty?"

"They didn't say, but if you step into the arena without that clearance, they'll arrest you."

"Lovely." Jackson flattens his lips into a hard line. "So let's not do that." He turns to the game keeper, waving him over. "Can you explain to me what's going on?"

The game keeper shrugs. "It's orders, I'm sorry. I just know what I've been told."

"Our options are to forfeit the match before it starts or submit a substitution within the next hour." Atlas turns to Valentino. "Blaise, go get the other division leaders." He looks at me. "Remus, you're part of this decision too."

"What do I think?"

"Yes."

"If we can find a substitution, I think the boys will want to fight. Even if we don't have a chance without Jackson, at least we'll crack a few ribs."

"That's my thinking."

"But also, we don't want to use up the boys on a fight we can't win," says Valentino, coming back. "We have to think of that side of it." He's trailed by Sampson and Danforth, their faces grim.

"So they're going to arrest Jackson Van, hm?" Danforth fixes him with a grim, sharp look. I can't tell if it's aimed at Jackson personally or merely at the situation.

"I say we go on," says Sampson. "Make it as hard on them as we can."

"I like that," Atlas strokes his beard. "Show them we've got fight." He looks at Valentino. "Who do you think would be a good replacement?"

"Use Cranston," he replies, though his face shows

he's not happy with the idea. "He's done this long enough, he can at least spot the other side a little. Give us a fighting chance. We'll protect him as much as we can. Fitch is young, but he can hold down the vanguard position."

"All right, then." Atlas looks at Jackson. "Don't worry too much. They can't do the same thing twice. For now, go see if you can impart some wisdom to Tom before we send him out there."

"Yes, sir." Jackson turns and leaves. To the man's credit, he's taking this calmly.

I go back to the equipment tables and heft my armor over my head. It's a familiar sensation and there's some comfort in it. I don't know what to do with politics and the bullying of the Guild, but I know what to do with a saber and my armguards. I'll take a few hounds down with me at the very least.

Nearby, I see Lucius struggling with his chest armor.

"Don't you ever have someone help you?" I ask, setting aside my armguards.

"Sometimes." He smiles sheepishly, and it lights his whole face up.

"In the Black Town, we'd always help each other harness up. Here." I motion for him to raise his arms.

Slowly, he does. I reach in and belt it tight.

There's sweat running down his collar already. One hand clenches at his side. He's trying to hold it together.

"How's that feel?"

"Better." He musters a smile. "Thanks."

I pick up my armguards and start strapping the first

one on. Lucius lingers. "Are they—taking Lieutenant Van from us?"

I look up and meet his gaze. "For this match."

"What are we going to do?"

"Tom is going to substitute as lieutenant. Probably change a few things for simplicity. And we'll go out and do what we came here to do."

I feed my armguard strap through the buckle, pull it up to the worn notch, reach down and grab the next one.

"Have you ever been in a crush-out?" Lucius's voice is low.

"A few times."

"Bad ones?"

"Once," I admit. I try not to think of that time. Shock-outs are more common; enough hits to the right spots, enough shocks, and you're out. Crush-outs are when you still have bars, but you're beaten up so badly you can't stay on the field.

Lucius swallows, the words come quick, low and breathless. "It happens a lot with us."

He's nervous, trying to hide it. In my time with the Black Town Stags I have seen something similar a few times, where men lose their nerve after a bad hit. But this is not quite the same thing. He's a man trying to be brave when again and again he's seen nothing but the worst happen.

"Has it happened to you?"

He nods. "But lots of boys. Lots who aren't here anymore."

I look him in the eye.

"Lucius. Your shoulder is going to be against mine. I will not let that happen to you. We might get shocked out together, but I swear as long as I'm next to you, there will not be a crush-out."

"I won't let it happen to you either," he promises solemnly.

I pick up my other armguard, slide it on. "Let's make them earn it, hm?"

"Sure." Relief spreads across his face.

Outside the gong sounds for inspection. The boys stiffen, hasten their preparations. I pull my laces tight.

Enough talk. Enough practice.

It's time for war.

Tom Cranston looks like a lost man, standing out in front of the phalanx with the lieutenant's armband.

He's a veteran and has done these things countless times, yet when the lieutenant of the Bloodhounds comes out to exchange formalities, Tom is late to clasp arms and forgets to say "prosper the Games." I hear laughter in the crowd.

I can sense it already. We're going to go down and go down hard.

We take our places and Tom gives the orders—a forward thrust up the right side, angling over and collecting the flankers on the way back. It's the best shot we have.

Sampson takes his place behind Tom for his final

orders. The exchange is brief, so brief I don't think anything worthwhile could have been said.

The Bloodhounds' lieutenant raises his fist and the countdown begins. I glance at Lucius, give him a nod, and make a slight motion forward. He slaps his armbands. We're as ready as we're going to be.

Godspeed, boys.

We rush, Lucius, Colt, and I, and Sampson falls in behind us.

Across the open arena we race, dodging obstacles, leading Sampson in the straightest path we can manage. This kind of maneuver is not for subtlety, but speed.

Ahead, I can see their phalanx making ready for us.

I give my saber a quick cut and spin and let loose a shout at the top of my lungs.

We clash. Saber upon saber with teeth-rattling force. Lucius catches one man in hand-to-hand, and I start fighting my man back, opening up a gap in their shields.

Sampson darts through. Up the mountain, towards the flag.

Lucius drops to his knees with another hit, his armband going dark. He's out.

We have just enough time to lock eyes before my hands are full with his attacker. We kept our promise.

A quick glance shows me Colt is one bar away from being shocked out as well. I have two bars. Enough to give Sampson some protection on the way back, maybe, if he hurries. I don't dare look behind me to see how the phalanx and Tom are faring.

Sampson, against all odds, has the flag. He dashes past

me and I drop the phalanx member I've been holding back and run for one of the flankers.

It's too late.

They've been waiting. They converge on him like a pack of dogs.

Sampson lunges, barely getting the flag to Isaac, the courier, before he's out.

Isaac bolts, tucking the staff up against his shoulder. But there's no way the flag will make it across so much open ground without protection.

One of their chasers slams into Isaac, sending him hard into the ground. The flag falls, touching the ground.

"No!" The world seems to still. We're done.

I see no one else of ours still on the field.

And then I know it for certain. I feel it in slow motion, five pairs of hands grabbing me from all directions. I brace against the rain of hits and shocks. Fight for the principle of it, while telling my mind *It'll be over soon.*

Seven seconds by the big clock across the arena.

I'm shocked out.

I drop to my knees, fighting for breath. The Bloodhounds walk past me. None of them reach out to give me a hand up, even though there's no one else nearby.

That's okay. I can get myself up, in a minute.

The medics are running out to Isaac, who isn't getting up. The flag twitches a little from the wind that's gotten in through the open gates. Sand kicks up beside it.

Over below their Captain's stand, the Bloodhounds laugh, arms over each other's shoulders, cheering like they've won a great victory.

I shake out the pain-tinged numbness from my arms and crack my neck. I haven't been shocked out that roughly in a while.

I stand up, wipe the sand off my cheek.

Crispin meets me as he's heading out to check on Isaac. "You all right?"

"Yes. Should be."

"They really swarmed you at the end."

I nod wryly. "Yeah, it's been a while."

"Never makes it easier." He shakes his head. "Go get to the medics, have them check you anyway. You're bleeding. In a couple different places."

"Isaac?" I hesitate before I head towards the gates.

"I'll let you know when I know something." Crispin's face is grim.

I trudge up to the center of the arena, which is full of blinding light and heady cheers. Tom Cranston, long shocked out, comes back to the field to have his emblem taken.

It's just us. The last man standing and the acting lieutenant. We, the pawns in the great War Games, echo the chant: "Prosper the Games."

Atlas looks tired when he speaks to us afterwards.

"Losing well is as much an art and tradition as winning is. You boys learn to lose well, and I promise you, we will better learn to win."

He doesn't keep us. We leave for the station as soon as we are able.

. . .

On the train back to the Iron City, I hear Blackstone talking below our bunks.

"He's leading us into death," he says, his voice lowered. "And what was bad in the Iron City will be ten times worse than before."

"You keep that talk to yourself," says Sampson, and I hear the creak of his bunk through the swaying and chugging of the train. "At least we ain't starving so bad. A man's got to live with certain things."

"Yeah, and do you care about the glory of the Games? What about upholding those?"

"I uphold everything better on a full stomach, and you know that better than anyone here. You stop with that talk now, hear? I ain't gonna listen to you if you're carrying on."

It's quiet for so long that I think they must have fallen asleep. But then I hear, softly, the sound of humming. A gentle song.

It's Phillip, his arms folded like he's keeping out the world. But his eyes are sad.

TWENTY-FIVE
BLAISE VALENTINO

WEAPONS MASTER, IRON CITY WOLVES

I RAISE THE COLLAR OF MY COAT AGAINST THE cold autumn rain and thrust my hands into my pockets.

It's been raining all day in the Iron City, a cold autumn rain that lashes down like punishment. Just a few weeks ago it was hot, and the storms that came were strong and brought relief.

This is the kind of chill that gets into your bones and stays.

I pass a newspaper stand on the street with a boy huddled next to it. He starts up as I walk by, but I wave him off.

I don't need to know what the papers are saying.

The headline beside him screams that the last three matches for the Iron City have been the worst they've seen in ages, that this William Bolton is a curse sent here to bring them all down. They're just as hard on Jackson Van, who they say should never fight in the Games ever again. They claim the bad luck and lack of skill—which have always plagued this city—are a direct consequence of Jackson's involvement. Off with his head, and so on.

They don't know me well enough to come after my head yet, but it's only a matter of time.

I step into headquarters, shaking off the rain.

"Mr. Valentino, were you walking around outside?" asks Susan as I walk by her desk.

"It's not that bad," I say, not slowing down. It's not the rain she means.

But as I said, they don't know me well enough yet, by name or face.

My office is locked; I take out my key and unlock it, pushing in and switching on the light.

My table and desk are both filled with papers and charts, everything I could find to give us an advantage against the Pompeii Vipers, our last match. It didn't do us any good.

We made history. The fastest full shock-out in the last ten years.

The only real bright spot is that our conscriptee, Laertes San Domingo, is catching eyes. He's given the other side real trouble the last two matches, and he took down a famous chaser in the fight with the Vipers.

"Mr. Valentino?"

My assistant is in the doorway. It is still so strange that I have an assistant now.

"Hm?"

"You wanted the doctor's latest report on Isaac Grafton?"

"Oh, yes."

He hands over the papers and I skim through them. It is as I feared. Isaac will continue out of commission for the next few weeks. He took a nasty crack to the skull in that first game, plus a fractured wrist.

At least we have more couriers.

I glance up to make sure my assistant is still here. "Is Jackson Van here?"

"Yes, he's been down at the barracks for a couple hours now."

"Tell him I'd like to see him. If he's drilling, tell him after."

"Yes, sir."

I toss the report on Grafton and start putting away my notes from the prior match.

We have the Hudson Jackals as our next match. They're savage. Dirty fighters, dirty tactics, and a hard city that loves to play rough. Hudson is an industrial town like ours, but economically on its feet. It makes for a hard match any way you look at it.

I think the Guild is feeding us to the hard ones on purpose. They're not too happy, I think, that Jackson Van is back in the arena so quickly. If we were the sacrifices before, we're now the scapegoats as well.

I pull out the annals, the books, and the histories. If anyone can find a weakness in the Jackals, it will be me.

There's a soft step in the hallway.

Jackson Van stands in the door, one hand on the frame. "You wanted to see me?"

"Yes. Come in." I step down my pen and stand up. My

office is a horrible mess and I'm only now just aware of it. There's really nowhere for him to sit, barely anywhere to stand.

"Here, you can have my chair." I vacate it, making it the one clear place in the room.

"I can't take your chair, Blaise. I'll stand."

He reaches down and picks up a stack of annals, setting them up on the table. In his little cleared spot he stands, leaning against the wall with one hand.

There's dirt on his neck; he's tried to clean up but missed a couple spots. I can't imagine the drills are all that clean today, what with the rain.

"I didn't expect you this soon. I figured you'd be drilling."

"I'm going back. Now is as good a time as any, since I'll be down there all day."

"In the rain?"

He shrugs, but I'm not fooled. There's conviction behind the movement. "We'll never get anywhere if we don't work, and the boys can't be expected to follow someone who won't work as hard as they do."

"Right."

He sticks by his principles, I'll give him that.

"I have two issues to discuss," I begin, picking up the top sheet of my stack of endless notes. "The first being that we seem to have some communication issues in the arena. I am not sure where it is originating from, but our signals seem to be leaking to the other side. As you know, I assume, this can be either deliberate or entirely accidental. We hope for the latter."

"Of course." His face is serious. He's looking straight ahead, thinking hard.

"It could be nothing, but I think I may see a pattern. And I want your thoughts."

"What's the pattern?"

"It usually happens right after formation. I watch the other side adjust to new orders. It's happened twice."

"Well, do they have couriers in scout?" presses Jackson.

"I haven't seen that. But sometimes they're disguised."

"They can't be using oculars?"

"I haven't seen anything. Those catch light, and the keepers shut that down quickly."

Jackson nods slowly. "I will keep a sharp eye out. Perhaps someone is taking formation too quickly or motioning too soon."

"Perhaps."

"And the second issue?"

He moves on quickly. Maybe he just wants to get back to the arena. Still....

"Laertes. San Domingo. How's he shaping up? I want to use him in scout, since Isaac's out. I've been watching him, he looks good. But I need you to like him."

"I do." His answer comes quick and sure. "He's young. Fresh, a little raw, but he hasn't stepped a foot outside where I've asked, and that's a lot for a conscriptee."

"Good. That's what I was looking for. Do me a favor and don't tell anyone about this conversation. Either of them, I mean."

"No. Of course not."

I pick up my notes and straighten them. "I'll be down later this morning with some scenarios to put to the boys. I want to be prepared for the Jackals—they're rough."

"Yeah, they are a lot of things," Jackson answers wryly.

I chuckle. He should know. "All right, get out of here."

He gives me a nod and leaves, shutting the door behind him.

My smile fades.

I hadn't told him the extent of my suspicions, of course, since he's also a suspect. But the patterns aren't nothing. On the contrary, they are strong. I think one of our boys is selling us out.

TWENTY-SIX
JACKSON VAN

LIEUTENANT, IRON CITY WOLVES

I WIPE THE SWEAT AND DUST OFF MY FACE WITH my heel of my hand.

"All right now! Take a break!" I wave the boys down.

It's not a hot day—the Iron City is set between the mountains and the coast, so it cools down early fall and the heat doesn't come back—but we are all hot, and we gravitate toward the autumn grass under the tree.

I loosen my armbands so the sweat on my arms can dry. The boys are doing the same, some of them taking them off to patch up cuts and scrapes.

Eddie has perched on a raised tree root, staring off at the busy, clustered city buildings. Above them comes the perpetual smoke of the factories.

I tear my gaze from them and turn to the kid. "So, I'm told you sing, Eddie, to make extra money. In those clubs with tuxedos."

"Where'd you hear that?" It's probably as many words as I've heard the kid string together at once.

"Is it true?" I smile, watching his face. I know it's true.

"S'pose so."

"I bet you're good."

"I dunno."

"You've got to be, if you sing there," says Colt, who should know something about culture.

"C'mon, let's lighten up. Sing something, Eddie." Laertes tosses the roll of bandage at him.

The men of the phalanx pick up on it, cupping their hands and shouting.

"Come on, Eddie!"

"Let's hear it, kid."

"I don't know, boys." He lifts the bandage up, hiding his face, partly in jest. But his ear, still visible, blushes.

"Just one song!" calls out Remus.

"What would I sing?"

I lean back, hands around my knee. "Anything you want."

He puts down the bandage. His face grows still and solemn.

This is the promise, the promise I made to you.
No matter how long I'm gone, how far I stray, I will not forget you.
When the sun falls over the slanting mountains that separate us,
when the sea pulses like your gentle heart,
when the birds sing their love songs, I will remember.

No, I will not forget, no, I will never forget,

> *no matter how the world works between us,*
> *and the weary days linger, I will come back for you.*

> *I will fight for you, I will bleed for you, I will die for you.*
> *For this is the promise, the promise I made to you.*
> *I will come back again to you.*

There's a hush as he finishes. He's got a sweet, warm voice, and it hangs around over the boys like a spell.

Sampson breaks the silence. "Where'd you learn a love song?" he grins wickedly. "You ain't never had a girl."

Eddie blushes hard and starts fiddling with the buckle on his arm strap.

"Every boy that sings in those rich-person clubs has to learn love songs. That's the law," teases Danforth, pushing back.

"That was real fine, Eddie," says Laertes, with no hint of teasing. "Real fine."

Eddie continues to fiddle with his armguard, growing increasingly shy and uncomfortable. "Aw. Ain't nothing," he mumbles.

It's time to come to his rescue.

"Break's over. Come on, boys." I slap Laertes's leg and get up. "We're going to Hudson in the morning."

We file into the preparation room in Hudson. It's old, kept deliberately run-down for their enemies. I never liked playing the Hudson Jackals; they're dirty fighters and extra good at rubbing your nose in your defeat.

I've been lucky in the past to avoid too many defeats at their hands. Now—

I set down my gear bag.

"Where is Laertes?" asks Chauncey.

"One of his bags got left in the automobile he was in. He went to go get it before they drove off." Danforth is wrapping his wrist.

"How did it get left?"

Danforth shrugs.

"Someone check, he's been gone too long," says Remus, casting a glance at the door.

I set down my second armguard and head up. I don't like the feeling I'm getting. Something's off.

I scan the hallways as I walk, and I see no sign of him. My pace quickens as I head for the door we entered—it's an alleyway at the back of the great arena.

Through the door, I see nothing. My hand goes to my one armguard, finger over the switch to turn the shocker on.

I step out into the alleyway, throw a glance up and then down. There are no automobiles. But at the far end, I see a group of men, all gathered around something, or someone.

Voices raised in laughter. One of them lands a kick.

"Hey!" I shout.

I take half a dozen steps in their direction and pause, trying to get a better view.

My shout seems to have had some effect. They're looking up, looking over at me.

"It's the lieutenant," one of them says, quickly.

"Is he alone? We should get him."

"Nah, man, we got to scram. You don't go touching Guild property."

"We just did."

I press forward, emboldened by their indecision. "Yes, you scram!" I shout. I quicken my steps.

Two of them take one look at me and run off. A third fellow was ready to run as soon as I came out the side door, and I catch a glimpse of him disappearing around the corner. The others, three or four of them, hold their ground.

They have San Domingo.

He's held halfway up by a couple of them, swaying a little. He has a gashed forehead, two black eyes, and he's bleeding from his nose and mouth. What's visible of his arms is black and blue.

"This your courier? You shouldn't have left him wandering."

"You get out of here, or I will call the authorities."

"What are they going to do? This is Hudson. They're on our side." They let go of him and laugh as he staggers.

"Last warning."

They take off finally, their laughter echoing against the high stone walls.

I run out to him. He's stubbornly standing, but I think he's afraid to move.

"Easy, kid." I grab his arm and duck down to put it over my shoulder. "You think you can walk?"

"Yeah, I can walk," he mumbles. "I was afraid they

were going to keep me away from the game until it started. It hasn't started yet, has it?"

"Tee, I don't think you're going to play."

"Just take me to the washroom. Let me get some of the blood off, it's not that bad."

"I'm taking you to the medics."

"Come on." He rolls his head back and fixes me with a look that's almost a snarl. His lip's bleeding pretty badly. I dig in my pocket and pull out my handkerchief, pressing it gently to his mouth.

"The medics or I'm going straight to Atlas."

He doesn't protest this.

"I thought you were going back for a bag."

"It was a setup," he says. "Driver was in on it. I'm just lucky they didn't take me out for good."

"The driver?"

"It's not any good, you're not going to catch him."

"The Guild is going to hear about this."

"What are they going to do?" Laertes looks at me like I haven't learned.

We make it inside and down the hall to the medics without more than a couple people seeing us. The medics take him from me and immediately start washing out the gash.

I step away and let them do their job.

"I can play."

Laertes sits on one of the benches in the preparation room, hands folded, staring up at Atlas with defiance written across his face. He's got some stitches in his head now, and one in his lip, and his black eyes are getting darker by the minute.

Atlas shakes his head, regretful. "Not with that face you can't."

"Captain, I've been beat up in the arena before. Here and before the Conscriptio."

"In the arena, it's part of the job. My job is sending you in ready, and tonight I'd be handing you over for a crush or shock-out. It is not up for debate."

"I wouldn't shock out quick, sir."

"It doesn't matter. You are not going into that fight today."

Laertes drops his head.

One does not win a fight with Atlas.

"I swear," he mutters under his breath. One fist pounds softly into his other hand.

Atlas turns his gaze to the rest of the team. Most of the men are gathered around watching the conversation. They break up and start to get ready again, even before Atlas says anything.

"Boys, we've lost enough preparation time as it is. Finish getting ready, inspection's in fifteen minutes."

In the rush of preparation, no one else notices Atlas step away to a quiet corner just outside the door to the arena. He presses his fist to his mouth, jaw hard, and I see him glance away, quick.

He clears his throat hard, then composes himself and steps back in, again unnoticed.

The other couriers give Laertes their well-wishes as

they go by. With Isaac out for a while, we're down to just Winston and Chauncey.

"Tough luck," says Winston. "We'll bloody a few mouths if we can."

"I'll kick their teeth in," says Chauncey. "Was any of them there?"

"Watch yourself," says Laertes. "You focus on the match, now."

"No reason we can't do both." Apa comes over, putting his huge bear paw hand on Laertes's head. "Just you rest easy, boy."

"Inspection in three minutes," warns Crispin.

Atlas calls the room together. "Look, boys, none of us wanted this. Especially Laertes. This city wants to intimidate us. They think they can push us around. I want you to show them that they can't. We are going to fight for this match, for our flag, in a way that makes them think twice before they try it again. You are going to show them that we are not afraid. But I want you to fight within the rules and within the traditions. We never dishonor the Games, in victory or in defeat. Go fight with honor, and you can hold your heads up around any man."

I lead the boys in clapping, then step out in front of them. "You heard the captain. We fight with honor, no matter what they do."

"Yes, sir!" comes from a dozen throats.

But I see the look in Apa's eye. He's out for blood. And if he gets it, I don't think I'm going to stop him.

· · ·

I sense the dangerous hunger the minute I step out into the arena. The crowd wants spectacle. The Jackals already smell blood.

And we're the entertainment.

I get my orders from Atlas, implementing any changes based on the setup of the arena. This one is fairly basic: large obstacles in the way, something like a five-foot river down the center, marking the center line. I kind of like it.

We walk to the center to fulfill the pleasantries, where a couple game keepers wait. They're watching us. They can sense the tension in the air.

"Hey, Golden Boy!" One of the Jackals' fighters calls to me.

It's Parker. Of all the men in the Games, he's one of the dirtiest. Any of us can hit a man and hurt him, but the dirty ones know where and how to hit to keep you down and crush you out.

He signals me, crossed wrists and two fingers twisting in front of his eyes, to show he's watching, then walks by close enough to brush me.

"We've been absolved of any wrongdoing. It wasn't us," he says, his voice dropping. I can smell his sharp, expensive cologne. "You should have heard him scream."

He backs away, laughing. "It's going to be you next, Golden Boy."

"You talk to me!" Apa throws himself between us and shoves his finger into the man's chest. "You want to talk that way, you say it to my face!"

Parker's face darkens. "Fine. But when the match starts, see if you can protect him from us."

Apa gives him a savage grin. "I'd like that. Come try, won't you?"

I lean in to him. "Don't antagonize him. Honor, not revenge."

"Oh, it's not going to be revenge." Apa licks his lips. "Not revenge, no sir."

We do our duty at the center line and then fall back into position. Both sides want this to begin. I take a deep breath and wipe the sweat from above my lip. Listen to the countdown.

Go.

Our boys break like fire over dry ground. Remus knocks a man flat at first contact. Colt gets two shocks in, immediately. Sampson is on their heels like a deer.

The Jackals' chasers are coming. We're fighting with traditional tactics tonight: a good old forward charge.

"Come on!" roars Apa, pounding his shield. Peter readjusts his grip and grits his teeth. Danforth is steady as ice, his eyes locked on the coming onslaught.

"Step back!" Peter shouts to me. It's about to get ugly.

I double check my armguards to make sure they are working.

Impact.

Winston comes running around the long way, up behind me. "Orders?" he pants.

"Where's Sampson?"

"On his way up. It's a fight all the way."

"Tell Chauncey to be ready for a relay. And you—get ready to use your armbands. I want you covering."

"Yes, sir."

"Only come back if there's a change past saving. Godspeed."

He grins, a willing, crooked smile. "Godspeed to you."

He dashes off.

They're beating down our defense. The phalanx is getting pushed back, even though they've taken out one of the enemy chasers.

Then their flag-bearer is up, around our phalanx and dashing for our mountain. I break and run after him, shocker ready, but I only get one hit in before he shoves me into the sand.

I follow after him, dogged, but he's built stronger and faster than I am.

Eddie cuts around me and grabs our flag just as the Jackals' flag-bearer pulls it from its stand.

They tussle—Eddie scrambling to hang on, afraid to let go lest the man get away, the Jackal kicking and biting at him to break free.

They go down into the sand and I come running to his aid just as a blow falls beside me, barely missing my body.

It's Parker. I dodge, throwing up my hands to protect my head.

"No, you don't!" Apa's voice roars in my ear. His knee brushes past me, almost knocks me down.

Apa's fist catches him in the nose, felling him hard. "What do you say now? Did I protect my lieutenant?" he demands.

Parker doesn't answer. Blood seeps through his fingers as he clutches his nose.

I don't like to see men get hurt in the arena, but today,

I can't find it in my heart to feel sorry for the man. It's a nose. And he brought this one on himself.

But there's little triumph in the moment. The great gong sounds above us and the match is over. The Jackals have made it to their mountain.

Eddie is on his knees over at the foot of the enemy's mountain. Our flagpole is in his hands, the flag gone. He's got blood smeared on his face and arms where he was dragged through the sand, hanging on.

The boy hasn't a quitting bone in his body.

I meet their lieutenant in the center of the vast arena. The steep upcurve of the Hudson arena is almost dizzying from the middle. Your fingers tingle just looking up.

He cuts the emblem from my chest, but I look in his eyes the whole time, and he sees I am neither defeated nor humiliated.

They know what they did.

I turn and join the boys that are left. There's only a few —Eddie, Remus, the phalanx.

Eddie still clings to the empty flagpole, his dark eyes hollow. I know that look. He's going over and over the moment, blaming himself.

I reach out and take the flagpole from him gently. "Take it easy, kid. You did good."

"I didn't," he says, low and soft. "I failed."

"You were put in a situation you've never been in before, and you still put up a fight. We'll get 'em next time." I slap his shoulder.

It doesn't seem to do any good, but I've seen this too. Good words and bad words plant themselves in these men's minds. It'll come back to him later with some measure of comfort.

I fall into step with the phalanx. Apa is still feeling pleased with himself after laying Parker out.

"You're bleeding." Danforth reaches out and swipes at Apa's head.

"Where?" He feels the spot. His fingers come away bloody and he checks again. "Huh." He peels off his shirt and presses it against his head.

His hair's too short, otherwise it would have matted. Instead, there's a sticky patch up along the front left side of his head.

"Here—" I grab the signal scarf off of my belt. "This is cleaner."

He tosses his shirt into the dirt and takes my scarf. "Thanks, brother." He grabs me against him and rubs my head roughly.

I'm warmed. He hasn't done that to me before.

Laertes is waiting for us when we get back. He still looks rough, but more than that, upset. A dark cloud seems to hang over his expression. I assume he watched the match.

"Parker said he was there when they beat you," says Chauncey, who seems to have a knack for saying the wrong things at the worst times. "Said you screamed."

Oddly, the glowering expression disappears. It seems to bring him back to himself.

"He wasn't there. And I didn't scream." He slides back in his chair with a groan. "You really thought I could take hits in the arena and I couldn't take a few from some Hudson men? Pitiful."

"Was any of the Jackals there?" Chauncey seems disappointed.

"I think the Jackal's vanguard was there. Hooker. The others were just men from Hudson, not fighters."

"So Parker wasn't there," Chauncey persists.

"No."

"You don't have to worry, Tee, I broke his nose for you." Apa comes in, released from the medics with a fresh plaster on his head. He's gingerly touching it.

"Thanks, Apa. You didn't have to."

Apa gives a rough laugh and rubs San Domingo's hair gently. "That's alright. I wanted to."

A light steals into Laertes's eyes. "That's what he gets for taking credit for things he didn't do."

"Yes, sir. He'll think twice next time." Apa chuckles to himself. "Wish I'd gotten Hooker too."

"Colt got Hooker," pipes up Lucius. "Almost a crushout."

"Colt?" Laertes raises himself on one arm. Colt's peeling his uniform off. His raises a couple fingers in salute.

Atlas comes into the room. He regards us for a minute. His eyes fall on Laertes, then on me. I'm still in my gear—there's a big hole in my uniform where they took the emblem.

His eyes gentle.

He just gives me a nod. And that's enough.

TWENTY-SEVEN
BLAISE VALENTINO

WEAPONS MASTER, IRON CITY WOLVES

THE DOOR SHUTS BEHIND THE HIGH commissioner of the Iron City. I have never seen her before today, but I can see why she's held her place so long.

She carries herself with the weight of history and precedence, tucked neatly into an expensive suit and an iron expression. Her assistant takes her coat and stands behind her, holding it.

She takes a seat at the table across from Atlas and myself and folds her hands. She smells of expensive perfume and cigarette smoke.

It's silent for the space of a few heartbeats. Long enough for me to hear mine, pulsing in my ears.

"Tell me, William, why should I keep you as captain of the Iron City Wolves? Everyone, including the Guild, is asking me for your head. I, however, never take things on another person's word. The decisions I make are for the city, regardless of what's said."

Atlas looks almost foreign to me. His hair's damp and combed and he's forced himself into a suit. It's perhaps the second time I have ever seen him in one. He looks dreadfully hot and uncomfortable in it.

But fear? He has none.

He leans forward, hand on the table. He's brought in the newspapers, the worst ones that call him every sort of name, the very ones that call for his head.

It's a gutsy move, but Atlas is no typical captain. He will not cringe before power, throw others into the fire, and beg for his place.

"Mrs. Hilton, I already respect you deeply for asking for this meeting. Know that whatever you decide, I respect you as a person."

"I'm flattered." She's not convinced.

"No offense, ma'am, but I don't mean to flatter. I want to tell you exactly why I should be here and why I am your best chance."

She folds her arms. "Go on."

"I know how the Iron City is viewed. I have seen it. The Games disrespect us. They use us as fodder for their heroes, not as heroes ourselves. Resources are scant here. That goes for the people in the city and it goes for our fighters. With less than enough, sure, we're beaten. Yes, we get the dregs of the Games. Do you expect castoffs who've been told they're no good to have the heart to beat the well-fed fighters in every other stable? Yes, the people are clamoring for my head. But they've wanted the heads of every captain for the last two hundred years. What do you expect? Old habits die hard."

I can sense it. She's curious now.

"What these boys need is someone who believes in them. And someone who won't abandon them when the going gets tough. Someone who will stand next to them as the tide rises and help them keep their heads above water. Do that long enough, and we might have a fighting chance."

"And why are you the man for the job?"

"What other captain looks you in the eye and doesn't lie to you? Tell me that."

She unfolds her arms slowly. "You speak with a great deal of arrogance."

"With all due respect, I think you're mistaking candor for arrogance. No one speaks the truth to you because they're afraid. And they have every right to be. But I tell you right now, I care about those boys in those barracks more than anyone else you or the Guild will be able to find, and you can take it or leave it."

She turns her iron gaze to me. "Does he?" She raises her eyebrows.

"Not a doubt, ma'am." I'm surprised I'm not afraid, looking this much power in the eyes. But there's a rush going through me. I enjoy it.

She holds my gaze a while and I hold it back.

Then she reaches for one of the newspapers and looks over it. Lifts another and reads it too.

"Hm." She sets them aside and takes her time before she looks up at Atlas.

"William, it is clear to me that you mean what you say, whether or not you are able to accomplish what you hope. You might be able to stand with our men in a rising tide, but who's to say you won't drown next to them?"

She stands up. Motions for her coat. "That said, I like your spirit. Go, try, and break your head if you want. I will stand up for you to the Guild, and to the city and its powers-that-be, for now."

She puts on her coat, buttons it up deliberately, and goes to the door. With her hand on the handle, she pauses, and turns back to Atlas.

"But let me warn you. Watch your back, especially in the streets. The Iron City is good at manipulating the outcomes it wants, against even its own."

She gives him a small, comforting smile, and departs.

Once the door closes, Atlas smacks his fist into his hand. "See, Blaise? I told you. Nothing to be worried about." He immediately loosens his tie and starts to unbutton his collar.

"She just warned you that you could get shot in an alley."

"Didn't say shot." He gives me an amused look, but I see deep down he's not taking it lightly. "Either way, I knew what I was getting into when I signed up for this. You're still with me, aren't you?"

"What, me?" I laugh, shoving away any worries. Glory is not for faint hearts. "To the hilt, Captain. To the hilt."

TWENTY-EIGHT
JACKSON VAN

LIEUTENANT, IRON CITY WOLVES

THE PREPARATION ROOM IS BUZZING WITH NOISE this afternoon. We stay in the Iron City for tonight's match, and the boys are happy to avoid a long train ride.

We are matched against the Carthage Battle Hawks tonight. They're all the rage right now in the Empire due to the meteoric rise of their young lieutenant and his flag-bearer. They are in the papers, in the magazines, on the television, on billboards lit over streets and city buildings.

They are darlings of the Guild, and that bodes ill for us.

The door opens, letting in a blast of cold late-autumn air. Atlas shoulders his way in, one hand in his pocket, and he goes over to the ice bucket to fill a cloth with ice.

"Is Blaise here yet?" he asks.

Quietly, he takes his hand out of his pocket and presses the ice against it. It's red and his knuckles are bloodied up.

"Just. He's out talking to one of the game keepers about something, I don't know what. He wasn't clear. You know how he's been before the matches—no smiles or small talk."

Atlas nods.

"What happened to your hand?"

He looks at me with a cryptic expression. It's clear he doesn't want a big deal made over it. "Just ran into a little trouble, down a couple streets."

"What kind of trouble?"

He just smiles.

"They came after you?" I lower my voice. "Who?"

"Probably some kind of gang affiliation. Bets and such. Not sure."

I look at him hard. Other than the hand, there's no detectable injury on him.

"You beat them." I feel bad for being incredulous.

"They weren't arena fighters." He shifts and readjusts the ice on his hand, then looks at me and Laertes San Domingo, the only two paying attention. "Don't spread it around to the boys."

"They'll notice," I say.

"Let 'em guess." He winks and walks out, I assume to find Valentino.

Laertes leans in, his voice low. "Boy, I'd like to have seen that." A sly little grin steals over his face. "Yes, sir, I'd like to have seen that."

Since our match against the Jackals, Laertes has improved greatly. His black eyes and bruises have faded, the stitches are nearly ready to come out, and he's chomping at the bit to be back.

"They're learning that wolves have teeth," I reply.

"Sure." Laertes rubs his hands together and cracks his shoulders. "Sure they are." He stops himself and looks at me. "Jackson, I didn't know you had a way with words."

I look at him with a straight face, but I let a smile out in my eyes. "You just figured that out, hm?"

Our arena is packed with locals and with fans from Carthage. The place hums with energy as we run out.

The Battle Hawks are waiting for us. Felix Garner, their lieutenant, stands with folded arms, a thin smile on his face. He won't look me directly in the eye, like he can't deign to associate with any of us.

It hurts, for a moment; I have been to glory far more and far longer than he. But beside me, Peter Hope clears his throat, and the sting dies.

These are my boys. I'd rather associate with them than anyone else in the Games.

Beside Felix stands Cassius Demarco, his flag-bearer. He looks at us with amusement in his face, his eyebrows slightly lifted in that expression a young man makes when he's trying to look good for every photograph.

This is what our glorious Games have come to. I want to laugh.

Everything is prepared before the countdown. Strategy, communication, formalities—Felix is forced to acknowledge us there—all leading to the moment when I raise my fist for the countdown.

I glance over at my boys, give them a steadying look. *Let's show them.*

The countdown begins. Hits one. We break into motion.

We're not far into our plan when Tom Cranston goes down hard, hit by an enemy chaser. One glance shows me it's a crush-out, and not in a good spot in the arena. I lift my arm, signaling for a stop.

I hate to give up the bar, but I've got to think about him. If this comes back to bite me, I'll take the responsibility. We need to get him out of here.

I go down on one knee beside him. Some of the other boys are starting to gather around. "Tom, talk to me."

"My shoulder, I think. It might be out." His face has gone pale and sweat's pooling on his forehead and neck.

Crispin comes down, his face all business. "Can you get up?" he asks.

"With help, maybe." Tom explains his situation again.

"All right." Crispin glances up, rubbing at his stubbly chin. There's a hawk-like expression on his face, but when he turns back to Tom, he looks gentle. "Tom, I'm going to put it back in. Tell me when you're ready."

"Let me catch my breath."

I stand up. Crispin has help right now and I don't need to watch.

There's a grunt—I think it's Crispin—and a sharp release of breath from Tom and they're getting him up. The crowd stands for him, chanting *virtus*.

That's another man down. I glance up at the board above the arena. There are nine of us and eleven of the Hawks. We can't afford to lose more.

I reform my phalanx; they're all still here. Peter Hope's had almost half his uniform torn off. I can see his shoulder and bare neck under his chest armor.

"What happened to you?"

"Cassius Demarco. He's using his knife on the sly. I shocked him and he backed off."

Jim Danforth comes around and looks at the tear. "Put on some clothes, brother."

"No, I was just hot. Ventilation, you know."

"They're going to put a forced out on you with that," Remus comments, walking by. "Not even joking. Just declare you out for equipment violation."

He flips his saber up onto his shoulder.

Jim Danforth laughs out loud. It's shared, shakily, by the rest of us. I lean into it, let myself laugh. Sometimes that's the best way of getting over something like this.

None of us can help Tom now.

The game keeper signals us—our allotted time is almost up.

I wave the boys over, get them gathered around. "Their flag-bearer is using his knife. If you can catch and expose him, try. He should get thrown out. As for the match, change of plan. They've seen our strategy now, so we're changing to a feint. Chasers hang back, let the flankers get up and engage the couriers. Their lieutenant is leaning heavily on the couriers so we'll see if we can't disrupt their communication."

Our flankers salute.

I look over at Laertes. "You are backup for Sampson tonight."

"Yes, sir."

"All right." I glance up at the clock. We have seconds left before the game resumes. "Get to your places."

Against all odds, we hang on. The chasers put up a fight at the Battle Hawks' mountain. Sampson takes several hits but gets the flag. And Laertes, who has followed orders, is there to take it up when Sampson is finally shocked out.

Our phalanx is locked in battle with the Battle Hawk's chasers now, as our flag's been stolen too. At the moment, it is almost an even match.

And Laertes is coming, running so fast he kicks up dust with each footfall, with no one around him as Remus and Lucius hold back the flankers. A whisper of hope rises in my heart.

I raise my arms and signal Laertes to angle in. There's no one there. He's coming in hot, and our men are closing in around the Hawks' flag-bearer.

Victory could be seconds away.

The great horn sounds, stopping the match.

I look around, confused, and run out to meet the phalanx.

"What's happening?" Peter straightens, his face confused. "No one signaled. We didn't signal."

I scan the arena, looking for each head. I see every one except my flag-bearer. No one is signaling. It's not us.

I turn my eyes to the Battle Hawks' fighters, but they're all standing with folded arms.

Atlas is down on the sand now, talking to the game keeper. There's a disagreement going on. Even the crowd gets quiet.

It must be something big. They call me and Felix over to listen to the head game keeper.

"It has been determined by the game keepers that in removing the flag from the mountain, the current flag-bearer used a form of carry not permitted in the arena. The flag-bearer is removed and the flag recaptured by the Battle Hawks."

Felix Garner smacks his fist into his hand with excitement.

It's over. The game's been handed straight to them.

"Since the Battle Hawks' flag-bearer has already set foot on his own mountain with his flag, the match will be considered over. We see no need to continue it."

Words of protest rise in my throat. The flag is in Laertes's hands. There wasn't a single man of the Battle Hawk's fighters close to catching him.

And tradition. Tradition forces the fighters to fight for every inch. Men have been permanently injured in the name of fighting to the end. Never have I seen them shift the heavy walls of tradition like this.

I can barely muster the words to answer the game keeper. "Prosper the Games." The irony in the words is heavy. It takes all my willpower to turn and walk away.

I don't know how I'm going to tell Laertes.

He's waiting for me, brows knit, eager and hesitant all

at once. I think he can tell from my face it's not good news.

"The match is over. They've given it to the Battle Hawks."

"How?"

"They say you carried it in Haskins' reverse."

"I what? You know, you saw—right?"

"It doesn't matter to them. It's over. There will be no appeal."

He's stone-faced. His anger is a cold, simmering silence. White knuckles grip the flagstaff as he lowers it slowly. "I'm sorry I let you down, Lieutenant," he says stiffly, forcing the words out.

"It's not fair!" cries Chauncey, glancing between me and him. He reaches for the flag as if he can stop it somehow, carry it forward.

"Easy, Chauncey." I reach for the flag and take it up. "It wasn't your fault, Laertes."

"But he—he didn't do it!" Chauncey thrusts out a long arm in protest.

"It's over. There's nothing we can do now." Laertes slides his gaze over to his fellow courier. "It's over."

Only then do I see the mask waver—a hint of dull pain in his eyes.

Tonight is going to be a long night for us all.

"Go home!" A glass bottle sails through the air and smashes at San Domingo's feet. He ignores it and keeps walking. There's a whole crowd of half-drunk, angry workmen who are just as upset by the outcome of the match as we are, but they have someone to take it out on.

The walk from the back alley to the waiting bus is short, but not so short that they couldn't find us and bombard us.

"Go back to the Golden City! Sellout!" Something hits the wall behind our head.

Danforth knifes in between me and the voices.

"Try that again!" he thunders.

"It's okay, it's okay." I try to pull him back.

He pulls his arm out of my grasp and stalks towards the shouters. "Say it again if you dare!"

The group goes quiet, cowed for a moment, and then someone shouts, "Sellout! The Iron City shoots sellouts!"

The jeers break out afresh, emboldened by the instigator.

"You're no true son of the Iron City, shouting at the ones who represent you before the face of the Empire," shouts Apa from behind me.

This has no effect on the man. He is laughing.

Apa wades straight into the crowd and the heckler ducks. "Come on! Stop hiding, coward! Show your face!"

Apa throws men aside left and right until his hand grabs the man's collar. He drags him out.

The man's fighting like a trapped cat, but it does him no good. Apa is built like a freight train and he's battle-hardened. One of the other workmen tries to rescue his friend, but Danforth steps in the way.

The man swings at him—I think the local pub must have something to do with this, because the man's not nearly of a size to challenge Jim Danforth and can hardly be in his right mind. Danforth lands a blow that sends the man flying ten feet back on the pavement. It's a stupendous hit.

A hand suddenly seizes my collar and almost drags me to the ground. I can smell the whiskey on the man. Peter Hope whips around and collars the fellow, breaking his grasp.

The volume of the voices is growing, the urgency heightening.

We're on the edge of an all-out street fight. I've never really seen one before, but I know with hard certainty I'm about to be in one if nothing is done.

"Boys, leave them!" I shout. "It's not worth it, leave it!"

Apa give his man one more shake and drops him. Laertes and Sampson step back, though their eyes stay trained on the workmen still lining the alley.

I lead the way down toward the bus, but Peter gets in front of me. The men in the street are following us, refusing to drop it.

Something flies through the air and hits the back of my head with a smack. My hand goes there instinctively. An egg, or what's left of one.

It's the last straw.

"Who did that?" demands Peter, putting himself between me and the assailant.

The response is only laughter and more objects thrown.

"Enough!" Danforth roars.

The alley falls silent. In the silence, I hear footsteps approaching.

"If it isn't the Iron City Whelps." Cassius Demarco appears from around the corner, a few other Hawks in tow, Garner included. They have their gear bags over their shoulders and their medals around their necks. Cassius laughs, finding his joke funnier than anyone else does.

Felix Garner takes the next shot. "What? Our beating not enough for you boys?"

Laertes launches himself at him. Danforth grabs at his arm, but it's too late. Garner hits the cold, dirty pavement and lies there gasping.

I think it's just the wind knocked out of him, but it doesn't matter. It's a split second, slowed to a clear, terrible thought.

This place is a powder keg. He's going to get killed.

The rest of the Battle Hawks roar up to meet our boys and the hecklers join us against them, united by the insult. Men are dropping into the gutters, with bloody mouths and white starched shirts stained and ripping. Hats are knocked off and blown down the road. As many oaths as rough men know are pouring out of mouths.

"Stop! Stop it, cut it out!" I press my back against the wall and watch, half horrified and half fascinated as the men tear each other up. The freezing brick chills me straight through my thin jacket.

I want to step in, but I know what a frenzy looks like. I've seen mobs. These men will not be parted by the likes of me, and beyond that, I can't help feeling the sense of a wrong being righted. The Hawks are getting the worst of it, by far.

I don't know what tips me off, but I'm suddenly aware that we must finish this fight and get out of here before someone gets killed or we get arrested.

"Peter!" I shout. He listens to reason best of anyone. "Peter, get out of there!"

He raises his head from the fight and extricates himself with a few blows and a kick to someone's head.

Calm, like it's nothing. This side of the Iron City is entirely new to me.

It's just in time.

Whistles blow. Police are running into the fray, pulling men back, hitting indiscriminately with their batons.

The men are parted. A few don't get up.

"You boys are from the Wolves, right?" A well-dressed officer comes up to me.

"A few. The rest are Battle Hawks and local men, I think."

"Your name?"

"He wasn't fighting," interjects Peter quickly.

"Your name?" The man's voice turns steely.

"Jackson Van."

He takes our names. Others are taking names from the Carthage boys and whatever men from the street they can stop before they run off.

An ambulance arrives for the men who didn't get up. I don't think anyone's dead, but it's not pretty either.

One of the Battle Hawks is hurt, a wrist or hand or

something. The others are crowded around him and around the ambulance, all talking, all pointing at us.

"We should leave," says Jim, turning around and starting to move us in the opposite direction. "No good's going to come from sticking around."

He herds us away toward our buses, just around the other side of the arena. No one follows us this time.

Once in the relative safety of the moving bus, we can breathe again. I'm sore where those couple flying objects hit me, but I'm not about to complain.

Peter's nursing his arm, Apa's tearing bandage with his teeth to put on his bloody knuckles, and Sampson and Danforth are sharing a bottle of witch hazel from the medical bag.

Laertes sits himself down the bench beside me. "The Battle Hawks don't come here much, else they wouldn't have said those things out loud in the street." Laertes has a new shiner where his old one from the Jackals had started to heal. "The Iron City might hate us, but they also won't stand for anyone else hating us."

"Is that how it is here?" I raise my eyebrows.

"Yeah, Golden Boy. Isn't that how it is in the Golden City?"

"No. I don't think many people hate us—them." The Toros.

"Well, we do." Laertes folds his arms and lifts his chin. "We hate them."

"Us against the world, hm?"

He looks at me like I'm saying something I should know already. "Well, of course."

. . .

Two days later, each one of us who was present at the fight is called up from drilling to Atlas's office.

We file in to find him sitting behind his desk, writing in a ledger. Stacks of records sit around him, on the desk, on the ground beside his old chair.

It creaks perilously as he looks up and sets down his pen.

We're crammed in around the edges of the room. There aren't enough seats—there's almost not enough room for us, period.

"Do you know why I called you here?" His face is serious.

"Because of the street fight." Jim Danforth is the elder spokesman. "I assume that's why."

"Yes, because you each have a fine from the city and from the Guild, since you engaged in street fighting, which is illegal."

There's a grim silence.

Laertes looks like he wants to protest—there's indignation all over his face—but he's holding back.

"There's never been a fine before," says Jim, confused.

"You incited a fight against the Battle Hawks, and Carthage has pull with law enforcement."

"Did they get fined?" Apa asks. Danforth shoves his arm.

Apa turns on him. "What?"

"What do you think?"

"It doesn't matter whether this sanction is fair. I am

taking the fines out of your pay. If you don't have enough, you'll owe the city until you do."

"Yes, sir." Peter Hope is the first one to speak up.

Atlas looks at me. "I heard you didn't have a part in the fight, Jackson, and I believe it. But that's the way they're going to treat you now."

"Captain, you don't need to explain," I say. "I understand. I am glad to take the fine with the rest."

He nods, and for me, there's a slight gentling of the steely exterior. "All right. That's it. From what I heard, there was some unacceptable loss of temper, but you boys were provoked. You understand this will not happen again."

"No, sir," I answer for us all. "Never again."

Atlas looks down at his papers, hiding a small smile. "I have also heard, unofficially, that the Battle Hawks got the worst of it. I believe they will think twice before they try something like that again."

Danforth guffaws and turns it into a cough.

"You're dismissed, men."

Peter Hope hangs back. "Sir, can I talk to you a moment?"

"Sure."

The rest of us file out, and the moment the door shuts on Peter and the captain, Laertes opens his mouth. "Curse those Battle Hawks. The Iron City hasn't ever cared before about street fighting. They only break you up if you're damaging too much property."

"And after that game too." Jim shakes his head. "Those men honor the Games in name, when there are eyes on them, but I wouldn't be surprised if one of the game keepers was paid."

"They don't need to pay a keeper," says Sampson. "The Guild loves them."

Apa closes his fist and smiles to himself. "I can't wait for the next calendar games," he whispers. "Give me the Hawks and I'll wring their necks like chickens."

Peter Hope steps out just then. "What's that about chickens?"

Apa looks at him with furrowed brows. "Nothin'. Let's get out of here, we've got drilling to do."

TWENTY-NINE
REMUS BLAKE
CHASER, IRON CITY WOLVES

POMPEII! POMPEII! POMPEII!

The crowd's chants fill the open arena. A storm is brewing and still they've filled it. It's a hostile crowd and we love it.

We stand close in the tunnel, shoulders brushing. Thunder rumbles over our heads. A hard wind sweeps down over the arena, blowing up sand, and the cheers double. It's considered good luck when the elements come to a fight.

We're crowded tight and the noise from the crowd and the coming storm is so loud we can barely hear Jackson as he shouts to us.

"It's us against the world, men! Let's fight for the Games tonight, fight for each other!"

"Us against the world!" we shout back. Our breath stands on the cold, damp air.

We don't have Tom tonight. He won't likely be back

until the final tournament. So young Trenton Fitch is our vanguard.

Besides that, it's a strong lineup: all of us boys who have taken the beatings out in the arena this year. I have a good feeling about tonight.

We're all hot and ready to fight, and that gives us a chance. A chance is all I'm looking for.

The gates open with a heavy clang and we burst out, fierce and strong. We may have paid a heavy price for our scuffle with the Battle Hawks, but the word of it precedes us now.

We may get beaten down, but everyone knows we're not weak.

Above us, the heavens let loose. Rain pours in sheets down over the sand. Even if it packs eventually, that sand is going to stick to us and weigh us all down.

Instructions are brief and clear. With the rain, we'll have some cover. We'll keep to the right side, not too close to the crowd, but out of the middle. With any luck, they'll have trouble seeing our maneuvers.

I go down to the base of the mountain and put my saber under my arm so I can tighten my gloves. I like being barehanded, but with rain, I don't want my hands slipping on the grip of my saber, or off a man's slick arm.

I check my armguard. It's going to be a match, all right. Shocks hurt double when you're wet.

Colt and Lucius come and take up their positions beside me. Colt is spinning his saber in his hand.

"Blake, what'd they call you? Back in the Black Town?" he asks.

"Aw." I chuckle and rub my neck, rather shamefaced. "I wasn't good enough to have a name."

"Well, I've thought of one. I'm going to call you War Hound."

"War Hound, huh?" I grin.

"Yes, sir. Because you run full tilt into a fight, even one bigger than you."

"If that's so, you make a pretty good war hound yourself. And you, Lucius."

Colt's eyes get warm and Lucius looks away, a dimple in one side of his cheek, he's so tickled with the inclusion.

"Well, there's no one I'd rather run into war with," Lucius says.

I reach out and rough up his hair. "Then let's do it."

The clock above us strikes the countdown. We share a look, the three of us, and I glance back to Sampson.

He tips me a salute with two fingers.

Here we go.

At the signal we break into a dead run. Angling to the right, switching back, keeping our forward motion just vague enough that hopefully—if they catch sight of us at all—we'll have them spread thinner than they'd like.

We meet one flanker. Lucius tackles him, doesn't even bother with the saber. The right attack and a hand over the mouth will buy you just enough time to keep the element of surprise.

Sampson runs up the mountain in leaps and bounds, deer-like in his agility. He whips past the flag pole and down the other side, barely breaking stride. Colt and I angle off to meet him, sabers ready for pursuit.

And it's coming.

My heart's pounding, and not just from the running. I've seen this before, felt it too. Everything going right in sequence, every second bringing you closer to the possibility of victory.

"Colt, get ahead!" I shout.

I deliberately slow and cast a glance over my shoulder.

One of the Vipers' chasers is coming, barreling towards us. I turn at the very last second and grab him hard around the waist.

We go down together in a tangle of sand and arms locked against arms. Trading blows, shockers smacking over the pounding of the rain.

The lights go out on our arm bands. Our struggling stops immediately. The man spits contemptuously and picks himself up.

He begins to curse, but it's drowned out as a deafening cry rises from the crowd. Shock. Horror.

I stand up, brushing sand and hair out my face.

Laertes and Sampson are standing on top of our mountain, in each other's arms, pounding each other's backs. The Vipers' flag is thrust into the ground beside them.

Atlas and the masters are rushing the field. Jackson meets them halfway, and Atlas catches the younger man in his arms.

They're laughing, crying, jumping in the air.

It's been so long I'd nearly forgotten what this feeling was.

We've done it. We won.

. . .

The night's a blur. Standing and watching as Jackson gets to take the Vipers' emblem, the way his whole face lights as he holds it up, the way the arena hisses at it and it's like music. Our walk back to the preparation room and the laughter and shouts that fill the place as we change out of our soaked, sand-covered uniforms.

We make toasts: Jackson to the Iron City; Colt, whose charge had led Sampson in, to the War Hounds; and Atlas to all of us. Sampson toasts the memory of this night, now and forever.

We troop to the buses, thoroughly exhausted. The Iron City is not far from Pompeii, so the buses will take us back to headquarters, and first thing in the morning, we'll go home.

As I lean back against the musty, cracked leather of the bus seat, Lucius slides in beside me. We don't say we're sore; it's a given. But he smiles at me, his dark eyes large in the dim light, his smile white.

"War Hound," he says softly, genially.

"Back at you." I smile and close my eyes.

In the dark, over the loud motor of the bus, a voice—Apa's, I think—starts to sing:

> *It's a long way we've traveled to here, to here,*
> *and a longer way still to go.*
> *But the sun's to our face and the roadway is clear,*
> *so let's whistle a tune full of cheer.*

It's a drifter's song. I don't know it well, but it's popular with working men, especially from the railroad and mining towns. A couple voices join him in the chorus.

> *Let's whistle a tune full of cheer, yes,*
> *let's whistle a tune full of cheer.*
> *The sun's to our face and the roadway is clear,*
> *so let's whistle a tune full of cheer.*

By the second verse, a half-dozen throats are singing. Beside me, Lucius starts. I hear Atlas, too. He grew up on the rails, so I've heard.

> *I've got only pennies to my name, to my name,*
> *and I can't even pay for an inn.*
> *But we'll sing and we'll dance and we'll share what we have,*
> *and sit round the fire by the way.*
> *We'll sit round the fire by the way, yes,*
> *we'll sit round the fire by the way.*
> *We'll sing and we'll dance and we'll share what we have*
> *and we'll sit by the fire by the way!*

"Don't you know it?" Lucius asks.

"I guess I do."

"Come on then, sing!"

I join in, and it seems the whole bus is singing now:

> *We've been on hard times all our lives, all our lives,*
> *but that doesn't matter, my friend.*
> *For water's more sweet and sleep all the more deep*
> *because of the life that we've led.*

Because of the life that we've led, we've led,
because of the life that we've led.
For water's more sweet and sleep all the more deep
because of the life that we've led.

It's true, in the War Games, that it's better to win much than to lose much. But with my head leaned back against the cracked leather, eyes closed, singing with these boys—I'm thinking it's true.

This one really is all the more sweet because of the life we've led.

It's still raining in the Iron City the next morning. It's one of those dark mornings where the sunrise is so obscured by the storm clouds that you're not quite sure when the day has actually started.

The bus pulls up to my stop, its dirty windows blurred by the steady, cold rain. I pick up my gear bag and sling it over my shoulder, moving carefully past the passengers seated around me.

I step down into the wet street, the water rushing past my boots, and see a figure waiting for me at the stop under an umbrella.

"Lucia!"

She reaches out her arms to me and I pick her up, spin her around. The umbrella falls to the broken sidewalk.

We're immediately soaked. Her eyes are sparkling, her sweet face transformed in a beaming smile. She presses her face against mine, laughing. "You did it."

"We all did."

"It was in the papers. There were pictures, descriptions, everything."

I wrap my arms around her and hold her close. For this moment, whatever else comes my way, I am happy. Insanely, inexpressibly happy.

Nothing can take this moment from us.

She takes my face in her hands. "You look so tired."

"I am. I want to dry off, warm up, and sleep."

"I'll put the kettle on when we get home."

"And we'll sit and I'll tell you all about it myself, every detail."

"And you'll sleep," she urges.

"That too." I reach down and pick up the umbrella, then offer her my arm, since my hands are full.

THIRTY
JACKSON VAN

LIEUTENANT, IRON CITY WOLVES

THE TOURNAMENT IS OUR LAST MATCH OF THESE calendar games. It's in Stonington this year, down in the south of the Empire where it is warm. Tournaments only come around every four years, and they're really for show. They rely heavily on momentum and intimidation, and upsets and beatdowns comprise half the spectacle.

Fighters, as a general rule, don't enjoy these tournaments. It's a typical format: you win one match, you get another; win that one, and you get a third. It's all for glory and domination.

But there are more injuries in a tournament—even fatalities, sometimes, because of how quickly one must go from match to match.

No good comes of asking exhausted men to fight over and over until they collapse.

The only two cities exempt from the tournament are

the Golden City and the Leister Bloodhounds. They will play their ultimate match here, but for a Wreath.

The preparation room is subdued. Many of our boys are young and have never been through a tournament. I, Remus, Danforth, Sampson, and Heath have.

I find Remus sitting on the bench, staring at his hands.

"You good?" I pause beside him.

He looks up and gives me a small smile. "Do you remember where we were this time last year?"

"Fighting for a Wreath. Or almost. The matches before."

"I was with the Black Town Stags, up against the Wolves in a sacrifice match."

"That's the Games for you."

He nods. "That's the Games."

It doesn't make it any easier when it's your turn to face defeat, but there's a gravity each of us must grapple with when he joins the tradition of the Games. They will always be far bigger than you and your ambitions. Even the men that are raised to the heights of heroes and gods must have their day and pass on into history.

Nothing lasts forever but the Games.

"Prosper the Games," I say, putting my hand on his shoulder.

He reaches up and grasps my wrist briefly. "Prosper the Games. If we must be the sacrifice, let's make it a brave end."

I am coming to understand this about Remus—he feels

the same sense of leadership, the same protectiveness for the boys that I feel. There's a comfort in that.

The other unpleasant thing about tournaments is that your opponent is drawn at random. You're told in the gate right before the match, so you don't have time to prepare a strategy tailored to your enemy's weaknesses.

We've drawn the Jackals, something I'm not entirely sure was random. The Guild likes a spectacle, and they know what happened last time.

I warn the boys not to get into fights, not to do anything that will get them thrown out. The Guild's looking for that. I tell them that I believe in them, that I'd die for them, and to bring honor to our name.

The gates open and we're turned loose.

The match is over shockingly fast. One of their strategies was to target me, to tie up the phalanx. It's a dishonorable tactic, to my mind. Not fighting to win, but rather to make us lose. The phalanx goes down fighting for me, man by man.

It takes them a long time to finally get to me, and I fight them with everything I can. The match has multiple medical intermissions, and though none of them are for me, I'm bleeding heavily from a cut on my arm and during the later intermissions a medic comes out to me and tries to get it stopped.

"Maybe you should let them take you," he tells me on the last one. My fighting's making it worse.

I don't mean to listen, but they get me on the next start.

They don't even try to take our flag until we're all shocked out. And then they run it up and down the arena, laughing, taking detours, dipping it in the mud.

It's disrespectful, but most of the crowd loves it.

Since we're all shocked out, we all come back for the end, the emblem-taking. Culpepper, their lieutenant, steps up.

"Didn't think I'd even see you again," he smirks, stepping up closer than he needs to be. His eyes flick to mine, and they're full of mockery.

I hold his gaze calmly.

Nettled by what he doesn't see, he draws his knife and takes my uniform in his fist, hard. There's a murmur behind me. The boys don't like what they see.

I keep a neutral face. Last thing we need is my boys getting in a fight. They'd be the ones in trouble, not Culpepper.

He saws at the emblem on my chest—it's a much easier task when you pull the threads tight and cut them bit by bit, but he either doesn't know or isn't interested.

Finally it tears loose, and he finishes the job with a jerk.

Only then does he look at me again, this time turning the emblem in his fingers, flippant. "Don't worry, it's not worth much anyway."

He drops the Iron City emblem in the dirt and grinds it

in with the toe of his shoe. The arena breaks out in a cheer.

"I'd say see you next time, but I don't know. Even the Wolves might dismiss you before next year."

I don't answer that. He's hoping for a reaction, so that's what I won't give him. I salute him, then turn and lead my boys away.

As we're walking, I see the Jackals' captain come out and point at our emblem, his voice scolding.

"Pepper, get that out of dirt. We have to put it on the wall."

I'm sent to the medics right away for my arm. Since I'd soaked through a few bandages before they got the bleeding stopped, they want to clean it out properly and probably stitch it up.

"Let's take a look," the medic says, businesslike.

It's an easy fix, a few stitches and a good solid bandage. I'm warned to carry my gear bag with my other arm, a warning that's not needed.

I go to the washroom to get the blood off my arms and the sand off my face. The medics have taken up the time I would have used to clean up properly and change, so it's straight to the press, disheveled as I am.

Atlas is out there before me. He gives me a look I can't quite read, but there's reassurance in it.

I step out in front of the newspapermen and the photographers, who are loud and blinding and insistent.

"In this tournament, there was not an active attempt to

reach the flag until after your fighters shocked out, Mr. Van. What was the strategy behind that?"

"I'd like to make a small correction to that statement." I clear my throat. "We were made an attempt to reach our flag. We had a shock-out and a crush-out in the process."

"Who was at fault in this loss?"

I can see in their eyes that they're hungry. They're waiting for me to say it, that I'm to blame.

"It was my fault," Atlas cuts in. "I let my boys down. They all fought like heroes down in that arena, Jackson Van included, and they deserve every bit of credit for getting the Iron City as close to victory as we were. In the end, the responsibility lies with me. I did not do enough."

I drop my gaze. What is he doing?

"And do you think your head will be on the chopping block? You know the Iron City's got quite a reputation for axing their captains." The man who asks this question stands, pencil poised, so close I could reach out and take it from him.

Does he not understand that this person he speaks of is flesh and blood and standing inches from him? A man with a heart and feelings?

"That is not my decision, so I choose not to speculate," Atlas answers. Iron. Unmoved.

"And Jackson Van, seeing how this year's games were disastrous even by Iron City standards, do you think, if you and Captain Bolton survive to the Games next year, that this year can be improved on?"

"I know it." I look over at Atlas, then back at them.

"With a man like Captain Bolton at our head—well, we boys would follow him anywhere."

I step back into the room. The air is heavy with disappointment, the boys slow in stripping their gear. They're beat, not just physically but in spirit.

Sampson King and Phillip Blackstone sit near each other. Sampson, who got shocked out halfway across the arena, swarmed by enemies, and Phillip, who'd taken things into his own hands with a valiant run and gotten crushed out halfway up the mountain.

He's tough; he's going to be all right. His wrist is in a cast now.

"I'm sorry, boys. I let you down." I say it loud enough to be heard.

Eyes go to me. Tom and Sampson with their arms folded, faces grim, the couriers with confusion, the chasers with skepticism.

"They came after me to stop you, and they succeeded," I press on. "It wasn't fair to you and I am sorry that I didn't do better. I will not fail this way again."

There's some mixed protest from the phalanx. Peter Hope stands up.

Laertes is wrapping up his ankle with a thick bandage. He looks miserable. "It wasn't your fault, Lieutenant."

"Then whose was it?"

"Ours. All of us." He ties off the bandage with a small jerk. "I'm not letting you stand up here and take the blame when there's others—myself as one—who should be sorry too."

I put my hand on his shoulder and give him a little shake. "Well, Tee, I appreciate the sentiment, but I'm not worried about you. You never make the same mistake twice."

My words hit. A small light comes into his dull eyes.

I go to strip my armor. I let the buckles go with a deep sigh of relief and heft the weight of the armor over my head.

This is light armor. I don't know how the fighting men do it.

I take off my gloves and set them next to me, then peel off my uniform shirt.

Peter Hope sits down next to me, his red hair dark with sweat.

I look over. "I'm all right, Peter."

He doesn't say anything, just starts undoing his armguards slowly. I put my foot over my knee and start undoing the tight laces on my war boots.

I don't know why it's the boots that always get me. My mind always goes straight back to putting them on. The dread, or the hope, or the anticipation I had pre-match.

I stop, weighed down with the disappointment and humiliation these boys just went through. And not one of them pointed a finger at me. "Just wish I could have done more."

"We all do." Peter sniffs, wipes the sweat off his forehead.

"You did what you could. I just hate that they came

after me and it worked. And it wasted you three, and Tom."

"But it's you people point the finger at first. You don't need to point it at yourself too."

"It's my place to take it. You get the glory, you take the dishonor too."

He doesn't meet my eyes this time. "We should have protected you and Sampson better."

Chauncey bursts into the room. "Did you hear? The Toros have won the Wreath! They shocked out the whole field and stood by to watch Luke Sheppard run the flag up the mountain and plant it with his own hands. A commanding win, they said."

"Chauncey!" Laertes's voice is indignant. He indicates subtly towards me.

"Oh."

Slowly, I finish taking off my boots and put them away. The tone of the room, already down, is now tight.

I stop beside Chauncey on my way out.

"I'm fine," I tell him, mustering up a smile and putting my hand on his shoulder. "Those boys in the Golden City all deserve it."

I walk out and head for the roof.

I lean against the cool railing. Up here the wind is thin and fitful, sometimes carrying the sounds of the city below, sometimes bringing nothing.

The city lights stretch out in front of me in a thousand blurred colors.

It's rather comforting to be up at night—the darkness has a way of wrapping around you and letting you be still. You don't have anything to hide, anything to be.

Not that my situation has changed.

I have to come to terms, in the end, with losing the Golden City and my dreams there. All the things it meant to me. Carrying on my father's legacy, those other boys I loved and fought with, the city that had crowned me their next hero.

I can't deny that this feels like a blow. I know what the celebration room would be like. I know Trey is going to think of me—once, maybe—and wish, as I do, that things had worked out differently.

That thought breaks me almost worse than all the others.

I hear a footstep behind me. It's Peter, changed into his street clothes, hair damp, a paper cup in his hand. "The medics thought you should have some." He holds out an iron drink.

"And you knew where to find me." I look at him wryly.

"I had an idea."

I take a swig of the tepid, slightly bitter orange drink. "You'd think they'd find a way to make these taste better." I hold out the paper cup and tilt it a little, looking at the dregs shifting in the bottom. Nothing for it.

I swirl it around and take the rest all at once. Fight against the urge to gag, manage to get it all down. I crush the cup in my hand.

"I suppose you want to be alone."

I don't say anything. I did, but I kind of like his presence right now. I move over a little to give him room.

He leans his big arms on the railing and looks out at the city with a sigh. "I've always thought Stonington was pretty."

I nod.

It's coastal, like the Golden City and the Iron City, but this sea is warm and clear. Some people live on boats here because it's so calm.

Peter looks at his hand. He's missing a nail, probably ripped off in the tournament.

"I'm sorry, Jackson," he says, finally.

He means a lot with that, and I appreciate it.

I sigh and rub the edge of the metal railing with my thumb. "We'll be back to get 'em next year."

"And the next one, too."

I look over at him, and he's smiling.

I smile back, the first one that's come naturally in a while. "And the next, and the next, and the next."

Normally I'd find this kind of talk ridiculous, but tonight it feels different: set in stone somehow, like the Games themselves. Just waiting for us.

THIRTY-ONE
BLAISE VALENTINO

WEAPONS MASTER, IRON CITY WOLVES

"No more trains tonight," the station master tells us when we arrive.

"What do you mean?" Crispin's face darkens. He's acting stable master for now, as Atlas is still caught up in formalities and meetings with the Guild. He'll head home in another day or so.

"No more trains are leaving tonight. Which were you expecting to be on?"

"The nine-thirty to Wachton," I speak up. "We're making a connection there."

"There is bad weather up north, delayed a whole bunch of things. We've had five trains out cancelled because they can't take us and they can't get to us."

"Well, what about tomorrow?"

"We're expecting some to make it through by early morning. You'll be wanting the express at six fifteen."

"All right."

Crispin turns to the boys to break the bad news, but most of them have heard. It's a tough thing, getting humiliated in the arena, being sore and beat up from it, and then being told you can't go home.

I can sense the disappointment and sour mood spreading. Jim Danforth throws down his gear bag and someone swears.

The station master raises his voice. "I'm sorry, there's nothing I can do, but you boys are welcome to sleep in the train station. It'll be an early train out."

We don't have a lot of choice.

I glance at Crispin, but it's Jackson who steps out and raises his arm for attention.

"Boys, we're going to bunk in here. Get as comfortable as you can. At least it's four walls."

The boys are trying to get comfortable. The station floor is hard, but even so most of them have opted for that with their heads on their gear bags rather than try to cram on the benches.

These benches weren't made for the kind of men the Games produce.

Laertes San Domingo has already fallen asleep. Poor kid wiped himself out trying to win us that match.

A handful of others are also asleep—the ones who grew up in hard cities, mostly.

I can't sleep. The tournament replays in my head: the

failed feint, the crush-out of Chauncey. At least he's okay now.

In truth, the whole match was my fault. I got too clever.

A coal train rushes past, letting its horn loose as it passes. Three long blasts. Not too unlike the horn in the arena.

Eddie stirs and turns over.

I pull out my pocket watch. Atlas hasn't come back yet. Not that I'd expect any different from the Guild. They are not respectful of others' time nor energy. They don't care that he hasn't slept in days.

This train is a long one, rumbling on and on.

Above its rumble I hear the high whine and pop of fireworks. From the far window, facing the city, their edges can be seen, and the colors.

Red and gold, for the Golden City Toros.

Jackson Van is lying down, his hands behind his head, staring at the faint bursts of light against the high window. I guess he can't sleep either.

"Are those victory fireworks?" It is Blake's voice, half asleep.

"Yeah."

"One thing's for certain," murmurs Danforth, "they'll never be ours."

"Don't say that." Jackson sits up, looking over at him. "Don't you say that. They will be ours, mark my words. And not too far in the future, either."

I smile to myself, suddenly heartened. Jackson Van once tasted victory in spades, and then he was given a good taste of the dirt. And still, he talks like this. He and Atlas both.

"You say that, Van," says Danforth, "but you've got to face the real world. They don't let guys like us win."

"Just wait." Jackson lies down again, hands back under his head. "I'll get you boys there."

THIRTY-TWO
JACKSON VAN

LIEUTENANT, IRON CITY WOLVES

It is dark outside the curtained windows of our Iron City barracks, and the tentative songs of the birds are the only hint that morning is approaching. I roll onto my back and thrust my arms under my head. I've been awake for a couple hours already, running over and over the last ten minutes of the tournament game in my head.

Most of the boys stayed overnight in the barracks last night. We'd traveled all day yesterday, meeting delays at almost every turn. If it wasn't weather, it was fellow travelers who'd gone to Stonington to watch the tournaments and the Wreath match.

There's never enough room in the barracks, so like last night at the train station, we're all strewn across the floor, but this time on cots and bedrolls.

Over by the wall someone rolls over and sits up. It's

Peter. Slowly he rubs his eyes, shoves off the blanket and reaches for his boots.

I listen as he quietly dresses and folds up his blanket.

He sees me as he passes my cot and I raise myself on my elbow. "Have you been awake?" he asks.

"Yeah."

"I'm going up to the roof."

"Can I come?"

He nods, a brief movement in the dark.

I roll over and shove my boots on.

"Where's your coat?" he asks.

"I'm fine."

"Bring the coat."

Reluctantly, I take my jacket from its peg as we head out of the barracks. The stairs to the roof are down the hall. I don't think I've ever bothered to go up there.

I follow him up the narrow steps through a passageway barely big enough for his broad shoulders. Above my head, he pushes open a door, and pale morning light pours in.

"Watch your step." He holds the door for me as I step over the high threshold and out onto the wide, high roof. There are railings, mostly used by the birds, and old, disused equipment is strewn here and there.

The wind blows strong, pushing against my jacket flap and blowing it open. I button it up. Peter's right. In the early morning, without the sun's warmth, the wind bites.

"Here's my favorite spot in all the Iron City." He folds his arms, wrapping his coat tighter around himself. "Take a look."

The snow-capped mountains in the distance are laced with pink. And between us and them stretch first the city, with its factories; beyond that, the mines; and then forests, rising on the ever-growing hills, upwards and upwards to the mighty peaks that stand wild, beyond the control of anything manmade. It's like you can watch as the grip of smoke and industry loosens and falls away completely.

"There." His whole face is lit with a kind of wonder. "That right there."

For a moment I don't feel any of the things that mattered so much downstairs. That Blackstone was crushed halfway up the mountain, the way Culpepper smiled as he cut the emblem from my chest, or how Atlas stood up in front of the press and told them it was his fault when really, it was mine.

It's just me and the wild mountains, impregnable, free.

We are silent. Words are not needed. We simply watch as the sunlight spreads across the sky, painting the peaks red-gold.

The noise of the city waking and setting to work begins to fight against the birdsong. But it cannot quite steal the silent beauty of the watching mountains.

"Do you come up here often?" Our breath stands on the cold air.

"If I'm in the barracks, every morning. The mountains, they—they have a way of melting your troubles."

I feel that now.

"I have dreams, you know, of running away." He sniffs and rubs his nose. "Out there into the hinterlands where they can't follow. I'd take my mom. Sometimes I think I will, when all this is over."

"But not now?"

"I've got you boys to think of. I wouldn't leave you. But —sometimes the city presses in on me until I feel so crushed I can't breathe. And then I dream. Of those." He nods towards the mountains. "Every night for a week, sometimes."

I reach out and put my hand on his shoulder.

"Don't tell anyone, will you?" He looks over at me.

"No one." I turn my gaze back out to the open view, try to soak in as much as I can before we have to go back down.

Peter's doing the same, a little smile on his face as his eyes roam over the distant ranges.

"Peter—"

He stops and looks at me, expectant.

"Thank you."

His face lights with small, genuine pleasure. "It wasn't your fault the other night," he adds. "Don't believe that for a minute."

"It's my job to take the blame. Everyone has places they could improve, of course. Except you. You, Pete, are perfect."

"No, I'm not." He protests, grinning. But he's blushing.

"Do you have a home elsewhere? For the in-between?"

He shakes his head. "It's the Iron City all the way. What about you?"

"I'm not welcome anywhere," I chuckle. "Unless I go

back to my parents. And no one would like that except perhaps my mother."

I sigh. The world has slipped back onto my shoulders. "I should go. I have to meet with Atlas this morning."

"Already?"

I give him a glance. My part in the tournament was not flattering. In most cities it's grounds for dismissal. I can only guess that what it's about.

"Atlas isn't going to give you the sack."

"We'll see."

"If he does, I am going to fight him on it, inch for inch. You are my lieutenant."

"And what about Luke?"

"What about him? He was good. I loved him and I'm happy for him. But I'll fight for you."

I give him a smile—he's trying to be comforting—and head for the stairs.

"I mean it, Jackson Van," he calls after me. "Whether you believe it or not."

I stare out at the slow falling of the snow. It's a new thing for me, not being raised in the north or near mountains, and the way the people on the street keep on walking through it, tolerating its presence, is amazing to me.

"Have you been waiting long?" Susan the secretary asks, slipping into her seat.

I pull my gaze from the window.

"Hi, Susan." I grip my hands together. Might as well get it over with. "I'm here to see the captain."

"Yes, he's expecting you. You can head down to his office."

Atlas is sitting behind his desk. As I come in, he stands up.

"Shut the door, please. And—have a seat." He indicates to a chair across from him.

I shut the door and come over.

"If this is about the tournament—" I begin. "I will make it up to you. If you decide to let me continue. I understand if you don't."

"It is about the tournament." Atlas's face is grim, sad even. "But none of that matters right now. Look, there is no easy way to say this."

He takes a deep breath, turns the handle of his mug. And then he fixes me with a direct look. "Someone's been selling us out during the Games. Passing information to our opponents. And they did it in the tournament, too."

Cold shock washes over me. I'm the one the finger will point to first, the easy answer. There's no way they'll believe me a second time.

"Captain, I—" No words come out. I'm not going to break. I am going to take this too, with dignity.

Atlas sees my face and he must see some of what's written there, because his expression suddenly softens. "Jackson, we know it isn't you."

"You do?"

"We'd be having a very different kind of conversation if that were the case."

I exhale, my body goes weak with relief.

"We're almost certain we know who it is."

My mind races over the men, over the ones in the tournament, over this past run of calendar games.

It can't be Peter, no chance. Not any of the phalanx. Sampson? Unlikely.

I want to get it over with. "Can I ask—?"

"It's Tom."

Our vanguard.

"He's been leaking signals and plans, for payment, I think, most of the year. We believe he is trying to pay off a debt to some shady lenders in the city."

I'm sick to my stomach. I've just been through tribunal myself, and even though this is different, making the choice to sell us out over and over again while looking your comrades in the eye—I can't help but feel some horror for him over it.

"We plan to dismiss him quietly. I am not looking to involve the Guild in this." Atlas's face is sad.

"Why did you call me, then?"

"Because you are our lieutenant and you have led that man in the arena. You have a right to know beforehand, and you have a right to speak for or against him before it's common knowledge. I should have warned you. Naturally, you're going to be gun shy about the issue."

"I just don't know why you didn't come after me first."

"We looked into everyone. But knowing you the way I do now, I didn't believe you'd done it the first time, either."

I nod. "That was a personal matter. One I had little control over," I say. "Captains, as you know, must fight to keep their places."

"I do. It's a necessary evil this beautiful game brings about. I am sorry for it, for your sake."

He stands up with a sigh. I follow suit and move towards the door.

"One more thing, Jackson, since you're here—"

"Yes?"

"I've been retained another year by the Iron City, despite the wreck of these Games. I've put forward a recommendation that you be paid a full lieutenant's pay this year. No docking for the scandal."

"You're going to keep me?"

"I paid a lot of money to let you back in the Games." Atlas smiles, his blue eyes wry. "I expect you to pull your weight."

"Thank you, sir."

I duck out quick to hide my smile.

"It's all right," his voice comes after me. "You can smile, you've earned it."

THIRTY-THREE
BLAISE VALENTINO

WEAPONS MASTER, IRON CITY WOLVES

THESE ARE THE DOLDRUMS OF WINTER, WHEN everything is perpetually gray, something Susan assures me will be permanent for at least another month.

Snow is piled high against the walls of the headquarters and barracks. Most days you can't even tell if it's morning or afternoon. And night—night comes early.

I pull my collar higher around my neck and duck my head against the sting of the winter air.

There are men drilling in the indoor arena, their breath standing in the cold, heavy air as they run and cut and wrestle each other down.

I walk on past and step up into the barracks.

The four-legged stove in the corner is blazing hot, and a dozen men fresh from the practice arena are gathered around it, thawing hands or helping each other out of their armor.

"It's the weapons master!" shouts Ami Pritchard-

Allen, halfway through stripping his gear. "Come on in, out of the cold!"

I shut the door after myself and go over to the stove. Lucius and Remus step aside to make room.

I hold my hands up against the warm air. Pretty soon final inspections will happen and most of the boys will go their separate ways, at least for a few months. But for now, the place is still bustling.

"What brings you down here?" asks Peter Hope, coming in from the other room, carrying his boots and armguards.

"Inspection preparation. Doing my job."

He gives my arm a friendly push on his way by.

One of the assistants from headquarters comes around with deliveries from the office: letters, paper forms, payments, and so on.

"Mail," he says, passing out a few letters. Jackson Van, Trenton Fitch, Ami Pritchard-Allen. They take their letters back to their gear stalls.

"You seen Sampson?" he asks me.

"He's up at headquarters."

The assistant gives a nod and buttons his coat up high before going back out into the snow.

"My family got five feet of snow," says Fitch, showing the letter to Eddie and Laertes. They come and look over his shoulder.

Apa glances over his, turning it back and forth a couple times, and rips it in half, throwing it in the wastebasket.

A newspaper sits on one of the benches—not today's,

since it's about the Golden City Toros winning the Wreath.

Chauncey picks it up and looks it over. "This newspaper got nothing but praise for that Luke Sheppard. Was he that good here, really?"

"He was that good," says Danforth. "The Guild just never gave him time of day because the Iron City didn't make them money. Until that night against the Black Town."

"Luke was like that," says Peter Hope. "The hero type. More hero than man. I think we all figured he could be more than we could give him here."

Sampson comes in, humming softly to himself, and starts to clean up his laid-out things.

"So there weren't any hard feelings, then? When he left?" Chauncey persists.

Sampson stops his humming and looks up. "Look, kid, it's like this. The Iron City's one of your one-way streets. Only one direction this thing goes, and that's down. If you get lucky—real lucky—and that street goes two ways for even a split second, you go. You don't stop, you don't think, you don't hesitate. You run for it."

"Have you ever seen it do that?"

"Only once since I've been here, and that was our boy Luke." Sampson's eyes stray to Jackson Van. "Just Luke."

"You think he ever thinks about you?"

"I hope," cuts in Phillip.

The question seems to strike Sampson strangely. His eyes get a faraway look. "You know what, kid? I think he does. More than anyone guesses, more than he might admit to himself."

He looks around the room slowly.

"You all have a good night." He gives us a nod and throws his bag over his shoulder. He walks out, whistling.

The next morning, it's snowed so much that the drifts are up to the windows. Inside, the windows are fogged from all the activity. Inspection is today.

The equipment's all laid out and the men are milling around, finishing up any last repairs or polishes.

"Has anyone seen Sampson?" I ask. I haven't seen him all morning.

"No, he was here last night. Has anyone heard? Has he taken sick?" Phillip goes over to the equipment tables. "His things aren't here."

Atlas comes over quietly. "Didn't you hear? There's been a transfer request for Sampson. The Vaqueros want him."

"Does he know?"

"I told him yesterday. I thought you knew already. Susan was supposed put the request on your desk."

"I went down to the barracks late afternoon and went home straight from there."

So all that last night, the way Sampson talked to the Chauncey, the way he packed his bags nearly full, the way he wished the boys goodnight. That was him saying goodbye.

"He's gone?" Phillip demands.

"Yes. He called me from the station. The transfer is complete."

"He didn't tell us. Didn't even say goodbye," says Phillip quietly.

It had all happened so fast.

"Guild is going to be here in five minutes! Last checks," calls Jackson. Atlas goes into the next room with the other men.

He'll be telling them the news.

The wastebasket stands next to me, empty except for a single letter, ripped in half.

Suddenly curious, I reach down into it and pick up the letter. It has Ami Pritchard-Allen's name on the front. I unfold it and hold up the two sides. It's a transfer request, put in by the Bloodhounds. For a sum we'd never be able to pay him.

He hadn't said a thing. He'd only looked at it for thirty seconds.

Through the door I can see the men lining up for inspection. Laughter swells as Atlas says something I don't quite catch. Apa is standing along the wall, sharing the laugh, and sobers up as Atlas goes down the line, checking.

They'll never know. He's thrown away a lot of money and his chance at making something of himself, to stay with us.

A man like Atlas will do that to you.

I drop the letter back in the wastebasket.

THIRTY-FOUR
CHASE BIRMINGHAM
STREET BOY, ISTANWICK

THE ARENA IN ISTANWICK TOWERS OVER THE dirty streets around me. The clang of trolley bells and the shouts of the street sellers fill the cold air. A bus rushes past, swaying, loaded down with too many people. It rattles and scrapes against the pavement.

These are the streets I've lived in my whole life, and finally they've led me to this place.

The Games.

I pull the cap down low on my forehead and stick my hands deep into my jacket pockets. It took almost the last of my money to get these clothes, and they're secondhand.

It's now or never.

I go to the corner drug store and buy a roll of bandage and some antiseptic. I pause to look longingly at the sandwiches in the trays beside the counter, but I resist. I don't have enough for one.

I walk down the street with the paper bag until I find

an alleyway that's quiet and has lots of boxes and trash-cans out. Glancing around quickly, I duck behind the cleanest looking set and roll my pant leg up over my right knee.

The dressing is soaked through and smells bad. I tear it off and fling it into the nearest can.

My knee's not looking very good. It's swollen and red, half scabbed, half draining. I open the antiseptic and grit my teeth as I douse my knee.

It hurts like fire, but it sure works.

Breathe.

I give it a minute to dry in the cold, early-spring air, then open the roll of bandage with my teeth.

This has to hold all night with me on my feet and maybe into the next morning. As tightly as I can without losing all movement, I bind my knee up again.

I haul myself to my feet. Bounce a little on them, gritting my teeth. It'll hold.

There's a gate at the side entrance to the Istanwick arena with a temporary sign someone's painted *Conscriptees.*

I walk up to the gate. In a little window to one side is a man with a dark uniform and a white mustache.

"I am here for the Conscriptio."

"Conscriptee or with a city?"

"Conscriptee."

"Name?"

"Birmingham? Chase Birmingham."

"Chase?" The man looks at me over his spectacles.

"It's a name, right?"

"Not like any I've heard."

"Well, it's the only one I got."

"Fine." His eyes relent a little and he looks vaguely amused. "A name's a name."

He looks down his register, his finger tracing down the list of names. "You're here. And under Chase, too. Here's your number. Once this gate opens, you'll head straight down this road here to the first door. There will be someone to direct you. Welcome, and good luck."

He lays down an armband with a number and reaches his hand out to shake mine. I wipe the sweat off my palm and take his hand.

I'm number fifteen. That's high.

My heart quickens. It means I will be wanted. Considered valuable by the cities, maybe even swapped if I land in an unfavorable one.

I wonder what they'd do to me if they found out I was hiding an injury.

A cold shiver runs down my back. It's one thing to hide an injury on the streets, when weakness can cost you your life—but once you're conscripted to a city, you can't leave unless they dismiss you or trade you off. You're theirs.

To hide the fact that you're damaged goods is a serious offense. But this is my one shot, and I'll risk everything to take it.

True to the man's instructions, there's a man at the first door who ushers me in.

"Put on your number," he instructs. "That way they know you're a conscriptee."

He waves me through.

I slip my arm through the armband and slide the thing up until it rests comfortably over my upper arm. The hall is long and my feet echo loudly against the polished floors.

This place is old.

A pale light pours through the doorway ahead; I step through and stop short. The ceiling is higher than any I have ever seen, held up by white columns, and the floor's covered in white stone. The banners of the twenty-six cities hang from the high columns across the floor.

Feels like I'm in the presence of something terribly powerful and ancient.

"Excuse me." Someone pushes past. He's wearing number thirty-five.

I step forward. I ain't seen anything like this in my life.

I follow thirty-five across the wide floor and down to the conscriptee area.

The conscriptee area has no seating. It's just a pit, where we'll stand for the whole night. My heart sinks.

But I'll do it. I've always survived. This is no different.

Torches light the expectant faces around me, lifted to watch the words of the man drawing the names and the cities.

The drums, which have been pounding like my heart, stop.

A murmur runs through the conscriptees. Only twenty

have been named, so we're still crammed in down here, sweating and brushing shoulders.

"The Iron City!" he announces. He moves down and they pull a name from the great urns.

Another one. His eyes go to the conscriptee pit, to me.

"Number fifteen! Chase Birmingham!"

It's happened.

I swallow, wiping the sweat from my forehead with my sleeve. Straighten my face to a blank mask before I step forward on my bum knee.

The other boys part to let me up, and I walk over to the stand microphone. I've never been near one of these things, suspended on their coiled wires.

I lean down to speak into it and hear a ripple of laughter as it makes a high noise. I step back.

"I hear the call of my captain, and to the Iron City I swear my allegiance."

They welcome me with handshakes and a good hard slap on the back. The big one introduces himself as the captain, William Bolton. If not for the gray starting in his beard, he'd still pass for a fighter. The next is Valentino, the weapons master. He's got a lean look to him, like a street man in good clothes. And the last is Crispin Teller, Stable Master. He's young to be a stable master, I think, but his dark eyes have the look of a fighter.

I take my place under the banner, clenching my jaw as I shift on my knee, and clasp my hands behind my back. I've done it.

THIRTY-FIVE
REMUS BLAKE

CHASER, IRON CITY WOLVES

THE BARRACKS HAVE BEEN SCRUBBED OUT FOR the new conscriptees and the windows are wide open. The place smells of lye soap and morning air.

I stand in the doorway, my gear bag over my shoulder.

"You're the chaser. Welcome back." The janitor emerges from the storage room, a stack of blankets in his hands. I rather like the man—he's got a sensible face and spectacles, and he dresses well. Vestiges of better times, perhaps.

"It's looking nice in here. I don't remember it being this clean last year."

"Crispin's had a big hand in this," says the janitor. "He has been hard at work in here since Atlas made him stable master. Can't say I'm mad."

"He's stable master now?"

"Made him that right after final inspections. Did you hear we lost Tom and Sampson?"

"I heard. I'm happy for Sampson. He deserved it."

"Did you hear Tom signed with the Vipers?"

"After we dismissed him?"

The janitor raises his eyebrows and gives me a knowing look. "There are different rules for the Iron City."

I lift my bag. "Will there be a place for me to unpack a little? For drills?"

"Anywhere that doesn't have a name on it." He nods to the other room where the equipment is usually laid out.

I step into the other room and see the handwritten signs with the names of the fighters who stayed on over the break.

Trenton Fitch. Phillip Blackstone. Three out of the four conscriptees from last year. Jackson Van.

I find a gear stall that's empty and set my bag down.

"Remus?"

Lucius Shanahan is standing in the doorway, his bag over his shoulder.

"Lucius!"

He grins and drops his bag, throwing his arms around my shoulders, slapping my back hard. "You're back with us, War Hound."

"Nowhere else for me to go," I laugh.

"Were you here this whole time?" he asks.

"No, I was able to go down and stay with my brother and his wife. Just a few weeks, but my wife got to see her family."

"I got married," Lucius says, shyly. "Just last week. Went back to Leister to my folks and married up."

"What? That's great news! Is she here?"

He nods. "The house isn't much, but it's ours."

I slap him on the shoulder. "When you're settled, bring her over for dinner some night. Lucia and I would love to have you."

"Sure." He smiles, his whole face lit up. The Iron City may still be the Iron City, but I can already feel the difference this year. Lucius is a new man, for a start.

We help each other armor up and we head out to the practice arena. Jackson is out running pace drills, the only other person here.

"What were you planning on doing?" Lucius asks.

"I was thinking of doing pace drills and contacts, but since you're here, my saber hits could use some work."

"Saber hits." He grins and spins his saber.

"A couple pace drills to get warm, and then saber hits. We'll try and stick to the main points for now, hm?" I point to my shoulder, chest, and hip.

"Don't worry. I got no problem hitting you," he laughs.

We break from drills a few hours later, sweaty and bruised. The dust's gotten everywhere, sticking to our sweat and running down our faces and arms, so we run the pump for each other and take turns sticking our heads under.

At the back of the barracks is an old stone wall that's been abandoned. We sit down on it and pull out our lunches.

When you drill before the elimination trial period begins, you're on your own for food.

"Lucia packed me sandwiches." I pull the brown paper-wrapped package out and set it on the wall beside me.

"They look fine, too." Lucius pulls out an apple and shines it up on his shirtsleeve.

"Is that all you got?"

"Nothing is unpacked," he says with a little smile, his mouth full of apple. "House is less organized than a hayloft."

I hand him a sandwich without a word.

We eat in amicable silence, staring at the distant mountains that just peer over the tops of the factories.

He looks down. "I want to say thank you."

"For the sandwich?" I laugh.

"Uh-huh. No." He looks up, out at the city. "No, for fighting next to me, and, you know, watching my back last year. I guess I was afraid of—what could happen to me in the arena."

"I think that's natural."

"If it's natural, then, why'd I feel like such a coward?"

"Fear doesn't play fair. Lots of men lose their nerve." I look over at him. "And just so you know, I don't think you were losing your nerve. You'd seen a lot. That eats at a man, especially when he's trapped."

He's staring straight ahead.

"Well, I couldn't face Margaret before, because I hated myself for being a coward. And she told me she didn't want to marry a fighter. But we loved each other, real bad."

I reach down and pick up another sandwich.

"When I went back home to visit, she was there, and I

found I could look her in the eye again. That was enough for us both, this time."

"You earned that. That was you, not me."

"I don't know. It all changed when you came, I mean it. But she's still afraid I'll get hurt. She works in a hospital, sees all kinds of things. And I don't want to let her down."

"Well, I've still got your back. Now and to the end of the Games."

"And I've got yours."

"Let's start by turning this cohort upside down, hm?"

"Yeah. And win the Wreath, maybe." He grins.

I laugh and take a deep breath. The Iron City always smells a bit of automobiles and chimney smoke. We're not quite close enough to the harbor to smell the salt air.

"You done?" I ask.

"Ready to work, if that's what you're asking."

I drop my hand onto his shoulder. "That's the spirit."

THIRTY-SIX
CHASE BIRMINGHAM
FLAG-BEARER, IRON CITY WOLVES

I PUSH MYSELF UP ON ONE ARM, LISTENING carefully. Above me I hear soft snoring. From the beginning of bird-sounds outside, I figure it's about four in the morning.

No sounds other than the breathing of the other conscriptees. I slide out of the bed, gritting my teeth against the pain as I put weight on my bad knee. My head's started to hurt the last couple days, in addition to the knee.

I stick my hand under the mattress and pull out the roll of bandage I've hidden there. I've been redressing the wound myself for the last week, but soon someone's going to catch me or I'm going to stumble and not be able to get up.

I sneak out into the hallway, into one of the storage closets. Behind an old box of bootlaces I've kept a candle stub and a box of matches hidden. I light the candle and peel up my pant leg. It doesn't look good. Blood and infection have seeped through the bandage.

A footstep creaks in the hallway.

I freeze. Someone's out there. If I blow out the candle now, they'll know for sure someone's in here.

I let my breath out softly, trying not to make any noise, and reach down slowly to roll my pant leg back down over my knee.

The door opens to show Phillip Blackstone framed in the doorway.

I pull down my pant leg hastily.

His expression darkens. "Kid, what are you doing in here?"

"Nothing." My mouth's gone dry.

"It's something, let me see."

I back up, but I'm trapped. I've got nowhere to go. I could probably rush him, knock him down, but the noise would certainly bring more witnesses.

He comes over and gently pulls my pant leg back up, revealing the bandage. I stiffen. Watch his face for his reaction.

I can't read his expression. His brow's just furrowed as he's looking at it.

"How long have you had this?" he asks.

"Right after the conscriptee inspection."

He raises his eyebrows. "Let's see it." He takes my feverish knee in his hands, moving the wrapping gently to look underneath. I grit my teeth, trying not to flinch.

"Kid, this is bad."

"They can't know. They'll dismiss me and no one else will take me. I won't get a chance."

It's on the tip of my tongue to say that fighting in the Games on this knee gives me a better chance at survival than going back to the streets, but he's occupied now with pulling up the bandage, rolling down the pant leg.

He's moving slowly, gently. "You go into the arena on this, it might be your last time."

"I can, though. I've done it before. I've beaten these kinds of things before in the cheap arenas."

He looks at me slowly. "I bet you have." He sighs, leaning his hands on his knees.

"Promise you won't tell anyone?" Sweat pricks the back of my neck.

Phillip looks up at me. "Chase. I can't let you keep working on this knee. We've got two, three weeks until eliminations. You have to stay off it until then. I'll talk to the captain, I'll find an excuse. Say you're sick—"

He straightens and touches my forehead. "You're feverish, so that won't be a lie," he mutters.

"But I can't hide—"

"I'm taking you to my place. You won't be on the streets and you won't be in the conscriptees' room. We'll get you healed up."

He grabs my arm and hoists it over his shoulder, pulling my weight off my knee and onto him. Together we steal softly through the barracks and out into the dark.

We pass under a street lamp; there are cracks in the sidewalk, and then it suddenly ends. There is no pavement at all. It's dirt. We continue to limp down the street.

"Are we walking there?"

"Yeah. I live close."

It's quiet again between us.

I fight the urge to put my head on his shoulder. I'm not feeling good at all. I'm afraid, so afraid to put myself in anyone's hands, but part of me was relieved to be found out.

"We're almost there," he says, glancing back over his shoulder. "I'm going to get you in, get you to bed, and clean out that wound. Then I'll have to get back. I don't want them starting a manhunt and getting us both in trouble."

"I don't understand."

"What?"

"I could be your replacement."

He sniffs and seems to hunch up his shoulders against me. "Don't see what that has to do with anything."

He leads me up a winding little front walk that's all scattered stones and up a couple steps to the front door of an old, small house.

He opens the door softly and keeps his voice low. "The bed right there, use that one."

It's against the wall in a small sitting room of sorts, facing the kitchen. It's all the same room, really. Two doors stand in the back of the house, both closed.

I ease myself down and take off my shoes. I wince.

"Easy. Just lay yourself down."

Phillip puts on a kettle of water to boil. The stove is old—most everything in here seems to be—but it's clean.

I ease my legs up onto the bed and lay back. The sheets smell good and fresh.

I'm cold and my head's pounding. A shiver goes up my back and I brace against it.

"I'm going to have you drink this." Phillip brings over a cloudy-labeled bottle and a glass. He pours out just enough to cover the bottom and then tips in a little more. "Take it slow."

"What is it?"

"It's just brandy."

"I don't know."

"It's not going to put you out. But it's going to help with the pain. You have to rest, and I need to see what I'm working with."

Reluctantly, I take it and drain the glass.

"Just lay back. Try to relax." He goes and takes the kettle off the stove as it starts to rumble and squeal.

From the kettle he fills a bowl and brings it over beside the bed. He leaves me and seems to be digging around in some closet; from it he brings out a medicine bottle and some clean cloths.

He puts a blanket under my right knee, folded thrice. "Okay, I'm going to be as careful as I can be."

He starts peeling away the stiff bandages. Between the brandy and the fever, I'm fighting to keep my eyes open, breaking out in a sweat.

He peels away the last bit of bandage that's stuck on. "You're doin' fine." He dips a cloth in the water and wrings it out.

I hiss as he touches the warm cloth to my knee. I push

myself up on my elbows to watch. There's something about seeing it that helps me brace against the pain.

It takes him a while to get it clean to his liking. The blanket underneath my knee is soaked with water and stained red.

"It's going to be all right, I think," he says. "But you've got to beat this fever. I'm going to bandage this up, and I need you to sleep. I'll bring back something to cool you down if I can."

I lie back, but everything in me screams I shouldn't trust him. He could do all this and then go straight to the stable master to turn me in.

"It's okay." He presses the back of his hand against my forehead. It's too cold. A second later, there's a cool cloth against my skin and I can feel the fight leaving my body. I'm fading.

"Don't fight it," he whispers. "You're not going anywhere."

Instinct is trying to keep me awake. I hear ragged breathing that echoes in my ears. It's mine, I know, but it doesn't feel like it.

"I've got you, boy," Phillip whispers. "I'll take care of you. You can let go."

A feverish spasm seizes my back. I want to let go and sleep so badly.

A gentle humming eases itself over my fighting breaths. Every instinct is screaming for me to hold on, to stay awake, but I can feel my grip loosening. I give up and let the blackness reach in and swallow me up.

· · ·

I wake up with no idea where I am. I scramble up and push off the covers. My shirt's missing, and my pant leg has been cut off, the knee swathed in clean bandages.

I'm in Phillip Blackstone's house.

Late afternoon sun filters through the closed curtains. Slowly, I fall back onto the pillow.

I can tell immediately that my fever's broken. I'm so weak I can't move.

A little face peers around the corner.

I raise myself on my elbow, wincing at the movement in my knee.

A loud squeak and the face disappears. Little voices whisper just outside the door.

"Hey," I say, shifting myself into a more comfortable position. "It's all right. You don't have to hide."

Two little figures shuffle in. A little boy and a little girl. Big dark eyes, dark curly hair, shy expressions.

"Who are you?" asks the little girl.

"I'm Chase. Who are you?"

"I'm Nora."

"And I'm Charlie," the little boy pipes up.

"Where is your shirt?" Nora asks.

"I don't know. Do you know where Phillip is?"

Charlie wrinkles his nose. "Who Phillip?"

"The man?" I try to indicate height with my hand. They just stare at me with shy little smiles. "Is anybody at home?"

They both point to the back of the house. I hear the sound of a door opening.

"What are you two doing out here?" It's Phillip, buttoning up his shirt.

"It's a man," Charlie tells him solemnly, pointing me out.

"Go on." Phillip scoops the child up and walks him to the end of the room. "Run along and play, both of you. Let me and the man talk."

"Who are they?" I ask.

"Those are my kids."

"Yours?"

"Not born mine, but they're mine now, and what else are you going to call them? Kids should feel they belong with someone."

I know that well.

Phillip drags a chair over to sit next to the bed. "How do you feel?"

"Better than before. No fever. How long's it been?"

"A day and a half. You slept hard."

"My knee?"

"It's closing up a little. Still a bit early to tell."

A knock sounds at the door. Phillip gives me a brief, grim look and goes to the door.

"Yes, sir?" He opens it a couple feet.

"Is he in here?" It's Atlas.

I scramble to sit up. Reach for my shirt. I can't find it. I pull the sheets up as far as I can, hiding the scars on my chest.

He sold me out.

Atlas shoulders his way in, ducking to fit under the low entryway.

"Captain Bolton, I—" Excuses fly to my lips but none of them suit. I'm caught, and it's going to be over before it's begun.

"Chase, son." Atlas crouches down beside me. His bulk dwarfs the modest room. "This is exactly the kind of thing I need to know about."

"I'll be ready," I protest, my strength pouring back into my body, as it always has, to save me. "I swear. You can work me just as hard as the others, and I'll be just fine—"

"No, no." He reaches out and puts his hand on my shoulder. "There's no rush. You're a good fighter. I wouldn't let you go back. Not to the cheap arenas, and certainly not out on the street."

"But you said you needed me right away."

"I'll worry about that. That's my problem."

"You mean that?"

"Yes. And I'll prove it to you." He pulls an envelope out of his pocket with my name on it. "There's your first month's pay."

I open the envelope. It's more than I've ever had in my life.

Relief washes over me and I'm suddenly weak with it. "I'm sorry, sir," I manage. "I should have told you."

"I know. And I expect you to if this ever happens again. But I also know you've come from places where you can't trust anyone. It's all forgiven."

He stands up. "You rest, and we'll send an automobile when it's time for you to be back."

Phillip sees him to the door and they spend a few

minutes outside, talking quietly. I slide back down in the bed and close my eyes. I have no strength.

The door closes.

Phillip comes back in, not quite meeting my eyes. "I'm sorry about that." He gestures to the door. I can hear the automobile starting up in the street outside as Atlas leaves. "I've never been a good liar."

"I thought you snitched."

"Not on my own, I didn't. But once he knew I knew where you were and you hadn't run—and trust me, you don't want them thinking you've run."

I nod. Breaking the code is one of the worst things you can do. They'll come after you like a fugitive.

"He says you can stay another day. Then the medics want to work on you at the barracks."

I've never trusted medics nor hospitals. Anyone I knew on the street who went to a hospital never came back.

"They won't send me to a hospital, will they?"

"I doubt it. Not now that the fever's gone."

I look down. "No one's ever done something like this for me."

Phillip just shrugs.

"They could have come after you too."

"Yeah." Phillip drags over a chair and sits down. "That wouldn't have stopped me. But I figured Atlas wouldn't dismiss us for this. Some captains, stable masters, they treat their fighters like cattle, but he don't."

I sink deep into the sheets. Just this short time being awake has exhausted me.

Phillip stands up and pours me a glass of water. "Drink this before you sleep. You need to get fluids back in you."

I take the glass from him and prop myself up enough to drink half.

"So they call you Chase, hm? Where'd you get your name?"

"The street. If you get food or money, you got to be tough or fast, otherwise they'll catch you and beat you and take it."

"And you were fast."

"I am fast." I hold out my water and he takes it, sets it down.

"When you wake up, you'll feel a lot better," he says. "You ever play cards?"

"No, just street shuffle."

He laughs. "That's a swindler's game. I'll teach you a real one."

THIRTY-SEVEN
BLAISE VALENTINO
WEAPONS MASTER, IRON CITY WOLVES

Atlas walks in front of me down the elimination line, his broad shoulders blocking the blinding morning sun, in and out. I see the faces that have become familiar as we pass and Atlas pulls them out.

Jackson Van, solemn, but with a settled look passing between him and Atlas, the sort shared by equals.

Remus Blake with a flash of a smile, Laertes San Domingo with that fierce light in his eyes. The men have started calling him Lightning.

It's the same on down the line—the tap on the shoulder, the nod, the small smile. The relief in the men's eyes as they are chosen.

Standing together are our flag-bearers, Phillip staring straight ahead, stiff and drawn up, and Chase with his hands clasped behind his back, his eyes following us down the line.

Atlas pauses beside them.

"Chase." He sets his hand on the boy's shoulder. "Step out."

Chase glances at Phillip and obeys. Behind his back, his fingers are working with anxiety.

"Phillip."

Blackstone steps out.

We move down the line, Atlas, myself, and Crispin, until the whole line's been passed. Nearly all the men have been chosen, and we may still turn out a little short-handed.

The absence of Tom and Sampson stands out, but young Trenton Fitch seems to be taking his promotion to vanguard very seriously. He is out training with the phalanx constantly.

He stands now with a little smile on his face, hands behind his back, squinting against the sun. He stayed at the barracks over the winter and spring, and I happen to know that all but a meager amount of his pay gets sent off to another address.

Susan seems to think it is younger siblings he's supporting. It's the common story here, I am learning. Most of these men are sending their pay to family, living on little to nothing, trying by these games to raise their family's circumstances.

It puts things in perspective. In Stonington, and in most of the more affluent cities, the goal is glory and fame. These men here are just trying to survive.

Atlas comes back around to face the line.

"Men, we are on the eve of our next calendar games. I am impressed by the work you have put in here. I drive you hard, and I do it to give us a fighting chance. And no, things aren't perfect here. We are still swimming against a powerful current that will try and drag us down, but at least we aren't doing it with one hand tied behind our backs. What we've done is give ourselves a chance. And in the Games, that is really all you can ask for."

Jackson is nodding, Remus listening with a little smile on his face. But they are not the only ones. I can see in the men's faces that they believe what he says this year, most of them.

"Let's bring honor to the Iron City and to each other. Prosper the Games."

"Prosper the Games," I echo with the others.

THIRTY-EIGHT
JACKSON VAN

LIEUTENANT, IRON CITY WOLVES

WE ARE IN HUDSON AGAIN. CRISPIN HAS HIRED bodyguards to follow the team for the short time we're out on the streets, not wanting a repeat of what happened last year, but I don't know that it's necessary.

These people, they play you dirty one way and leave it like a seed to grow in your mind while they come up with the next trick.

The boys grab their bags from the old truck they filled up at the train station, throwing them over their shoulders, making their way into the dark, iron-barred halls of the Hudson arena.

The Jackals have been circled on the calendar for a long time. The fourth match of the season, the one the boys are waiting for.

Our last three have been an improvement. Anytime you lose, it's a punch in the stomach, but I can feel we're close to the surface. One of these matches, we're going to break through.

The boys, they have fight in them. They're no longer beaten down and hanging their heads at the end of every match. And here in Hudson, it's personal. No one's forgotten what they did to Laertes or the way their lieutenant tore the emblem from my chest.

These boys are not walking into this arena like lambs to the slaughter. They smell blood and they're ready for it.

We all are.

We're up against the metal gate, old iron with a coat of fresh black paint.

The Jackals are chanting *Golden boy* at us—well, at me. Since my fall from grace, the term's become a derogatory one, and here in Hudson, there's no question what they mean by it.

"Boys!" I shout, gathering the men around me. "We are taking that mountain. Hear me, boys? We're taking that mountain. That team, they think they're going to rip this emblem from our chests tonight. This is the night we prove them wrong."

The roar that meets me matches the chants over my shoulder. The gate opens with a hard clang and we run out like we belong.

The Jackal's captain stands watching us with cold eyes. There's something snake-like about the man.

I run over to Atlas, who's had a chance to look over the

arena. His orders are brief. Element of surprise, but within a system. We watch each other's backs.

"Go get them," he says, smacking my shoulder.

The crowd's started their chants of "golden boy" again.

The Jackals have come up to the center line for the opening formalities. They're shouting taunts.

"Come on!" roars Laertes, lifting his head and striking his chest. "Come on and take it from us if you can!"

"Easy," I say to him under my breath.

Our whole line is staring them down, daring them to overstep. Even Chase, who hasn't had any experience with Hudson, has a glint in his eye.

Lieutenant Culpepper and I clasp arms and bow toward each other. Today, it's more of a slight inclination of the head.

"Prosper the Games," I say solemnly.

"Prosper the Games," he echoes, and there's a wolfish eagerness in his eyes. "See you again soon."

We retreat back to our starting positions. I give the orders. A surprise thrust up the side, with a hook to the left of the main attack. Eddie will lead one, supported by Winston Heath and Chauncey, and Chase the other, with the chasers behind him. One's brawn and the other's speed.

We'll see which one gets the enemy to bite.

From across the arena, one of the enemy chasers locks eyes with us and signals that he's watching.

Apa spins his saber and clashes it against his chest, shouting a taunt across the field. Peter and Danforth smile, then look back at me. "We've got your back today."

I salute them.

Laertes starts beside me today, balanced on the balls of his feet, ready to run. But I don't think I'll use him much. I want him in reserve, in case the flag needs to be relayed. And I'm not giving the Jackals a chance to try to crush him out.

Culpepper raises his fist for the countdown.

I look over at Laertes and give him a nod.

This one's personal.

The beginning of the match is fast and hard. Men whipping past, phalanxes roaring to meet chasers.

Two of the Jackals' chasers tangle with the phalanx. I get stepped on and go down, only to have one of the chasers fall half on top of me. It's a crush-out for the chaser. The Jackals are forced to give up a bar to get their man out of the arena.

I drag myself out of the mess, unhurt except for my pride.

In the melee, Peter's had one of his armguards ripped off. Apa's been hit in the mouth pretty hard with the handle of a saber.

"Easy there," Danforth laughs, and he holds out his hand to help me up.

Peter is strapping his armguard back on.

"Apa?"

He spits blood. Wipes his mouth. "I'm good."

On the other end of the arena, it seems to be going better.

Chase's attack has had some success. Our flag is secured, and the Jackals have backed off from their positions, but there will still only be a small gap where he can run without any of the Jackals' fighters near him.

The gong sounds again and we move back into action.

Sure enough, on the far end of the arena, below the Jackals' mountain, I see Remus and Colt and Lucius holding back the phalanx and the couriers, giving Chase his chance to dash back down the mountain.

For a moment, there's a hitch, a tangle where the fight is thickest.

And then he breaks free. Streaking across the arena with the dust kicked up behind him, flat outrunning the flankers behind him. He tears into our territory and our phalanx closes in behind him to protect his retreat.

He's up the mountain, faster than I've ever seen a boy run, planting the flag as he falls to his knees. He scrambles up and looks around, breathing hard but grinning. He seems unphased, unaware of the rarity of what he's just done.

The great horn sounds. The match is over, and we've won.

For a moment, the arena goes silent. A smile starts to steal across my face. I can't help it. The other boys, they're running for our mountain, incredulous joy on their faces.

Nothing makes me happier than seeing their faces like that.

They swarm Chase, shaking him, clapping him on the shoulder, teasing him.

Up above us, the board reads ten men for the Iron City. They only took out two of us before we planted our flag.

The place roars with boos and jeers, and I do not care. It's music.

I draw my war knife and step up to take the emblem from Culpepper's chest. He's glowering at me, and I know he remembers the last time, and his words.

"Good to see you again," I say mildly. My greatest pleasure will be in taking it quietly and respectfully. I'm not playing his game.

I've already cut half of it when I realize what I should have done in the first place.

"Laertes!" I call, jerk my head for him to come over. "This one's yours."

Solemnly, Laertes takes the knife from my open palm and steps up to Culpepper. His face is serious as he takes the emblem in his fingers and cuts a neat hole around it. He turns it in his fingers and gives Culpepper a long, deep look. "Prosper the Games," he says.

Culpepper maintains a bitter silence.

Laertes turns and holds the emblem high.

The boys break the line and go over, roughing him up, casting looks of triumph at the retreating Jackals.

"Keep the emblem," I tell Laertes, throwing my arm across his shoulders. "You deserve this one."

THIRTY-NINE
ATLAS BOLTON

CAPTAIN, IRON CITY WOLVES

MY FIST'S AROUND A HOT MUG OF COFFEE, BUT I haven't had the chance to drink it. The orange lights of the street lamps go out one by one as the sky outside my office window lightens.

Valentino has worked like a machine on the strategies for our match against the Riverton Vultures tomorrow—I even think the man's excited—and they're all sitting on the table, spread out. I've spent all night looking at them.

Arena maps, fighters' rosters, strengths, weaknesses, the strategies employed by their captain and lieutenant and weapons master in the last year and the few previous.

Everything a man could want.

But there's always an elusive element in the arena, something intangible that doesn't show in battle plans.

The human will. And these Games are the ultimate test of it. Who is more desperate, who wants to win more badly than the man across from them, who loves the man fighting next to them more.

To my boys, the Vultures are another challenge, another step towards victory. A chance to celebrate rather than hang their heads.

To the captain of the Vultures, I know it will be more.

Aaron Gerard and I knew each other, back in our fighting days. We fought on the same side for a year and we worked well together, but he was transferred the next year and that goodwill soured. He was out to get me every chance he had, and to make it worse, I often had the better of him, playing vanguard to his courier.

The Vultures are his team now. Win or lose, I know Gerard will take this one personally.

I rub my tired eyes and finally lift the coffee mug to my lips, take a large gulp and then another. The sun's making an appearance now. Soon, Susan will be back in the office and have another pot of coffee going.

I am going to need it.

I've considered telling the men about it, to warn them that Riverton may be coming straight for their throats, but they shouldn't have to carry the burden of someone else's vendetta.

I stretch, cracking my shoulders.

These men are something. The way they fought for Laertes in that last match. And the way they take getting beat over and over with dignity—I would do anything for them.

I glance at the calendar: three matches lost, one—the

match in Hudson—won. Hudson was a hard win, and Riverton is going to be hard, and then Wachton.

Wachton is strong and hard-hitting.

What we have before us is a gauntlet, and compared to the rest, we're underfed and underequipped.

I recall something Crispin said, back when I called him in to tell him I was not packing him away with the rest of Ed Barbara's men.

He told me how these men took beatings and refused to complain. And I see it now in all of them. In Jackson, and in Remus and Laertes and the other recent conscriptees.

I swirl the coffee in its mug and swallow the rest down.

There's a reason I stay up all night. Because if there's anything I can find anywhere that will give these boys even a little more of a chance, I have to find it.

I grab the mug and head out into the hallway to refill my coffee. A narrow bar of light stands under Valentino's door, and at the end of the hall, I can see someone has lit the overheads in the practice arena.

It's Jackson.

He's running pace drills, his shirt already soaked with sweat.

FORTY
CHASE BIRMINGHAM
FLAG-BEARER, IRON CITY WOLVES

THE HIT KNOCKS ME STRAIGHT TO THE GROUND, winded, staring at the stars above the open arena. For a split second I'm frozen.

I block my head as another hit falls, hard, on my shoulder.

I try to roll over, get to my feet, save the last bar, but one of the chasers puts his foot down hard on my shoulder. "Not so fast."

He leans down and I fight his arm away, but it's only delaying the inevitable. I can't get out from under him.

I get in one shock—eliciting an oath—and then he shocks me, harder than necessary. I guess I kind of brought that one on myself, but a man's got to fight to the end.

The chaser leaves me where I lie and goes running after his comrades. I press my hands against the firm ground and push myself up.

This arena is a little different today; it's been set full of grasses and branches and brambles, perfect for ambushes.

Which is why I am walking myself out of the arena now.

Phillip Blackstone meets me at the side next to the medics. He's been shocked out for a few minutes already.

"You fought hard," he says, points to my head.

I touch and my hand comes away with blood on it.

"Must've caught one of those brambles."

It's been a rough night for all of us. Jackson is standing with his hand on one hip, gazing out at the arena with a grim face. They got him out fast. Cut him off from the phalanx and went right to town on him. The phalanx took some hard hits trying to get to him, and by the time he'd signaled for them to abandon him, they didn't have enough bars left to stop the onslaught.

The chasers had been ambushed, our couriers caught and pinned down and taken out, hit after hit. The Riverton Vultures have used this terrain to their advantage at every turn.

"Who's still out there?" asks Phillip. "The clock ain't stopped."

He cranes his neck to look down the line. It sure looks like all of our fighters are here and not on the field.

"Eddie's out there. He hasn't reported," Laertes says, his eyes on the arena. "Chase, you passed the flag off to him, right?"

I nod.

"Are you sure? I don't see him."

"His name's still up." Danforth nods to the sign above the clock where each fighter's name is listed.

Eddie Greenbriar, it says, standing all alone against the six names on the other side.

"Well, where is he then?" Phillip mutters.

The Vultures seem to be thinking the same thing. They're running about looking. It's not going to do us any good, since we have no real defense for our mountain, yet Riverton cannot win if Eddie remains in the fight with their flag.

And he must have it, because it is gone from their mountain.

There are two chasers going through the grasses and brambles with their sabers, beating it all down, trying to flush him out.

"You see him?" I lean close to Phillip. He gives me a tiny shake of his head.

We're looking, but we don't even want to look too close. The Vultures might be watching us, using us to find our own man.

I look up at the clock. Time is passing; the match cannot finish with the flag missing and one of ours loose, but to everyone it's looking like a decided finish.

The Vultures are losing their patience. They stalk around shouting insults and randomly whacking at the brush.

Nothing. If it weren't for the name up there opposite the others, they'd look like crazy men. Phillip starts laughing.

Right now, we're the ones with nothing to lose. We get

to watch them get themselves all worked up over one lone boy playing hide-and-seek. We've as good as lost the match, so it's kinda nice to see them work for it before they take it from us.

The only ones with grim faces are Atlas and Jackson. I figure they're thinking of the match and the fact these men are getting angry, fast. They'll go a-swinging at Eddie if they find him, and none of us are there to protect him from a crush-out.

The flag-bearer on the Riverton side is helping with the search. The other flag's with him, since they don't want to leave it undefended on the mountain with Eddie still at large.

He's poking at the brush with the end of the flagpole, looking for movement.

A head lifts from the brambles right behind him. Lowers again, so quick I think I've made it up. The barest tips of fingers reach out and unhook the flag from the enemy pole.

And suddenly Eddie's up, running for his life to our mountain, both flags, void of their poles, in his hands.

A shout breaks out and the chase is on.

"Eddie! Eddie!" Laertes is leaping in the air, screaming.

We're all screaming now, willing him to stay ahead. He leaps over clumps of grass, streaking across the distance, closing it bound by bound.

A courier's hand grabs for him, skates across the back of his armor, fails to grasp. None of the chasers are close enough to hit him. He nearly trips, takes a faltering step, and then leaps for the summit, collapsing at the very top, sobbing for breath.

The crowd goes mad with shouts of disbelief, boos, and screams of excitement from the pure rush of watching that unfold.

He did it.

It's the rules. If you plant your flag on your mountain and your side's got possession of the enemy's flag, you win.

We run to him.

He's curled up over both flags, sides heaving, gasping for air.

"Eddie! Eddie, you beautiful boy!" Danforth grabs him by the arms and pulls him up.

Eddie's arms and face are all scratched up from the brambles, his uniform torn. Leaves and pieces of vine are still caught in the buckles of his armor.

His eyes are wide and dark, full of disbelief. Then the beginnings of a smile start across his face.

We snatch him up onto our shoulders. Lift him, clumsily, up above the rush of jubilant bodies. Someone starts singing an old love song:

This is the promise, the promise I made to you....

Phillip's voice is in my ear. "Don't you know this song, kid?"

I shake my head.

"I'll teach it to you someday," he says, with a friendly shove.

I will fight for you, I will bleed for you, I will die for you.
For this is the promise, the promise I made to you.
I will come back again to you.

They're laughing, whooping, singing the love song in voices cracked from shouting. Eddie's overwhelmed by it all. He lifts a fist in the air finally, head tilted to the sky. When the song ends, they chant his name.

We Wolves have taken over the arena. Eddie's let down and Atlas wraps him up in a big, strong hug, roughing up his hair.

As I join in the chant, a kind of settled warmth comes over me. I think this is what belonging someplace feels like.

On the walk back to the preparation room, we're met by the enemy captain.

"William."

Atlas halts, goes still. "Gerard."

"You think you're clever, hm? Now that you're a captain?" The man leans towards Atlas, his eyes like hot coals. "The Guild will not allow you to keep getting away with these tricks. It's a disgrace. They'll crush you, and on a stage far more public than you expect."

Atlas doesn't move a muscle. "That what you've come to say?" he asks softly.

Gerard looks past Atlas at us. "Don't you think that you have something special here. It won't last."

"Aaron, not here," Atlas says, his quiet voice like steel. "You want to come for me, do it, but leave my men be."

"Right." Gerard gives a withering smile. "Leave your men be. It's not as if they won't be taking that beating too, when it comes." He casts us a glance as he strides away.

There's a hard, uneasy silence. Atlas turns slowly to us. "Boys, no one's going to take away your right to celebrate. No one."

Someone smacks Eddie between the shoulders, and the tone lightens again. Forget these captains, all pride and big talk and fear of being sacked.

Try starving. Now that's something to fear. Like Atlas said, no one's taking this from us.

FORTY-ONE
REMUS BLAKE

CHASER, IRON CITY WOLVES

Jackson Van gestures with his long arms, brings us in close.

"Wachton's got some of the best chasers in the Games, so we're going to create multiple diversions. Eddie, you're going to the far side, and you're going to run doubled back obliques. Colt, you're on him. Phillip, center. Straight up. Lucius is on you, and Trenton."

Trenton nods, and Lucius salutes with a couple fingers.

Jackson's eyes go to me. "Remus, you're shadowing Chase. Chase, it's a cut across the center, right wheel, and a charge. Do you need anyone else with you besides Remus?"

Chase shakes his head. "I'll do it better going light."

"Good. Laertes, you're undercover. I want it looking like you're running messages and then I want an abort and rush, at your discretion."

Laertes grins. "Yes, sir."

"Then we're set. You watch yourselves out there, boys. I'll be sending the other couriers to assist as I see fit. Phalanx and I will keep the mountain. Go to glory, prosper the Games."

"Prosper the Games," we echo.

"Looks like we've been split up," I said, as Lucius and I break from the circle. I switch off my armguard to clasp Lucius's arm. "See you after."

"And you, War Hound." He smiles.

Chase and I take up our place near the foot of our mountain. "Ready?" I ask.

He nods. So serious. But he turns on his shocker and touches mine in salute.

It's time.

The arena is instantly chaos. Attacks and counter-attacks all over. Chase and I tuck our heads down and storm a zealous flanker who's come too far over. I get in one good hit, and he's gone.

A glance down the arena shows that Phillip and Trenton have broken away; Lucius is engaged with a hard-fighting chaser, trying to buy them time.

The Wachton flankers are flying in and out, trying to get in hits on engaged fighters. One of them veers off and makes a beeline for Lucius's blind side.

He doesn't even see him coming.

Time slows as the hit lands. They go down together, but they're sideways, twisted with Lucius on his back. A loud, involuntary gasp breaks from the crowd. I'm in motion before a thought can even register.

It's bad.

Colt Bridgerton is the first one to him.

He seizes the Wachton flanker by the collar and drags him off. I can see from here it's a crush-out. His leg's twisted under him at a sick, unnatural angle.

I drop my saber in the grass and kneel down beside him.

He's already going unnaturally pale under his healthy, dark complexion. A cut on his forehead is trickling blood.

"Please, can you move my leg?" he whispers.

"Easy, now, I've got you." I take his hand from Colt, look him in the eyes. I know it's how the Games go, but this was the first time we'd been split up in half a dozen matches.

Of course he takes a hit like this on the day I couldn't watch his back.

Laertes comes scrambling over, throwing a glance over his shoulder. "The phalanx is moving up to give us a moment. Jackson wants to know if he should come."

"He shouldn't come, Tee. Tell him to stay. But tell him it's bad. We need to stop the match and get him out of here."

"Eddie's signaling," says Colt. "He's on his last. He'll forfeit if we need him to."

"Forget it, I have an extra."

I hit the bar on my armguard with my chin. Raise my fist high with the signal. I don't know if they can see it, in the middle of the fight, surrounded by our phalanx and Wachton's chasers.

"Remus?" Lucius's voice has gone up in pitch. He's pale and sweating. I can't let him go into shock.

"You've got my hand. It's all right." I turn. "Has someone called the medics?"

"Please, can you move my leg?" he asks again.

"Is the match stopped?" I ask Colt. "Are they coming?"

In response, a great gong sounds above us.

"Soon," Colt says, his eyes on the edge of the arena.

"I'm not going to leave you," I promise, holding Lucius's gaze. "But the medics are coming, and I am going to give them room."

"Sure." He tries to smile.

Crispin comes running, followed by the medics.

I give him a warning look as I stand up. "It's bad," I whisper.

Crispin takes my place and I kneel down by Lucius's head.

"Lucius," says Crispin, "can you feel your legs?"

"Yes, sir."

"Good. We're going to move you off your leg. We're going to do it as quick and gentle as we can. Bite down on this and breathe through your nose."

Lucius's eyes are on him, calm, patient.

"Are you ready?"

"Just do it."

Lucius can't see me from this angle, but I reach down and take his hand. The medics make eye contact with each other and lift. I grit my teeth as he crushes my hand in his.

I recoil, sickness immediately rising in my throat. The bone's exposed, and he's bleeding into the grass.

He'll be lucky if walks properly again, let alone returns to the arena. And he just married his girl.

"You did good, you did good," I whisper. I'm sweating terribly; I wipe my face against my shoulder, keep his hand in mine.

The medics work at stopping the bleeding while a stretcher's brought out.

I stand up. The men from both sides are watching.

One of Wachton's chasers stands with his fist pressed against his mouth. Our boys are standing with hollow, shocked looks on their faces.

It doesn't matter if you've seen it before. You never get used to it.

The game keepers step out, backing everyone away as Lucius is lifted onto the stretcher and carried out. I push past them, ignoring whatever they say, and take his hand for a moment.

"I'm coming to see you," I promise. "Don't worry, I've still got your back."

He gives me a ghost of a smile, and then we're parted for good.

I watch as they take him out and then turn back to take stock of who's left. Colt and Peter Hope were both shocked out while holding off Wachton after Lucius went down. That leaves six of us: Jackson, Apa, Danforth, me, Chase, and Eddie with his one remaining bar.

I'm also down to one.

These injuries happen in the arena. I've seen them before. Sometimes you come out of the situation fired up. Angry, ready to fight. And sometimes all the heart's been sucked right out of you.

My heart's gone right now; it's walked clean out of the arena and into the ambulance with Lucius.

Jackson does his utmost to rally us. We still have two men with a fighting chance at the flag.

The match starts again, but I can tell from the first five seconds it's no use. Eddie's taken out, then they swarm Jackson, and he and the other two phalanx are gone.

Chase and I make it, with the flag, almost to the center line. Half the Wachton cohort is waiting for us there. I engage as many of them as I can, try to give Chase a way out.

I'm swarmed. Out in seconds. Down on the ground. I'm not hurt, but somehow I don't have it in me to haul myself up quite yet.

A cheer breaks out, and I know they've caught Chase too. Above me, the attendants drop my name from the board. Chase's comes down right after.

"Hey, Iron City." One of the Wachton couriers pauses as he passes me. He hesitates and then holds out his hand to help me up.

I dust off mine and take it.

"You know, I kind of hate to see you guys lose like this. You fight hard."

I take the acknowledgement with a nod. That's a lot more than most men will give you in the arena.

The final formalities are a blur. I want to get out of here and talk to Crispin, to Atlas, hear what the doctors think.

I catch Crispin halfway to the preparation rooms.

"Have you heard anything?"

"Just that he's in good hands, but it's serious. His leg's a mess. They haven't ruled out the spine as another injury. We're lucky we're in Wachton—they're competent and they'll be good to him."

"Nothing else?" I sound more despairing than I meant to.

"I imagine we'll know more tomorrow."

"Have you called his wife?"

"No, not yet. I was going to do it as soon as we got out of here. Wachton doesn't have any telephones on this side of the arena."

"I can do it."

"Are you sure?"

I nod. "I think it'll be better coming from me, if you don't think that's overstepping."

Crispin sighs. There are shadows under his eyes; this night's been tough on him too. "Go ahead. She knows you, and you know him."

The streets out on this side of the arena are quiet and chilly. The sky is clear tonight, with stars visible even over the lights of the city.

I push a coin through the slot and wait for the opera-tor. "Margaret Shanahan," I tell her. "Norwood Hospital, Iron City."

"One moment."

"Hello?" A soft woman's voice comes over the line. I glance up, take a deep breath.

"Yes, is this Margaret?"

. . .

The rest of the Wolves have headed back home. It's me and the assistant stable master, a gruff older fellow they call Stan.

The nurse talks to us softly outside the room. "He is awake, but the morphine's dulled him a bit. We are keeping him on regular doses for the moment. They put the bone back into place, but there is still the chance the doctor might decide it's better to take the leg."

"What do you think his chances are?"

She shakes her head sympathetically. "Time will tell. It's early. But you can see him now, if you want."

"You go ahead," says Stan. He's not excited, I think, at the prospect of sickrooms.

I go in, met by the sharp tang of antiseptics and bleach.

He's lying with his eyes closed and his face drawn, but the ashy paleness from the arena has mostly subsided. He looks more himself.

"Lucius," I say softly.

His eyes open, move to me almost passively, and stay. But there is recognition in them.

"What are you doing here?"

"I stayed. I told you I would." I put my hand on the edge of the bed. I don't know what else to say. There are no answers to this, and I'm thinking of the way he was hit, on the blind side, no chance. The way we told each other "see you after," like it was the easiest thing to say.

"Is my wife coming?"

"She should be here any hour."

"Who told her?"

"I did."

I'm looking for words to reassure him that I broke it to her gently, but before I can say anything, he closes his eyes. "Thank you. I hoped you might."

He opens them again. "Can you stay 'til she gets here?" he whispers.

"Sure." I muster a smile. "Anything."

I bring over a chair and settle beside him.

The morphine seems to drag him in and out. One minute I know he knows what's happening, the next he's hazy-eyed.

It's the first chance I've had since the match to sit and rest my body. Adrenaline has kept me on my feet. Now it simply slips away as the terrible weight of the night comes over me. Exhaustion and guilt take its place. Hot tears fill my eyes.

If only I'd shouted something. If only I'd taken down that flanker when he passed me. It's happening again and again in my mind, the moment that can't be undone.

"Remus...." Lucius is looking at me with reproach in his eyes. "You ain't crying for me, are you?"

I wipe the tears away with my thumb. "I didn't have your back this time."

"I'd never blame you, Remus. We had our orders. We followed them. There's honor in that."

There's honor in that. Words that should comfort. They feel so hollow right now.

FORTY-TWO
BLAISE VALENTINO
WEAPONS MASTER, IRON CITY WOLVES

I REACH INTO THE TRUCK WHERE ALL THE GEAR bags are stacked and pull down my own modest carpet bag. Even after a loss, the men usually talk and joke with one another as they grab their things and part ways at headquarters.

Not today.

We're fresh off the train from St. John's after a brutal beatdown from the Tsunamis. Several of our men were injured. None the way Lucius was a couple weeks ago—he's still in a Wachton hospital, unable to travel—but we're going to have to call up some of the reserves. Everyone else is at the very least beaten up and in sore need of rest.

Remus reaches up and takes down Eddie's bag for him. He's going to drive the boy home. Eddie's arm is in a sling, broken. He took a nasty hit moments into the match, and they'd had to halt the game to get him out of the arena. Jim's limping along on crutches.

Atlas shades his eyes as he looks up into the pale mid-morning sunlight. I can tell from the set of his shoulders that he is bone tired.

Jackson comes over to clasp his arm in farewell, and Atlas musters up a smile for him. "Rest up, Lieutenant. I'll see you tomorrow."

I shoulder my bag and follow Atlas towards the head-quarters front doors. There will be no rest for us.

Susan meets us at the door as we walk into the build-ing, her face serious. "There's some men to see you, Mr. Bolton," she says. "They're up in the meeting room."

"What kind of men?"

"Guild men." Her pursed lips show exactly what she thinks of such men.

Atlas touches her shoulder gently. "Thank you. I will take it from here. How long have they been waiting?"

"An hour, nearly."

He nods. "Valentino, will you come with me?"

"Of course." I run my hand over my hair, smooth it down.

Stone comes into his face and he squares his shoul-ders. I'm not the only one who senses a trap.

"The Guild does not offer this lightly," says Reginald Barkley, the regional Guild officer, a bald man with a hard face and dead eyes. "In fact, it has been fifty years since the Iron City has been invited to a ceremonial match. It is an honor."

"I understand that," says Atlas. "We will be ready, of course. I am just curious why it's being offered now. We still have six matches left in the calendar games."

"These things are not for us to question. They are handed down from the highest authorities in the Empire. It pleases them to declare a ceremonial match now, and to invite you."

"May I ask who we meet in battle?"

The man smiles thinly. "The Golden City."

A wave of shock washes over me. Honor, indeed. They're going to make an example of us in front of the entire Empire. Two matches we've won, both upsets against dreadful odds, and the Guild is so bothered by it that they've come up with this scheme to put us back in our place. It's clearly contrived.

"And how much time do we have to prepare?"

"Three days. It is tradition, as you know, for the teams to be informed suddenly."

Protest rises to my lips. We only just got off the train from St. John's this morning. Our boys are all beaten up, and in the last two matches we've lost one of our chasers for good and two other men temporarily.

But they know that, of course.

Atlas's eyes are flint. "We accept," he says quietly.

He has no choice. There is no refusal allowed in these Games. You'll die beating against them sooner than make them move.

"Good. Arrangements have been made, and the

commissioner knows of our intentions to host the ceremonial game in the Iron City. It will be good for the economy, no?" He smiles, all false benevolence.

Atlas does not return it. "Well," he says instead, getting to his feet. "I am sure that you gentlemen are very busy men. Your dedication is commendable, coming all this way to deliver the news in person. I will not keep you any longer." He ushers them to the door with more courtesy and dignity than I think I have capacity for at the moment.

When he shuts the door, I see his face change. He's exhausted, beaten-down.

"They are setting us up to fail," I say.

He sighs heavily. "This is what you and I signed up for when we came to the Iron City."

"What are we going to do?"

"The only thing we can do. We'll meet them. I hate it, I'd die on my sword for these boys if I could. They mean to punish me, but it's the boys they're punishing, really. It's the fighters in the arena who have to go in there, take the beating, and get back up."

"Our boys will do it for you."

"Oh, they'll do it, but the question you have to ask yourself is: is it fair to them, to ask them to keep doing this? To ask them to go be ripped apart, again and again?"

It's silent for a moment before I answer. "Speaking realistically—we don't have a choice, do we?"

Atlas doesn't answer. He stands up. Closes his eyes a moment, drawing in a deep breath.

Then he throws open the door and strides out.

FORTY-THREE
CHASE BIRMINGHAM
FLAG-BEARER, IRON CITY WOLVES

THE ROOM'S SILENT. ALL OF US STAND gathered, our eyes on Atlas at the front of the room.

There was misery in his eyes as he told us, quite calmly, that the Guild had matched us to the Golden City Toros in three days.

Eddie's here with his arm in a sling. Danforth's on crutches. Winston Heath's got stitches in the side of his face. We're all banged up, many of us with stitches or wraps under our clothes. The least hurt out of us are still bruised and scraped and sore. I mean, I still wrap my knee every time before I run.

Atlas sees that as good as anyone. He knows what he's asking of us. Knows it ain't fair.

He breaks the silence. "If there was any way I could take this away for you boys, I would do it. I know who you are and I know what I'm asking. And it's not fair. There's no excuse for it. I am sorry. Sorry that I cannot give you what you deserve."

Jackson Van speaks up. "I am afraid I am partly to blame. Me being here puts a target on our backs where the Guild is concerned."

Protest rises immediately from the men. Atlas shakes his head.

"You may not like it," says Jackson, raising his voice to be heard, "but that doesn't make it any less true. And I am not going to stand here and let you pretend, all brave, that it isn't part of the issue."

Apa steps forward, head up, dark eyes blazing. "I am going to come up here and say it because no one else is, and I am certainly not letting Jackson Van put this all on his shoulders. Sure, they're coming for us because he's here. What right do they have to do that? We know why they don't like us. And you know what? I spit on them. I don't like them back. So what if they want to pick on us because they hate our lieutenant? Let them come try."

Beside me, Phillip speaks up. "Look, boys. I don't know if we make it—this match, or the Wreath, or out of the Games alive. But if I get a boot in my back every day for the rest of my life, I am going to keep fighting every day, to the very end. That's what I know."

Remus Blake steps out of line. He ain't much of a talker, that one, but I think that's why the boys quiet down to listen. "Some of you remember I was with the Black Town Stags before I came here. With Atlas."

Atlas meets his eyes briefly but can't quite do it a

second time. He shifts his feet, keeping his eyes down. Remus keeps on looking at him steadily.

"If this man told me to swim clean across that ocean, I'd swim it. If he told me to walk clear from here to that mountain ridge in the dead of winter, I'd do it. And I'd do it in a heartbeat, because I know he'd do the same. There's not another captain in these games that I can say would lay down his life for me. And because of that, I'll follow him anywhere."

Atlas is silent, looks too choked to speak. He clears his voice at last and coughs. "I won't let you boys down."

Remus raises his fist in the air. "Give me the Golden City. I want the Golden City." He looks at Jackson.

Jackson raises his fist.

"I want the Golden City!" Laertes shouts.

"I want the Golden City!" Peter Hope.

Phillips's fist is up, then mine.

We echo the shout: *We want the Golden City. Give us the Golden City.*

FORTY-FOUR
JACKSON VAN

LIEUTENANT, IRON CITY WOLVES

I HAVE NEVER SEEN THE IRON CITY PACKED THE way it is today. People from the Iron City, people from the Golden City, all streaming through doors, clogging streets, waving banners and shouting since the morning. All waiting for the evening match.

Whatever else happens tonight, it's not going to be easily forgotten.

A voice shouts to me in the hallway. "Jackson! Jackson Van!"

It's Mark Brissinger. I almost ignore him and keep on walking, but I slow my pace and turn to face him instead.

I shouldn't have. His eyes are hungry.

"Mark. I figured I'd see you around one of these days." I don't know if the subtlety of the remark is lost on him or not.

He's moving towards me, drawn up to his full height

to try and look me in the eyes. "How does it feel to be the laughingstock of the Empire, hm?"

He hasn't changed.

"Is that what you think we are?" I take a step towards him. "You can call me whatever you like. You tried to bring me down, you succeeded. Maybe I'm a laughing-stock. But those men in there are anything but."

"I will call them what I like when I beat them."

I stare him down. "Mark, I am not your lieutenant anymore. I am not your scapegoat, and I am not your rival. Humiliate me if you can, but I think you're going to find it harder than you expect."

"I can still break you." He's bristled up like a hound, his blue eyes like ice.

I smile. "Good luck with that."

I turn and walk away. It's good none of the boys were here. I can imagine what some of them would've done in response.

And I wouldn't have blamed them, honestly.

Preparation is beginning. Men coming in with their gear bags, assistants going over the equipment, making sure it's all legal for inspection. It's games like these when the game keepers are looking to hand out sanctions or for reasons to take men out of the matches.

Someone's ball is on the ground. It's one of those rubber balls that they use for jacks. Probably Colt's or Tee's. They'll go at each other's throats for little games—cards and jacks and playing catch. It reminds me of a couple of young bucks play-fighting. Just sharpening themselves on each other.

I pick it up and bounce it a couple times.

Peter settles down next to me. He's lacing up his boots, high and tight. Something I love about the man is he's calm. He could be watching a sunrise or facing down three chasers with sabers, and he'll have the same expression, same tone of voice.

"Do you know something?" I toss the little ball up and catch it.

"Hm?"

"Remember when we got in that street fight with the Battle Hawk fighters?"

He chuckles. "Sure."

"I checked my pay. My fine was never taken out of it."

Peter looks away. I love the man. He can't hide a thing.

"Is that why you asked to stay and talk to Atlas alone?"

"And if it is?"

"You paid my fine."

"And you didn't have any money."

"Not then. But a lieutenant is set to make a lot more than a phalanx member, all told. You know that."

He shrugs. "I had money then. And the fight wasn't your choice. They just wanted to see you go down with us. Besides," he grins, "we should have held on to our tempers better that night."

"I still don't see why you were so good to me. I hadn't done anything for you. In fact, I probably made it worse, in the beginning, just by being here."

"Why?" Peter laughs. "Because you had every reason

to hate being here. Every reason to sit down and feel sorry for yourself. You got dealt the worst hand a man could be dealt, and I never once saw you take it out on us."

"It wouldn't have been fair to take it out on you. You didn't do anything."

"But do you know how many men have? You say you're nothing special, but we've seen all kinds here, and I can tell you, that's rare."

Peter looks at me and I can see in his eyes what he wants to say is important. I cup the ball between my hands and look at him.

"I just want to say, Jackson. Regardless of how this goes, I'm with you. Win, lose, or draw. I'll go to war with you anywhere, any day."

"Even on just three days of rest," I joke.

But he's serious. "We're not going to let you down, Jackson. I swear."

"It's snowing," announces Trenton, coming in. He's bundled in a sensible sweater and coat, like a true native.

"How hard?" asks Phillip.

"Not bad. Why?"

Phillip mumbles something to himself.

"Phillip, where are you going?" asks Chase.

"I'm getting some air! It's too hot in here."

Trenton laughs. Good luck with that, and don't get locked out. They almost didn't let me back in, didn't believe I was one of the Wolves."

Phillip laughs good-naturedly, waving him off, and goes out.

FORTY-FIVE
PHILLIP BLACKSTONE
FLAG-BEARER, IRON CITY WOLVES

LAUGHS FOLLOW ME OUT OF THE PREPARATION room and the door slams, cutting them off. It's peaceful here in the hallway. Somewhere a door to the outside has been propped open; I can smell that sharp, freezing air that means snow.

I start in that direction and stop short. A figure's there, ten feet away, standing half in shadow, watching me. A figure I'd know anywhere.

Luke Sheppard.

The Golden City's been good to him. Gone is the leanness and weariness that used to hang about his cheeks and eyes. He's all filled out and muscular. He even has a beard.

"Hello, Phillip."

"Hey, Luke."

"How are you?" He seems unsure of what to say. I haven't spoken to him since he left.

"I'm well. You look well. Is your family good?"

"They're wonderful."

Do you ever miss us? I want to ask. But all I say is, "Sure. I bet."

He licks his lips, starts forward and stops himself. "Look. I have to get back, they don't know I'm gone. The Toros, or the Guild. But they're planning on changing the terrain. We've been told sand, but they're giving us grass, hoping you won't have time to change strategy."

He looks down, debating with himself, and then back up. "We've known about the match for three weeks, and I heard you were just told a few days ago. I thought it only right you should know that."

I nod.

"It's not fair or right, we both know that. I still plan on winning this match, but I wanted you to know."

"I'll tell the captain."

"Do that." He turns to leave.

"I'm happy you won a Wreath." I raise my voice slightly so he hears. "I know you wanted to, bad as any of us."

He turns back. Something conflicted crosses his face. "I thought of you all. It probably sounds poor coming from me, but I did."

"Nah. You're a good man, Luke. You deserve this, really."

He hesitates like there's more he wants to say, but seems to think better of it. He comes back and holds out his arm. "Sure. See you across the arena."

I reach out and clasp it firmly. "See you across the arena."

FORTY-SIX
REMUS BLAKE

CHASER, IRON CITY WOLVES

ATLAS STEPS OUT IN FRONT OF US.

"Gentlemen, I would like to read something to you this evening." He holds up a scrap of newspaper.

"This was published in the Golden City Chronicle a little over a year ago. *'Jackson Van has been rescued, as it were, by the flailing Iron City Wolves. The most interesting thing about this arrangement will be seeing which one will pull the other down faster. Or, perhaps, which will sell the other out sooner. Together, they can only sink further into ignominy and squalor.'"*

Eyes go to Jackson, but he's standing with his hands in his collar, a little smile on his face.

Atlas folds the paper up. "That was the last article in the Golden City Chronicle that—to my knowledge—mentioned our names and Jackson's together, until a piece two days ago about the impending match. I will not read that one to you tonight. My question for you gentlemen tonight is this: has what the article said would happen, happened?"

"No!" The shout resounds around the room.

"No. We have already proved them wrong. We know who we are. It's time to show them tonight."

Final preparations begin as Atlas takes Jackson aside to talk with Valentino. From the way they're talking, something's changed. New information, perhaps. It happens.

Beside me, Liam and Colt are solemnly painting each other's arms with a band of blue. Paint is allowed in the arena, and some cities carry its tradition stronger than most.

But the special matches, the ceremonials and memorials, they require it.

The Iron City's patterns are a ring or band of solid blue on the arm, with three streaks of black or gray down one side of the face.

I reach over, thinking to ask Lucius to do mine in exchange for my doing his. And then I remember.

He's still down in a Wachton hospital, facing the prospect of life without the Games—life without walking, perhaps—alone, except for Margaret.

I've had enough.

I pick up the box of paints left for me and take it to the cracked mirror across the room. I pick out the black, running a thick line down from my cheekbone.

Enough of Jackson taking insults because he'd rather swallow them than let them fall on his men.

The second line goes beside it, thick and hard.

Enough of the injustice in the arena, with the game keepers turning a blind eye to the abuses of the other cities.

The last line is a streak, tapering off at the end. I reach for the blue.

Enough of the pain these boys have gone through. Year upon year. To the point where Lucius thought he had lost his nerve.

I grit my teeth as I paint the thick blue band. Press my arm against the wall and turn to the mirror to get my blind spots.

Enough of the massive strain Atlas takes upon himself to protect us.

I throw down the blue next to the black.

It's time to go out and show the Empire.

Jackson's words to us, as he stands with his back against the gate, are simple.

"The Guild thinks they can make an example of us." His blue eyes are solemn as they search ours. "Today we are not fighting to prove them wrong. We're fighting for our brothers. For us. We who stood together against the world. So fight for your brother today."

The gates swing open.

The arena is packed to the rafters. It's the most people I have ever seen here. The shouts are so loud my ears ring.

And then they change, unite into words—a chant.

It's our people; they're shouting *Golden Boy,* and this time they mean it.

It's no longer the insult they hurled at him a year and a half ago when he was exiled to us. It's not what our enemies have thrown at us, taunting our leader. This is full-throated courage.

This is a declaration of war.

Jackson raises his fist to them and the cheers rise louder, if that's possible.

The formalities, the orders, and the place-taking are slow and clear. Every detail, every shaft of light from above and the dust caught on it, every glance between us men is as clear as if it happens in a spotlight on a dark stage. My ears ring with the noise.

Colt steps up beside me. "Let's get 'em, War Hound."

I smile, give his armguard a hit with mine.

It's strange to me that a boy raised like him would want to throw in his lot with us when he could have had anything.

But I guess I'm one to talk. I gave up the Black Town for Atlas.

Jackson raises his fist in the air to start the countdown. My heart matches each strike beat on beat.

It's time.

I launch forward, running with all my might towards the center line. I'm stride for stride with Colt and Liam, spread out at only a saber's length.

Colt spins his saber and brings it down as we meet the Golden City's roaring rush.

Blows rain down. Shoulders, legs, arms, we're fighting tooth and nail.

A shock takes me in the neck. I grit my teeth against it and get the man back. It's just enough. I see Chase dart through, low and fast, whip past a flanker and bound up the mountain.

I glance at Colt. He's seen it too.

"Liam!" I shout.

Liam's got his man down, he's shocking him over and over with a fierceness that takes even me aback.

He gets to his feet as the man lies back, exhausted.

Above us, the man's name is dropped from the Golden City side.

Liam dives into my man, wrestling him, and with two of us, the man's got no chance.

"Remus, arrow!" Colt shouts.

Chase is coming back. He's low on bars, but he's on his feet running, head low, flag streaming behind him.

The thought goes through my mind that I have no idea what's happening at our mountain, how many men are left there, if the flag's still there, or if we've as good as lost already.

I block it out. All I know is the task in front of us.

Colt has gone down with his man. Liam and I break away and follow Chase out, trying to guard him from attack.

Couriers and flankers come after us, passing us by and flying at Chase.

He hangs onto the flag as he's run into by a flanker. He stumbles, catches himself with the flagstaff, and stays on his feet.

Laertes is running to him, hands out, ready for the pass. Tee's got three bars. He'll survive more attacks.

Chase passes the flag and then catches at his pursuer, getting a hand on the man's ankle. It doesn't stick, but the man lost a second and Tee's off running like lightning.

Liam's panting, but he doesn't hesitate as he engages another Toro. They crash to the ground together. I continue my escort alone.

And then I see it.

Jackson is still standing on the mountain, Peter Hope beside him, guarding the enemy flag. They're the only two left, both bleeding, but standing.

The Toros don't have their flag yet.

A Toro shoots past me and I reach for him and miss. It's Luke Sheppard. The man has no quit in him.

I almost never see lieutenants on the wrong side of the arena, and here he is, taking Laertes single-handed.

"Jackson, Jackson!" Tee shouts, his voice ragged. The boy's been running for his life.

He thrusts the flag into Jackson's hands and spins on Luke Sheppard, who is inches from shocking him out. He catches Sheppard by the collar, dragging him to the grass.

And Jackson runs.

Twenty feet. Ten feet. He plants the flag on our mountain.

Jackson is caught in the haze of the spotlight. The crowd roars like a hurricane. His name thunders from a hundred thousand throats. But his eyes are on us.

He raises his arms—

You can't hear a thing the keepers are saying. It doesn't matter. We know those words well.

Colt jumps into my arms, shouting, screaming, tears streaming down his face, and I pound his back. We're caught in the blur of bodies.

The thought is a whisper of sadness inside a moment of blinding happiness: *I wish Lucius was here to see this.*

The boys surround Atlas, shouting his name, as he comes out. He's crying unashamedly, but we all are.

I throw my arm around his neck and shake him. He's buried in the mass of bodies swarmed around him, laughing, crying, roughing him up.

The Toros are leaving the field, heads down. Their captain's angry, shouting at the game keepers. There's nothing they can do.

Luke Sheppard pauses beside the gate and looks back, looks up at the rafters and the crowd like he's done it a thousand times before.

A little smile crosses his face. And he looks straight across to Phillip.

He gives him a nod.

Phillip presses his fist to his chest in answer.

When I look back, Luke's gone.

It was such a little thing to notice, yet I feel I've just

witnessed something final. A closing of a door that's been standing open, waiting to be shut.

Phillip's got tears in his eyes.

"You good?" I shout, clapping him on the back.

"Happy," he laughs, chokes. "I'm so happy."

Everything after is a golden blur. Speeches are made. Toasts are made, with the water pitchers and then with a bottle of champagne that someone found and snuck in. It's one bottle, so we pass it from man to man, each taking our taste.

We sing, we shout Jackson's name. We can't help it. We're all beside ourselves.

Outside, the streets are crowded. Iron City workers and families clogging the streets with celebration, even though there's snow all over the ground and the air is frigid.

I step out into the back alley, the one almost-quiet place in the city tonight. The sky's cleared up, a rare thing, but the snow must have been a short squall. The distant roars of cheering are dulled by the high brick walls outside the arena.

A bunch of the boys have gone on ahead and I need to catch up, but I want to pause for a moment and take it all in.

I close my eyes and take a deep breath.

"I wouldn't do it, if I were you." It's Audra Hilton, the Iron City's high commissioner.

She's standing in the alley. Too well bred to lean against the wall, but there is a lit cigarette in her fingers. A picture of the Iron City, complete. Even the highest here have their sorrows.

"What do you mean?"

"Throw your career away. They won't let us win, not in the end." She gives me a sad smile.

"Is it wrong for us to celebrate?"

She shakes her head, almost regretful. "But you're a good man. I know your story. I know a lot of things; it's my job. You don't have to stick around here, especially after tonight."

"I think it would be ungrateful."

"You say that now." She takes a small, dignified draw on her cigarette. "But they'll crash. You don't rise this high without a reckoning. You could save yourself. And you have to think of that in a place like this."

I can still hear their laughter. Filling the night air, coming up the alley to us.

I don't care.

"Then I'll burn. These are my boys, and I'm sticking with them."

She shrugs and takes one last, long draw on the cigarette before tapping it out on the rusted edge of the trash bin.

"You may think differently, eventually," she sighs. "But I respect that. Loyalty."

She moves past me, giving my arm a pat as she goes by.

It's strangely still in the alley. The cold wind swirls

down between the buildings, and it carries on it the far rumble of the trains and the rise and fall of the passing automobiles, the cheering of the people, as beside themselves as we are.

We're their heroes, finally. What they are tasting right now is hope. We're all breathing hope right now, thanks to Atlas.

In this moment, I can see everything clearly. Time, passing, and us caught in it, in a moment that is just for us.

It was no mistake that brought me here to the Iron City.

And live or die, it's my place.

FORTY-SEVEN
JACKSON VAN

LIEUTENANT, IRON CITY WOLVES

THE LEAVES HAVE FALLEN OVER THE STEPS TO MY house. I will need to attend to those. With the madness following our victory against the Golden City, I have been at headquarters far more than I have been at home.

I take out the key and unlock my door.

There's a single letter on the floor beneath the mail slot, and I know the handwriting immediately. With my thumbnail, I rip open the envelope.

Inside is a folded newspaper clipping from the *Golden City Chronicle*. I pull it out and hold it up to the fading golden light in the window.

The title splashed across the top reads "The Iron City Hails its Golden Boy." But it's the underlined section below that draws my eye.

The arena does not lie. Does the Guild? Perhaps. Do the captains? Certainly, at times. The Games do not.

The man we saw last night in the arena was not the boy who read his Guild-written apology with a dull, pained voice, nor the indecisive lieutenant who froze in the face of Coventry's fierce onslaught.

I would not be surprised if the Golden City wondered, last night, whether they judged Jackson Van too hastily, and whether, perhaps, in their zeal to do justice and honor the Games, the Games were in fact dishonored. Perhaps we did not know what we had until we let it go.

The truth will out. May it be a lesson to us all.

A small note falls from the folded newspaper to the floor.

Son, I am proud of you. The truth will out. Dad

My medal from the victory hangs on the wall above my shelf with the others, and the Golden City's captured emblem sits on the shelf beside it.

For the first time, I can look at that emblem—the one I'd once loved and fought and bled for—and there's no twist in my stomach.

Only a settled sense of purpose.

I glance at the calendar. There are five more matches.

Our work's not over. In fact, it's barely begun.

ACKNOWLEDGMENTS

Many thanks to all those who have by their hard work, discipline, and courage inspired me and made the themes of this book so dear to me. Keep at it.

To my street team who hang in there, help spread the word, and generally keep me moving forward with your hype. This one's for you.

My deepest thanks to James Egan at Bookfly Design. Your covers elevate everything and bring my words to life. I can't thank you enough for the

To those who have helped through encouragement, kindness, deep conversations, and lightening the load in any way, thank you. I won't remember everyone, but if you think it might be you, then yes, I am talking about you.

To, Elisabeth, my editor for her tireless work and her dedication to these stories. I am so lucky I get to craft stories with you. I couldn't do this without you.

To Lydia, the patron saint of writers on deadline (mine especially). Thank you for all the help, prayer, and encouragement you bestow on me.

To the One from whom all stories come. Thank you for the beautiful stories and for making me a storyteller. All glory to You.

ABOUT THE AUTHOR

EMILY HAYSE is an award-winning author and screenwriter with a love for nature, sports, compelling characters, and strong coffee. Originally from Michigan, she now resides in Southern California, where she can often be found baking, hiking, or bringing new worlds to life. *The Dogs of War* is her ninth novel.

ALSO BY EMILY HAYSE

Crowning Heaven

Seventh City

The Last Atlantean

The Rivers Lead Home

These War-Torn Hands

The Beautiful Ones

In the Glorious Fields

Yours, Constance

Kill the Dawn

www.ingramcontent.com/pod-product-compliance
Lightning Source LLC
Chambersburg PA
CBHW061622210726
48287CB00001B/241